THE BOOKSELLER

VALERIE KEOGH

Boldwood

First published in Great Britain in 2025 by Boldwood Books Ltd.

Copyright © Valerie Keogh, 2025

Cover Design by Head Design Ltd.

Cover Images: iStock

A CIP catalogue record for this book is available from the British Library.

Paperback ISBN 978-1-80549-450-8

Large Print ISBN 978-1-80549-452-2

Hardback ISBN 978-1-80549-451-5

Ebook ISBN 978-1-80549-453-9

Kindle ISBN 978-1-80549-454-6

Audio CD ISBN 978-1-80549-445-4

MP3 CD ISBN 978-1-80549-446-1

Digital audio download ISBN 978-1-80549-448-5

This book is printed on certified sustainable paper. Boldwood Books is dedicated to putting sustainability at the heart of our business. For more information please visit https://www.boldwoodbooks.com/about-us/sustainability/

Boldwood Books Ltd, 23 Bowerdean Street, London, SW6 3TN

www.boldwoodbooks.com

For my cousin, Joe Keogh, with love

PROLOGUE

I adored my father. He was a tall, broad-shouldered man with work-callused hands, his round face perpetually tanned from days outside as a labourer on a building site. On minimum pay, to make a decent income, he needed to work long hours, often seven days a week. The rare times he was home, he looked down on me and my two older siblings with absent-minded affection. And we – or I, at any rate – looked up at him as if he were a god.

There were times, especially in the long days of summer, when we didn't see him for most of the week. I used to imagine that he'd come to see us as we slept, that he'd bend to brush a hand over our heads, plant a kiss on our foreheads, perhaps even whisper that he loved us.

We children never questioned the long hours he worked. If our mother did, we weren't aware. Did he really need to work so hard? Or did he choose to be out in the fresh air with the gruff, cheerful camaraderie of like-minded men rather than spend time with his house-proud, slightly pernickety wife? She was a quiet, biddable, conscientious woman who prided herself in keeping a clean home and neat, well-behaved children. There wasn't a pinch of steel in her; she'd sway in the softest breeze, in the slightest waft of discontent from our father, or in the smallest sign of misconduct in her offspring.

We weren't bad children. At least, my siblings weren't. My older sister and brother, close in age as they were, were best buddies. They rarely tolerated their bratty baby sister tagging along and often vanished on some adventure, leaving me forlorn, lonely, and desperate for company. When my father was home, I would look up at this big man, idolise him, almost beg for the merest hint of attention.

That's how it started. My mother, unable to discipline us for breaking any of her many rules of good behaviour, would keep note of the slightest infraction and pour them out to her husband when he had time to mete out punishment. Frequently, this was days after the event, when none of us children could remember what we'd done wrong. It didn't matter. My father would use his large, worn hands on us. He would pull my soft, yielding body to him and bring his hand down on my behind. The pain would be intense. As would the pleasure of being held so closely. Of having this god-like man's complete, undivided attention.

Sometimes, if my crime warranted a more severe punishment, two or three wallops rather than one, he would mete it out, then wipe away my tears. He'd hold me in his arms, offer me comfort, and whisper into my ear, 'You mustn't be naughty, my little lamb.'

These were moments of bliss for a child desperate for affection. I became naughtier and sought for more ways to offend. I deliberately broke things, stole from my mother's purse and from the corner shop. I caused trouble in school: pushed my classmates, refused to do the teacher's bidding, answered back. Anything to draw my mother's ire in order to merit the punishment doled out by my father, and the pleasure that followed.

I was fifteen when my father left us... *me, he left me.* Not voluntarily, though. Not for him the slow fade into old age and frailty. My big, strong father died in a stupid, careless work-place accident.

His death left me bereft. Doubly abandoned when my mother retreated into herself. My siblings, now in their mid-twenties, had already left home: Sarah married and living in Bath, Doug living in Glasgow. They came home for a few days for the funeral, then left with promises to return. But they and I knew these were made for form rather than any desire to visit.

I desperately missed my father. The feel of his hand across my cheek, or the punch that would send me careering into the wall for some infraction of my mother's increasingly erratic rules. I missed him because his discipline was always... *always*... followed by words of comfort and love.

By the time he died, pleasure and pain were already inextricably linked in my head.

1

_____

Helen twisted under the duvet as the dream came. In full colour and stereo sound, as it usually did.

The snap of the leather belt before Toby held it taut between his hands, face set, mouth a narrow slash, grey eyes sparkling flint. She held her breath and waited for the sound of the leather cutting through the air, that distinctive swish that always preceded a bolt of pain. She braced herself but made no attempt to dodge out of the way. Why would she?

When neither the sound nor the pain arrived, she opened her eyes to look at the man who insisted he loved her, the man she loved in return, and saw that something had changed. He'd never make a poker player; every emotion was written clearly on his face. And sometime, in the preceding days, or weeks, or had it been months, his love had soured. There was something different in his eyes, something new... She wasn't sure, but she thought it might have been disgust.

She remembered her fingers closing around the handle of the knife. It was in her hand when she rang for an ambulance, still there when the police first hammered on, then burst through her front door.

'Drop the weapon!' someone had shouted, repeating it louder, as if she was deaf.

She'd looked at it, confused. Weapon? It was a kitchen knife. One she'd only bought the previous day. An incredibly sharp one, she'd already nicked her finger with it. It had bled profusely but not enough to cover the knife in blood as it was now, dripping from the edge, her hand covered in it, the cloying scent drifting up to make her gag.

'Drop the weapon.' More than one voice now, loud and insistent.

Finally, she did as she was told and released her grip, opening her fingers to allow the knife to drop to the ground. The point of the knife missed her bare foot by a hair's width and embedded itself into the wooden floor.

She couldn't remember if she'd screamed then, or if she'd looked down at Toby's cooling body, pleased to see his expression had changed, his mouth twisted in disbelief rather than disgust. Pleased that the bastard would never be able to hit her again.

The police refused to allow her to wash before they took her away. She sat in the back of their car with her bloody hands resting in her lap where they stained the thin fabric of the cream dress she wore.

In the station, they took photographs. They even took swabs which she thought was a waste of taxpayers' money. She wasn't denying it was Toby's blood. How could she when they'd found her with the knife in her hand? The very knife she must have driven into his belly with as much force as she could manage. Had she found it easier than she'd expected? She didn't know. Her memory of that day had a gap between when she picked up the knife, and when she saw Toby collapse at her feet with a ridiculous look of surprise on his face. She'd watched the blood gurgle up from the wound in his belly for a long time before she associated it with the knife in her hand.

In the two years she'd spent in prison, she'd had the dream almost every night. She considered it a part of her sentence. Perhaps she had been foolish to believe it would eventually stop. That once she was released on licence, half-free as that might be, she could start looking to the future.

The counsellor she'd seen as part of her rehabilitation said the dreams were caused by subconscious guilt. 'You have to learn to forgive yourself,' she'd said. 'Negative thoughts are detrimental to your well-being.' The counsellor always spoke in soundbites, as if waiting for someone to quote her. Helen had thought she was full of crap, but the sessions, although not mandatory, were a welcome diversion from the gruelling boredom of prison life.

During one session, she'd given the counsellor an edited version of her childhood, telling her about her siblings, not her parents. About the words that still rang in her head. *Stupid baby! Noisy brat!* 'My sister was ten years older than me. I still hear her sometimes, telling me I'm a nuisance.'

'Echoes from your past,' the counsellor had said, nodding as if this was perfectly normal. 'What I'd like you to do, when you hear this voice in your head, is to imagine writing whatever she says on a piece of paper, then tie it to the bottom of an imaginary helium balloon and release it. As it floats away, see your negative thoughts going with it.'

The next time the voice had sounded in Helen's head, she did as the counsellor had suggested. But as the balloon was floating away, taking all those horrible words with it, her sister came dashing up with a knife in one hand and burst it. The ensuing bang made Helen cry, and gulp, and her mouth fill with blood that had exploded from the pretty yellow balloon.

It was a dream. Helen woke in her prison cell, a film of sweat over her body, the echo of her scream still floating in the air, her cellmate glaring at her, and the certain conviction that the counsellor hadn't a clue what she was talking about.

Of course, Helen hadn't been able to tell her everything. If she had, if the counsellor had known the truth, the sessions would no longer have been an optional extra; they'd have been compulsory. And the poor deluded counsellor might even have suggested that Helen needed psychiatric help.

If they knew the truth... all of it... her sentence would have been far longer than four years.

So, Helen kept her secret. And if the payment for keeping it was to be continuously reminded of what she'd done, well, that was her penance.

2

After two years in prison, Helen was released to spend the remainder of her sentence on licence. Free, but tethered by conditions she had to live by, with a community offender manager appointed to ensure she did. It did mean, though, that she was entitled to pick up the tattered strings of her previous life. The civil service job where she'd worked for ten years was waiting for her. She'd have gone back to it, would have had to, except for the sadly fortuitous death of her mother the previous year.

Her mother's will, like her home, had been neat and tidy without any trimmings. Everything was to be divided equally between her three children. It didn't make Helen rich, but suddenly a dream she'd had forever, one of owning a second-hand bookshop, was made possible. The last few years, the two in prison, the one before, had been a struggle. Books, her escape as a child, proved to be just as effective when she'd been stuck behind prison walls. In an odd way, she'd benefited from the limited supply available. It meant she read whatever she could lay her hands on, reading genres she'd never thought would appeal: steampunk, science fiction, biographies, memoirs. It had broadened her taste, one way of turning what had been a horrendous, life-changing period of her life to a good advantage.

During the second year of her incarceration, it was one of the things that had kept her sane. The other, after her mother passed away, was spending her limited Internet access scouring the estate agents for suitable properties in Bath to house her bookshop. She intended to be sensible and pay off the mortgage on her home first, but it still left a very healthy four hundred thousand pounds to work with.

Her sister Sarah, who'd visited regularly since her imprisonment, was the first to be told her plans. 'I'm going to open a second-hand bookshop.' Helen watched her face as she took in the news. If Sarah thought it was a crazy idea, it wouldn't have changed her mind, but the sisters had grown close in the last year and she wanted her on her side.

For many years, Helen had harboured resentment for the way her older siblings had excluded her when they were children. The ten-year age gap between the sisters, which had seemed to be an uncrossable divide when one was five and the other fifteen, didn't seem to lessen when one was thirty and the other forty. But when Helen's world imploded, Sarah was there, and her unconditional support during the trial and since had brought the two together.

'A bookshop! You'll be in your element,' Sarah had said. 'I think it's a brilliant idea.'

'It'll be a bit like living between the covers of a book.' That's the way Helen saw it. It's the way she *wanted* to see it.

By the time she was released, she'd looked at hundreds of properties, but they were either in the wrong place, or priced way above her means. Or simply not the shop of her dreams.

'You'll find something,' Sarah said. 'It's just going to take time.'

Helen didn't want to wait. Her future was there, just out of reach; she wanted to grab it, hold on to it tightly, and fly with it.

She stared at the road ahead as Sarah drove her home on her first day of freedom. 'I'm so tempted to do a Mel Gibson.'

Sarah glanced at her. 'What?'

'You know. Like in that movie *Braveheart*, when he shouted, "Freedom!"'

'If I remember rightly, he died straight after.'

Helen shrugged and returned to staring at the road ahead. 'I'd better not tempt fate then.'

They were at the turn-off to the road where she lived, waiting for a break to cut across the traffic, when she saw something ahead. 'Look,' she said. 'There's a For Sale sign.'

Sarah didn't need to be told twice and indicated to pull back into the traffic, then immediately signalled to pull in to the side of the road and park. The For Sale sign was affixed to the front of a rather shabby, down-at-heel building.

'It used to be an electrical repair shop,' Helen said, peering out of the car window. 'Although I've never been inside.' She pointed to the neighbouring building. 'That pizzeria has been there forever. I used to get takeaways from it.'

'What d'you want to do?'

'Get out and have a closer look; hang on, I won't be a sec.' She pushed open the door and climbed out, her eyes fixed on the building. There wasn't much to see. It had obviously been on the market for a while. Weeds had lodged in the cracks between the building and the footpath. The bay window and the glass panels on the front door were boarded up, preventing any opportunity to see the interior. She stepped back to examine what she could. It needed a lot of work. The window frames looked as if they needed to be replaced. A gutter was leaning at an alarming angle. She'd bet the roof would need to be repaired too.

When she sat back in the car, Sarah's assessment was clearer. 'It looks like a right dump.'

'Perhaps.' But Helen's head was spinning. Stupidly, she hadn't considered this area, but wasn't it the perfect place for a bookshop? Although the road was a busy one, there was plenty of parking. The surrounding area was a mix of residential and businesses so the footfall past the shop would be good. 'No harm in having a look online when we get home, see how much they're looking for.'

Sarah was busy trying to do a U-turn, so it was a few minutes before she could reply. 'You're not seriously thinking about it, are you? Honestly, it looks like it would be a total money pit.'

A short while later, they were parked outside Helen's end-of-terrace house. She could feel herself tearing up as she looked at it. Home – was there ever a more beautiful word? Pulling a tissue from her pocket, she wiped her eyes before turning to Sarah. 'Thanks again for having looked after it the last couple of years. And for keeping the car ticking over.'

'No problem. I popped in yesterday and stocked your fridge up with a few things too so you don't need to rush out to the shops.'

'It's good to be home.' It was, but it was also the first time Helen had been there since Toby's death. The place had been cleaned by specialists. Sarah had been clear about that. But Helen still had to face where it had happened. Where her life had changed. Sarah must have understood, because her normally chatty sister was silent as Helen opened the front door and stepped inside. She dropped her holdall on the bottom step of the stair, then without a word, walked the few steps to the kitchen door and opened it.

She didn't move forward, not even when Sarah put a hand on her shoulder and said, 'You okay?'

If they had put white tape on the floor marking where Toby's body had lain, it couldn't have been any clearer to Helen. She could almost feel the cold handle of the knife in her hand, could almost smell a metallic whiff in the air. Worse, she could hear Toby's voice. 'You know you want it. You love it, don't you?' The crack of the belt as he snapped it, the swish of leather through the air, the pain.

'Helen?' Sarah's voice, more urgent now.

'I'm fine. It's just...'

Helen reached for her sister's hand and squeezed it.

'You don't need to explain. When I think of what that bastard put you through, honestly, I wish he was alive so I could kill him myself!'

It made Helen laugh and relieved the tension that had mounted as soon as she'd opened the front door. 'Killing someone isn't that easy to do, you know. It takes a special frame of mind.' One that had been warped in her childhood, and irreparably twisted in the years since. She caught her sister's concerned glance and smiled. 'Perhaps it's too soon to make jokes about it? Let's have a cup of tea to celebrate my release.'

'I bought biscuits.'

'Tea and biscuits. The perfect celebration.'

When they were sitting at the small kitchen table, Helen dipped a biscuit into her mug of tea and popped it whole into her mouth, then pointed to the mobile Sarah had left on the table. 'Have a look to see how much they're asking for that place.'

'You're not seriously thinking about it, are you?'

Helen stared into her tea. 'I've been looking almost a year. I haven't seen anything in my price range that's suitable.'

Sarah reached into her handbag. 'Here,' she said, taking out a mobile phone. 'I thought you'd need a new one when you got out.

Things have changed a lot in two years. Now you can have a look for yourself.'

Tears filled Helen's eyes again. 'I can't seem to stop crying today,' she said, picking it up. 'This was so kind of you, thank you.'

'You're allowed to be emotional. It's a new start for you.' Sarah nodded towards the mobile and smiled. 'I was going to make today's date the password, but I thought the year you were born would be easier.'

Helen had always been good with technology so it didn't take her long to figure out how to use it. A few minutes later, she sat back with a sigh. 'This is very neat, very clever. Right, now let's find out about that shop.'

She'd taken note of the estate agent's name and was soon checking their website. 'Here it is,' she said, unable to keep excitement from seeping into her words. 'Two rooms and a kitchen on the ground floor. Three rooms and a bathroom upstairs.'

'Are there photos?'

'Only one of the outside. None inside.'

'Ha!'

Helen looked up from the phone. 'What?'

'No photos inside because the place is a dump, just as I guessed. They don't want to put people off by showing how bad it is. They want to get you there and hope to persuade you.'

Helen scrolled through the details. 'It's in the perfect location. The size is just what I was hoping for. You're right though, it says it needs total refurbishment.' She put the phone down. 'It's been empty for two years, but it's still priced way above what I could afford considering it needs work.'

'Yes, if it needs a total refurb, you're talking a lot of dosh. It's what I said: a money pit.'

'Yes,' Helen said, dragging the word out.

'What's going on in that head of yours? I can almost see the cogs turning.'

'I was just thinking of the coincidence. It's been empty for two years. So has my life. Maybe it's a sign.'

She half-expected the reaction to be a laugh or some scathing remark. Instead, Sarah poured the last of the tea into her cup and sat back. 'Why don't you go and have a look at it? When you see inside, you'll realise it's totally unsuitable and then you can put it out of your head.'

'It's just...' Helen hunched up her shoulders. 'I want to get on with it, you know. Take control of my future. Get the shop. Fill it with books, start this new chapter of my life.' She let her shoulders drop. 'A cliché, but doesn't it fit?'

Sarah reached for Helen's hand and squeezed it. 'It does. And it will work out for you eventually. I don't think this place is the right one for you, but why don't we go and have a look at it? Rule it out, get it out of your system, then I'll help you look elsewhere.'

There didn't seem to be any point in reminding Sarah that Helen had been looking for a year and knew what she wanted. When she shut her eyes, she could see it as clearly as her reflection in a mirror. There'd be high ceilings, wooden shelving on every wall stacked tightly with books. A staircase to an upper floor – preferably a cast-iron spiral one but she would settle for a simple stairway. There'd be old, worn leather chairs for customers to sit in, wooden tables and old lamps. An oak desk, scarred by life and time, for her to sit behind. Every detail was carefully drawn in full colour in her head. And in those long days locked away, she'd even designed a logo to go with it. With a surname like Appleby, it wasn't hard. An apple, with a cartoon bee sitting on top reading a book. Twee perhaps, but it would make people smile. She'd have a stamp made, and every book in her shop would have the Appleby logo.

Her past – all of it – would be just that. Wouldn't it? The prison counsellor had advised her to forget the past and think of the future. What did she know about anything? Helen had crossed a line by killing Toby. On this side of it, she wasn't sure who she was any more. A victim? A murderer? An ex-con? A pathetic fool?

'What d'you think?'

Helen looked at her sister, confused. 'About?' Then she shook her head. 'Sorry, the shop, yes, why not? It won't do any harm to have a look. It's like when you see a dress in a shop window. You fancy it, but don't have time to go in to try it on. It sticks in your head, becoming the most perfect dress ever, until you give in and go back to try it on. And you hate it. But then it's out of your head. It'll be like that.'

'Exactly,' Sarah said, giving her arm a gentle nudge.

But it wasn't.

3

Sarah insisted on staying over that first night Helen was out of prison. 'Just to keep you company.'

Helen didn't think it was necessary. She wasn't a child. But when they'd both gone to bed, when silence fell on the house and all she could hear was her breath, she was grateful there was someone on the other side of the bedroom wall. Not that she was going to call out, or God forbid, go into her sister's room and ask if she could sleep with her. After all, she'd done that as a child and it had got her nowhere.

It wasn't that she missed the continuous rumble of sound that she'd got used to over the last two years; it was that in that ever-present noise, the sounds from her life before, were better concealed. And now, in the silence of the home she'd shared with Toby, they were back... his voice, hers. Loud and shrill, harsh and angry. They started quietly, increasing in volume to a crescendo, fading away to a sibilant whisper.

Sarah had asked, many months before, if Helen had considered selling up and moving elsewhere for a fresh start. As if she'd find it uncomfortable moving back into a house where someone had died.

Where someone had been murdered, the tiny voice inside her head corrected her. Where she had murdered her partner.

Earlier, in the kitchen, she'd stepped over the space where he'd lain, lifting each foot high enough to clear his body. If Sarah had noticed, and she must have done, she'd said nothing.

Perhaps it would be sensible to sell and move elsewhere, but Helen had fallen in love with the late-Victorian house the first time she'd viewed it. She'd stretched herself financially to buy it and had done renovations over the years as money had allowed. Although perfect for one, it had proved to be slightly too small for two. Had that been part of the problem? Had the six-foot Toby simply taken up too much space?

Annoyingly, he still was. Was this his revenge for what she'd done – to haunt the home she loved?

Helen linked her hands behind her head and stared at the ceiling. She'd left the curtains open but the nearest streetlight was quite a distance along the road outside. It barely impacted on the darkness of the room and did nothing to dispel the shadows in the corners. She could sell up and move elsewhere but what would be the point? The shadows would always be there.

The prison counsellor had advised her not to dwell on the past, and she tried not to, but the bastard kept insisting on tagging along for the ride.

She tried to concentrate on the future. As soon as she and Sarah had made the decision to view the dilapidated house, Helen had rung the estate agent and made an appointment for the following morning. This morning, she realised looking at the bedside clock, the 12.02 teasing her.

She thought about going downstairs for a cup of tea, but

alone, in the dark, she couldn't face opening the kitchen door. It was foolish. Toby wasn't there. He couldn't hurt her again.

But that was part of it, wasn't it? Being back here, in this bed they'd shared, she could finally admit that she didn't miss *him* – she missed the pain.

4

The following morning after breakfast, rather than driving, Helen and Sarah walked the ten minutes to the property. They were standing staring at the frontage when a car pulled up and a harried-looking man stepped out. He saw them, pinned on a smile, and extended a hand as he approached. 'Ms Appleby?'

'Yes.' She shook his hand and indicated her sister with a jerk of her head. 'And this is my sister, Sarah Drew.'

'Nice to meet you both,' he said, giving Sarah's hand a quick shake. 'My name is Giles Lambert. I'm the agent for this exciting premises.'

'Exciting premises!' Sarah muttered into Helen's ear as the estate agent pulled out a huge set of keys and searched through them for the appropriate one.

Inserting it into the lock, he jiggled it for an age before it finally turned and he pushed the door open. 'It's been empty for a little over two years,' he said, standing back to allow Helen and Sarah to enter. 'It was a small electric appliance repair shop. The owner ran it for almost two decades.' He sniffed and looked around, shaking his head. 'I don't think he spent much on repairs even when he was here, and there's been nothing done, as you can see, in the years since.'

He wasn't making much of an effort to sell the place, but he didn't need to. Even in the poor light coming around the edges of the boarded-up windows, there was something about the spacious room with its high ceilings that immediately appealed to Helen.

When the estate agent flicked a switch, the room's grandeur was slightly dimmed by the rotting window frame, the damp patch on one wall, the underlying stink of decay. Ignoring the negatives, Helen concentrated on the high ceiling and the space, her imagination already at work to transform it into the picture she'd had in her head for so long, the details etched during sleepless nights and long, monotonous days. She followed a beam of light to an even larger room at the back of the shop with windows overlooking a tangle of greenery that at one stage had probably been a pretty garden.

Helen peered through the dirty glass, trying to make out the extent of it without venturing outside to be attacked by brambles. Big enough, she thought. As she leaned forward, her fingers sank into the rotten wood of the windowsill. She ran an eye around the frame. It too was in bad condition.

'There's a pantry kitchen too,' the estate agent said from behind her, jerking a thumb towards a door. 'It's in need of a refit.'

'I'm surprised the place hasn't fallen down.' Sarah opened the door to the kitchen and screwed up her nose. 'A refit? It needs to be gutted. It stinks of mouse droppings too.'

Helen brushed crumbled wood from her hands and crossed to peer over her sister's shoulder. The one window in the small room had been boarded up, and what little light there was drifting through the doorway where they stood. Although Helen was searching for something positive to say, there was nothing to be said in favour of the mismatched cupboards with their doors either missing or hanging askew. Nor could she come up with anything nice to say about the ancient cooker that stood at the far end of the narrow space, almost completely blocking the back door. The grease and grime of decades had changed its original colour to a sickly beige. A row of dials near the top reflected what little light there was. It made the cooker look bizarrely demonic.

'You okay?' Sarah asked when Helen shivered.

She shook her head to dispel the macabre image of the filthy old cooker staring straight at her as if welcoming her into its space. Silly, stupid nonsense. 'It's the thought of the mice,' she said nudging her sister's arm. 'Shut the door before they come to investigate the intruders.'

Sarah hurriedly slammed it shut and took a step backwards. 'This place should be condemned.' She darted a disbelieving look at the estate agent. 'You're seriously asking four hundred k for this?'

He shrugged. 'Structurally, it's sound. It's in a good area, and could, with a bit of imagination, be converted into a nice family home.'

Sarah raised an eyebrow. 'A family home? Did you see the traffic on that road outside? That's the Upper Bristol Road. It's always busy. You wouldn't be able to open your door without breathing in car fumes.'

Ignoring them, Helen went back into the front room from where a stairway headed upward. The landing window, layered in years of grime, threw a soft-focused light that hid more than it showed. She stepped gingerly onto the first step. It squeaked noisily but seemed safe. The landing window, although dirty, hadn't gone the way of its downstairs relations and seemed solid. In fact, with a bit of prodding, she discovered that all the windows upstairs were in good shape. Two of the three bedrooms, with the same high ceilings she'd admired below, were each a good size, the third much smaller. The bathroom was also a decent space.

'Bloody hell, it stinks in here.' Sarah stood in the open doorway; her face screwed up in disgust. She pinched her nose with her thumb and first finger and spoke with a resultant nasal twang. 'Can we get out of here now?'

'In a minute.' Helen shut the door and headed back into the front bedroom. She tapped on the dividing wall. 'It'd be easy to take this down, make this and the back bedroom into one big space. I'd leave the smaller one to use as an office or storage.' When there was no comment, she turned to see her sister's appalled face, mouth opening and closing as if she simply couldn't find the words. 'Look past all the mess,' Helen said. 'The rooms are big, the ceilings high. There's plenty of light.' She tapped her hand on the wall again. 'With this gone, it would be amazing.' Her eyes sparkled as she waved a hand around. 'Imagine all the walls lined with bookshelves.' Another wave of her hand, lower down. 'Maybe hip-high, stand-alone shelves in the middle.' She frowned as she considered the logistics. 'Maybe on wheels, so we could move them out of the way to hold book talks, or for book clubs, etc.'

'You're serious!'

Helen was. Creepy cooker aside, it was exactly what she'd been looking for. 'It's perfect. There's free parking outside so people can park and come in. Student accommodation for Bath Spa university isn't far away. I could hand out flyers, advertise in university magazines. Plus, there'd be passing trade from people who live around here.'

Brushing past her silent sister, she returned to the ground floor where the agent stood, hands in his trouser pockets, boredom in the tight line of his mouth.

He looked resigned rather than hopeful as Helen joined him. 'Seen enough?'

'It's been on the market over two years, hasn't it?'

He shrugged. 'Twenty-five months.'

'And you've had no offers?'

He straightened suddenly as if smelling potential in her interest. 'Not correct, we did have one but it fell through.' He waved a hand around. 'It could be a little goldmine this, if it was done up right.'

'Why did the sale collapse then?'

She could see the wheels in his brain turning as he wondered if the truth or a lie would be of more benefit.

'An issue with planning permission, I'd say,' she said. It was a complete stab in the dark but she was guessing only an investor would be interested in purchasing such a run-down property.

The agent shrugged again. 'You're right. He wanted to convert it into three apartments but couldn't get planning permission for more than two. He said it wouldn't be financially viable so pulled out.'

'And no offers since.' She smiled. 'So would the owner be agreeable to drop the price for a quick sale?'

Sarah's jaw dropped. 'Are you crazy?'

'Subject to a survey, of course.' Helen might be a little crazy but she wasn't stupid. Her funds were limited. Cosmetically, the place was a dump but that could be fixed. If it was structurally unsound, it would be the money pit her sister had warned about.

'I'm sure they'd entertain any reasonable offer,' the agent said, his whole demeanour changing at the thought of a sale. He tilted his head in question and waited.

'It needs new windows. There's damp. The kitchen and bathroom need to be gutted. It's going to take quite a bit to get it into shape so I'm thinking three hundred thousand is a much more suitable price to pay.' Helen watched his face carefully, relieved to see he didn't immediately shake his head. It was a low offer; she might get lucky.

'Let me see if I can get the owner on the phone,' the agent said, reaching for his mobile and heading outside, shutting the door behind him.

Immediately, Sarah turned to her. 'Are you absolutely barking mad?'

'If I can get it at a good price—'

'If you got it free, it'd still be too expensive!'

'New windows, bathroom, and a small kitchen.'

'And the damp.' Sarah pointed to the ominous dark stain down one wall.

'Probably a leaking pipe.' Said as if Helen knew what she was talking about, not as someone desperate. And she was. This place was perfectly placed, the ideal size. She could make it work. She could put the past behind her and be happy.

She wanted happy. Had been searching for it for too long. She'd traded pain for it. But then, wasn't it always the way?

Happiness had a price. It came down to what she was willing to pay to have it. She'd paid with part of herself for too long. But the woman on this side of that line she'd crossed by killing Toby, wasn't going to pay that way any longer.

A run-down dump of a house, a wrecked mess of a life – she was going to fix both.

5

It took a lot of to-ing and fro-ing, nail-biting, floor-pacing, checking mobile reception, and a million doubts about whether Helen was doing the right thing or not, before an agreement was reached. The vendor came down to three fifty; she came up to three twenty-five. An agreement was finally reached late that evening at three forty.

'Three hundred and forty thousand!' Sarah opened the bottle of wine she'd insisted on buying to celebrate Helen's new venture. 'I hope you know what you're doing.'

So did Helen. 'After I've paid off the mortgage on this place, I'll still have thirty grand left from the money mum left me. It's not a lot but if the place is structurally sound, I should be okay.' She gave her sister a gentle thump. 'You and Devon will help, won't you? I can hire a skip and we can haul everything out, see what's what.'

'Of course we'll help. Devon's mate, Ivan, works for a kitchen installation company. I bet he'd be able to get you something at a knock-down price. He might be able to install it too.'

The kitchen was the least of her worries but Helen wasn't

going to look a pretty gift-horse in the mouth. If she was lucky, her brother-in-law might rope his mates in to do more than install a kitchen. 'I don't suppose he knows someone who does windows, does he?'

Sarah see-sawed a hand. 'He knows lots of guys; some are decidedly dodgy, but some are sound. I'll get him to ask around.' She took a sip from her glass before continuing. 'You are going to get a survey done, aren't you? It's not worth skipping that essential step.'

As if Helen was stupid. She hid the irritation in the wine glass she held to her lips without drinking. Her tolerance for alcohol had dropped after her two-year abstinence and it wasn't wise to get drunk. She might say things she shouldn't to the sister she needed. Say stupid things, not do them. She couldn't give that as an excuse for what she'd done. She'd been stone-cold sober when she'd killed Toby.

'Of course I'm getting a survey done. I was lucky; the fifth person I rang had just had a cancellation, otherwise I could have been waiting for a few weeks. He's coming tomorrow. Until he says it's structurally sound, there's no point in planning anything.' But she was. In her head, as she'd been doing for months. No, not months, she'd been planning this bookshop all her life. For as long as she could remember, she was happiest between the pages of a book. It was a happiness that came with no demands, no promises. *No pain.* And if a book disappointed, as happened, there was always another to pick up, another adventure waiting. Now, they were offering her a future, and she had to grab it.

'Helen?'

She dredged up a smile. 'Sorry, what were you saying?'

'I was asking if you needed to let your COM know.'

Helen's smile became fixed. Her sister appeared to think the acronym was better than the full title – community offender manager. As if COM sounded cute and cuddly. It didn't. Neither did parole officer, to use the more common title. Or supervisor, which was, to Helen, the least offensive. The conditions of her release on licence were fairly straightforward. Basically, she had to stay out of trouble, not go anywhere without telling the supervisor, stay in contact with her, tell her if she changed her phone number or email. Tell her everything. This last wasn't a condition, but it seemed safer to assume it was, safer to assume that this woman, Moira Manson, who already knew so much about her, was entitled to know the rest. Helen had no intention of inadvertently breaking the rules and being recalled to prison to serve the remainder of her sentence.

'I'll do it now,' Helen said, taking out her phone. She emailed Moira with the details of the property she intended to purchase and the business she hoped to start. 'It's best to tell her everything,' she said, putting the phone down. 'She shouldn't be surprised; I've already told her this was my plan.' She remembered explaining that she and her siblings had been left a considerable amount of money when their mother died, and she'd hoped to make her dream of opening a bookshop come true. She'd been surprised by Moira's reaction – a laugh of derision followed by a snort of disbelief. Helen wasn't certain, but she thought she'd also seen a sliver of envy flit across her face.

Putting the woman out of her head, Helen's thoughts turned back to her plans for the shop. It would depend on the results of the survey. With only thirty thousand pounds to play with, any structural repairs would put the premises out of her reach. Then she'd have to begin her search again, putting her life on hold once more, that new future she yearned for. A chance to put the past behind her. The thought made her give a weary sigh.

Sarah reached across and grabbed her hand. 'It's shocking that you have to live under these license conditions for two more years. I blame that useless blasted solicitor you had. He should have insisted they dismiss the charges against you.'

Dismiss the charges? Helen gave a soft laugh. 'A bit hard to do that. After all, I did kill Toby, remember? His family, and their solicitor, wanted me tried for murder. It was only thanks to my solicitor that it was reduced to involuntary manslaughter. And thanks to his argument that there were mitigating circumstances, my sentence was only four years and not longer.'

'You were defending yourself.' It was an argument the sisters had had time and time again. Helen had been grateful to be sentenced to only four years, Sarah incandescent with anger that she was serving any time at all. 'I don't think I'll ever forget the photos of your injuries. The welts across your back. The bruises.' She squeezed the hand she still held. 'I still can't believe you put up with it for so long.'

'He was so good to me, you know.' Helen's eyes filled. 'The first few months, he was gentle, kind, considerate. I thought I'd fallen on my feet.' She pulled her hand away from Sarah's, reached into the pocket of her jeans and pulled out a tatty tissue to dry her eyes. 'You know my track record with men was pretty crap. Toby seemed to be the answer to all my prayers.'

'He certainly put on a good show. And Devon liked him. Not that that's saying much; my idiot husband likes everyone, he's the most ridiculously undiscerning creature.' She hesitated. 'I haven't liked to ask before, but when did it all start going wrong?'

It was a question Helen had been asked by so many people – the police, the doctors who'd examined her injuries, her solicitor – but it wasn't something she'd been able to answer. Not then when it was all so fresh and raw, not now when she could look back and see how stupid she'd been. Because it was a lie, Toby had never been gentle, kind, or considerate. 'I'm not really sure,' she said.

'I suppose it started slowly, didn't it?' Sarah nodded in agreement of her own statement. 'That seems to be the way with most domestic-abuse situations.' Colour flared in her cheeks. 'I did a lot of researching before your trial, learnt a lot more about domestic violence than I'd ever wanted to know. Some of the cases...' Her voice trailed off and she shook her head. 'I still think you should have been found not guilty.'

'Buying that knife was my downfall. The prosecution said it showed premeditation.'

'It was unfortunate, but everyone knows coincidences happen.'

Helen took a small sip of her wine. Maybe she should drink more. Maybe if she did, she'd forget the expression on Toby's face that last day. Forget her disappointment when she didn't hear the swish of the belt sailing through the air, didn't feel the sharp, sweet pain as it connected.

Her sister believed she'd wielded that vicious blade to protect herself from him.

But that wasn't the way it had been at all.

6

To Helen's relief, the surveyor's report came a week later and showed that the property was structurally sound. She punched the air in excitement, hung up, then immediately rang Sarah to tell her the good news.

'So you're going ahead with buying it?'

Helen's excitement dimmed. She'd wanted her sister to share in her joy. There was nobody else. The few friends she'd had, old workmates mostly, hadn't survived the shame of her arrest. 'Yes, I am. It's the perfect property in the ideal location. It's just going to take hard work to get it sorted.'

'Well, congratulations then, if it's what you really want.'

Helen gritted her teeth. It appeared she'd be celebrating alone.

Sarah, blithely unaware she'd disappointed her sister, added, 'Devon and I will help you when we can. It'll be months yet though, won't it?'

Her sister wasn't jumping up and down with excitement, but she was offering practical assistance which was worth more. Helen wanted to reach through the phone and grab her in a tight hug. 'Thank you. With you and Devon helping, it will make it so much easier. I'm hoping the conveyancing will be done in about six weeks.'

She'd been stupidly optimistic. Despite constant phone calls to nudge things along, it was eight weeks before everything was signed and the property was hers.

The waiting days dragged. There was only so much she could do. She put up adverts offering to buy used books in the windows of local shops and in every free newspaper she could find. She had a couple of calls within a few days and drove to pick them up, adding them to the boxes sitting in the middle of her living room waiting to be taken to the shop.

When everything was signed and the estate agent handed her the keys, she went to have a look around the property on her own. Inside, it was better, and worse, than she remembered: the space bigger, the ceilings higher, the smell worse, the damp patch on the wall bigger, the clutter and mess more offensive. And yet, as she walked through the rooms, she could see it as it would be, and a thrill shot through her.

The following day, the hard work needed to whip the tired, worn-out building into shape began. She pulled in favours where she could, desperate to keep the cost of renovations to what she could afford. Devon's friends proved to be a godsend. Not only did they do both the kitchen and bathroom on a shoestring, but they helped out with stripping the decades of grotty wallpaper from the walls and with the repainting. The damp patch on the front wall had been caused, not by a leaky pipe as Helen had thought, but by a cracked gutter outside spilling water down the wall when it rained. It was easily, and thankfully cheap, to sort out.

Helen spent money where it was needed – on the electrics, and on triple glazing for the new windows to the front of the house. She wanted the bookshop to be a haven where people could disappear into books and not be disturbed by the constant traffic outside.

The cost of the refurbishment didn't spiral out of control, but it did nudge over the thirty thousand pounds she had, forcing her to dip into her credit card and use a hastily arranged overdraft. It was worth it, she decided, looking around. It looked even better than she imagined it could. A carpenter friend of a friend of Devon's had made the bookshelves lining the walls both upstairs and downstairs, using wood he'd recycled from old pallets that he'd sanded smooth and varnished. He'd also built some modular units on wheels for the upstairs space.

She'd been right about removing the partition wall between the two larger bedrooms. With light flowing from both sides, it was an amazingly bright space. She sourced some comfortable bucket chairs and a couple of small tables on eBay for a song. And had been lucky to have spotted an incredibly battered but beautiful desk in a local charity shop for the grand sum of twenty pounds. A couple of brass reading lights with green glass shades, found in yet another charity shop, completed the décor.

On the last day, when everything was done, she treated everyone who had helped out to pizza, beer and Prosecco, setting it all out on top of the modular units on the first floor.

'I can't believe you've done it,' Sarah said, lifting her glass in a toast to her sister. 'I have to admit I was sceptical, but it looks amazing.'

'I couldn't have done it without all your help.' Helen gave her sister a hug, then raised her glass to the others. 'You've been lifesavers.'

'This floor was a bitch to sand and varnish,' Devon said,

tapping a floorboard with the toe of his shoe. 'I don't know how many times I wanted to bugger off to the nearest pub and leave you to it.'

Helen's eyes swept across the walnut-stained floor Devon had worked so hard on. It glowed and contrasted perfectly with the pale wood of the shelves. When they were lined with books, it was going to look incredible. 'You did a brilliant job; I really appreciate it.' She waved her free hand around the little circle. 'All of you. It hasn't been an easy couple of years and now, thanks to you, I'm looking forward to my future.'

'You're still hoping to open on Monday?'

Helen lifted her chin at the hint of doubt she heard in her sister's voice. 'I *am* opening on Monday.' Nothing was going to stop her beginning this new chapter. She needed to put the last few years behind her and get on with living. 'I'm only going to open downstairs at first. I have enough books to fill most of the shelves there thanks to the adverts. I've still a few collections to do so I should acquire more over the next few weeks.'

Sarah put down her empty glass and stretched her hands over her head. 'You want a hand with the unpacking?'

It had taken three runs in Helen's hatchback to move the books from her house to the shop earlier that day. She'd piled the boxes up downstairs. Shaky towers waiting to yield up their treasures, books waiting to be released and given a home on the shelves. She'd been happy to accept help with every other aspect of the work but this, this unpacking of her precious books, was something she wanted to do herself. 'Thank you,' she said, giving her sister a grateful smile. Truly, Helen couldn't have managed without her. The ten years that had separated the sisters so dramatically, that had made such a difference when they were children, maybe they didn't matter any more. Maybe Helen could finally forgive and forget. 'You've done so much for me; I'll be forever grateful.'

'But you want to unpack the books yourself?' Sarah grinned as she leaned forward to press a kiss on Helen's cheek. 'You and your books. When I think of you as a little 'un, that's the way I picture you: a ragamuffin with her nose in a book.'

As a child, Helen hadn't simply been lost in a book. She'd been in a different world. One where she wasn't lonely or sad. A world where she was a princess, or a queen, where she was friends with lions, played with tigers, and had long conversations with honey-eating bears. Lost in a world where she didn't care that her older sister and brother didn't want her tagging along. *You're too small. You spoil our fun. Go away, baby!*

Lost in a world where she didn't care that her mother was more concerned in keeping her house tidy, than in caring for a child she'd never wanted.

Helen quashed down the squirt of anger she always felt when she thought about her childhood and forced a smile. Books had been her saviour then, and now looking around the space she'd created, she knew they would be again.

Sarah checked her watch. 'Right, well if you're sure you don't need us, we'd better get off.'

'Thanks for the pizza and beer,' the three lads said almost in unison, waving their hands dismissively when she tried to thank them yet again for all their hard work.

'They've enjoyed doing it,' Devon said, giving Helen a kiss on the cheek. 'Kept them out of trouble.'

'Kept them out of the pub anyway,' Sarah said, linking her arm in his. 'You too. Think of the money you've saved.'

Helen waved them off, then shut the door, leaned against it, and let her eyes drift over the space as a shiver of anticipation swept over her. Some of the towers of boxes waiting to be unpacked were filled with books she'd had for years. Old friends she'd be reluctant to give away but she would. There was no room for sentimentality if she wanted to make the business work. The remainder of the boxes were filled with books she'd gathered over the last few weeks as a result of the adverts.

She'd settle for getting all of these boxes done before her grand opening on Monday. Only one more collection was scheduled to be done before that. They'd go upstairs out of the way until she had time to sort through them.

She grabbed the stamp she'd had made to mark each book with the Appleby logo. Then with a dramatic gesture, she ripped the packing tape from the first box and reached inside to begin the task of deciding where each book should go.

The light faded as she worked. The wooden venetian blind that she'd had hung across the bay window shut out most of the light from outside, some creeping in around the edges to make strange patterns on the walls. She switched on a lamp, working in the glow of it until the corners of the room vanished into darkness. Looking up from the book she was examining, she was startled by the thought that the room had become an infinite space without borders, and she was suddenly overwhelmed by the notion that she was no longer alone.

The book she held fell to the floor with a thump that seemed to echo around the silent room. 'Hello?'

How stupid. Did she expect an answer? The front door was locked. There was nobody there. Nobody. She pressed her lips together to stop herself saying his name but when she stared into the dark corners, it came on a whisper. 'Toby.'

He was haunting her. It had to stop. His death had been the end of one part of her life and the beginning of the next. It was going to be different from now on. *She* was going to be different.

All she needed to do was to put all the lights on and chase the shadows away.

Her eyes were gritty with tiredness by the time she decided to call it a day. She got to her feet and frowned to see how little she'd achieved. It was taking longer than she'd anticipated and only a few of the shelves were filled. She ran her fingers along the spines, a slow smile forming. It was a start.

Her brain was rattling. Even after she'd driven home, eaten leftover pizza, and crawled into her bed, her mind was still grappling with clashing thoughts.

But they were mostly happy ones. It was all coming together. From now on, this would be her life. She'd derive pleasure from her business, find it between the covers of books, in the words printed on the pages, and never let another man into her life.

Toby's handsome face appeared on the back of her eyelids. For weeks after his death, it had seemed to be etched there, torturing her into sleepless nights where she was afraid to shut her eyes. The years in prison had dulled the image, softening the edges of it, until finally he was a soft-focus shadow of himself that returned now and then like an unwanted guest. One that lurked in the shadows, like he had done earlier that night. Always just out of sight. Watching her.

When he came to her in her dreams, he was always dead, always bloody. It was easier then because she didn't need to kill him again and again.

For a time, they'd been good together. Hadn't they? Or was she making the mistake of looking back through treacherous, rose-tinted glasses? She'd thought they were happy; kept thinking it long after she'd known it wasn't true, even when he'd looked at her in disgust before bringing his heavy leather belt down on her bare back.

7

Exhaustion sent Helen to sleep quickly, the tangle of thoughts waking her just as light slipped around the edges of the curtains at four the following morning. For several minutes, she lay with her eyes shut, hoping to drift back to sleep, but many of her thoughts had barbed edges and prevented the return. At four thirty, she wondered if she should simply give up and get on with all she needed to do. Deciding it was the better option, she threw the duvet back and got to her feet.

Over breakfast, she made mental plans for the day ahead. First thing, she'd get to work unpacking the remainder of the boxes. So far, it had been her books, and they were mostly genre fiction: crime, a few romance novels, and some old classics. All, unfortunately, were more than two years old. She was hoping to find newer books and a more eclectic mix in the boxes she'd acquired in the last few weeks. Apart from a quick look to make sure they weren't total rubbish, she'd accepted whatever was offered willy-nilly, unable to afford to be choosy. Not at the price she was offering to pay. Most people were simply relieved to get rid of excess books and were happy with the few quid she gave them.

The thought of all she had to do galvanised her. She grabbed her bag and keys and headed out. With a collection planned for that afternoon, it made more sense to take the car. She parked outside the shop and sat for a moment staring at it through the car window. It looked good. The hand-painted sign over the door with Appleby Books in bold print, had turned out better than she'd hoped for. She'd toyed with having a logo on the sign too but decided to keep it simple in the end.

Unlocking the door, she pushed it open. The bell she'd had mounted overhead to alert her to every customer's entrance, tinkled a greeting. It would have made her smile, if she hadn't looked around in a panic. There was so much still to do.

Despite her early start, by late morning, she'd emptied only two of the boxes. It was hunger that brought her to a halt. With a glance at her watch, she got to her feet. Eleven thirty. The pizzeria next door would have opened to get ready for the lunch trade. And they did pizza by the slice.

She'd already proven to be a good customer of theirs and had developed a friendly relationship with the two owners who weren't Italian but Londoners from the East End. When she'd met them first, they'd spoken in strong Cockney slang she was barely able to understand. When she got to know them better, she discovered they mostly put it on for the benefit of their customers.

She pushed through the door into the restaurant. It was small with only six tables, but she knew from speaking to them that the bulk of their business was from takeaway. 'Anyone home?' She crossed to the desk and picked up a menu.

The answer came from the back room. 'Keep your 'air on, we're coming.'

It was another couple of minutes before Helen heard footsteps approach and the broad, almost cherubic face of Alex appeared. 'I could have run off with all the silverware,' she said with a smile.

'Wouldn't be the first time that's happened.'

It was always hard to know whether Alex or his twin brother Zander were joking. She'd thought they were when they'd told her their names, but no, their mother thought it was funny to use one name, Alexander, and split it between them, adding a Z to make it easier. The two men, in their early sixties, had decided to begin a new life away from the East End where they'd lived all their lives when Alex's wife had died following a long illness. They sold the fish and chip shop they'd run for decades, moved to Bath, and looked around to find something to do. When they saw the pizzeria for sale, they had a eureka moment. That was a little over two years before, and they'd never regretted it.

'Food's food,' Zander had said to Helen when she'd queried why the change. 'There's been a pizzeria here for almost ten years. Don't fix what ain't broke.'

She liked their down-to-earth, no-fuss attitude, was glad to have them as neighbours, and more than happy to pick their brains for information on things she didn't know. She'd promised them free books in return. The offer had drawn guffaws from both.

'Read a book! Leave it aht, luv!'

For someone who considered reading as essential as breathing, that came as a challenge. 'I bet I'll find something you'll enjoy,' she'd said. So far, she hadn't succeeded.

She picked up a menu from the counter, then put it down with a smile for the man opposite. 'Why do I bother to look, eh?'

'One of these days, you might choose something different.'

'Not today. I'll have the usual mushroom pizza and a large

latte, please.' There was no point in only getting a slice or two. She'd eat most now; any that was left over she could have that evening. Save her having to cook. Save her having to go shopping for food.

It was a warm day. Rather than eating inside, she took her purchases into the garden and sat on a plastic chair she'd brought from home.

The pizza was good. So was the coffee. As she ate, she considered her neighbours. They were friendly, helpful, always had a smile and time for her. But friendly and nice as they were, there was something about them that made her wary.

Perhaps it was simply her experience with Toby that had left her so suspicious or was it their reaction when she'd asked, on the first or second time they'd met, why they hadn't been interested in buying her shop themselves. They'd laughed it off, said they hadn't been interested, that they had enough space for their requirements. They'd sounded honest and truthful, but she was almost certain they were lying. Or was it that she simply couldn't tell any more? Toby had said he loved her, and she'd believed him. And he'd been lying. Maybe everyone lied. She certainly did.

Alex and Zander were nice to her, they made great coffee and bloody marvellous pizza, so perhaps it was better to smile and say nothing. What was that old adage – keep your friends close and your enemies closer – yes, and she'd do that. She'd smile, play the helpless female, and keep her eyes open.

Toby had taught her a valuable lesson. Never trust anyone. Especially not a helpful, charming man.

Nobody was going to ruin her second chance at happy ever after.

8

Helen hadn't finished the work she'd hoped to get done by the time she needed to leave for a pick up that had sounded promising. The call had come to her mobile two days before and she'd answered with a breezy, 'Appleby Books.' The words were still new, and she felt a thrill of pride every time she said them so it took a few seconds to register the protracted silence on the other end. 'Hello? Is there anyone there?' She'd been about to hang up when she heard the distinct sound of someone clearing their throat. 'Hello?'

'I'm sorry.' The voice was quiet, low-pitched, with a distinct quaver. 'Dry, dusty air.' As if that explained everything.

Helen waited.

'I saw your advert. In the paper. For books.' Short sentences interspersed with loud gulps of air. 'I'm downsizing. Books need to go.'

Downsizing was one of the most frequent excuses Helen had received for those wanting to get rid of books. It was one that worked in her favour. They wanted rid; she wanted to acquire.

'Great,' she'd said. 'My shop isn't opening for another few days but I'm here almost every day if you'd like to drop them in.'

'I have quite a lot. Would it be possible for you to call around?'

The *quite a lot* had Helen perking up her ears. 'Yes, of course. I'm free on Friday, would that suit?'

'Perfectly.'

Helen raised an eyebrow as she scribbled down the name and address that was given to her in a stop-start fashion. It was in a very salubrious part of Bath. She hoped the books Mrs Clough wanted to give away wouldn't turn out to be a set of encyclopaedias. Or worse, two sets. Helen smothered a laugh and assured the lady she'd see her in a few days.

And here it was Friday afternoon already. Getting to her feet, she sighed. She should have asked Mrs Clough more questions. Like exactly how many books was 'quite a lot'. Optimistically, she opened the rear door of her car, unclipped the back seat and pushed it flat. If lots did indeed mean *lots*, she should have enough room. She climbed in and drove the short distance to Lansdown Road. Only a six-minute drive, but what a difference. Here, the traffic was lighter and the houses, set well back from the road, were huge detached and semi-detached mansions.

She pulled up outside Mrs Clough's house and stared through the open gate, then climbed out and walked up the short driveway to stone steps that led upward to the front door.

There was a bell set into the stone on one side. Feeling slightly, and stupidly apprehensive, Helen pressed once and heard it chime inside. Remembering the hesitant way the owner spoke, she wasn't expecting a quick response and jumped when the door was opened almost immediately.

It seemed to amuse the slightly built, elderly woman. 'I was waiting for you,' she said in explanation. 'I don't get many visitors these days.'

Helen felt herself being judged by small, blue eyes in a heavily powdered, lined face. She tried to look professional, trustworthy. Tried not to allow her gaze to linger on the woman's thick head of snowy-white hair. It had to be a wig, didn't it? Giving a nervous laugh, she reached into her pocket for a business card. 'Helen Appleby, Appleby Books,' she said, extending her hand with the card between her fingers.

It was taken and examined, front and back, before the woman nodded. 'I like your logo. It's clever. And cute.' Stepping backward in jerky steps, taking the door with her as she moved, Mrs Clough waved Helen into the house.

It struck her suddenly that nobody knew where she was. She hadn't told her sister or anybody else where she was going. The hallway behind the woman was poorly lit, gloomy even, all shadows and dark corners. It seemed to frame her and her oddly almost luminous white hair, making her appear unnatural and unreal.

Helen looked back towards the road. No cars or pedestrians were passing. If she shouted for help, nobody would come running. Her hand slid into her jacket pocket, fingers closing around her mobile. She could pull it out, pretend there was a call and quickly ring for help. But who would she ring? The police. And say what? That an elderly woman had invited her into her home. A woman Helen had made an appointment to see. Or she could ring her sister? She'd be more likely to understand but even she would raise one of her fashionably thick eyebrows and tell Helen to get a grip.

As if she was hearing her sister's caustic words, she mentally thumped herself on the forehead. Honestly, first Alex and Zander and now this poor old soul! Her experience with Toby had left her doubting everyone's motives. Everyone's actions. She had a sneaking suspicion she was drifting into paranoia. Convinced that every person she met was out to get her. She had to stop. Thanks to Toby, she'd lost years of her life; she refused to let him wreck any more. She also refused to listen to the little voice inside her head when it sniggered and asked, what about all Toby's years, the ones Helen had stolen? Guilt, with its loud, insistent voice that echoed painfully in her head, was a constant companion. She'd learnt not to ignore it, but to live with it. She had no choice.

Inside, the spacious hallway was not only gloomy, but chilly too. A mahogany coat rack sat in one corner, laden down with hats and coats. Helen shivered to see cobwebs stretching from the collar of one to the sleeve of another. Against the other wall, a dresser was laden with china figures. Dust lay thickly, lacy cobwebs swaying gently between them in the draft from the open door.

When it slammed shut behind her, Helen squealed, immediately rushing to cover her embarrassment by holding a hand over her mouth and coughing loudly. 'Sorry,' she said, waving her other hand in apology. 'I have a bit of asthma.' Did asthma make you cough? She'd no idea but her excuse seemed to have been accepted, Mrs Clough's powdered face now creased in concern.

'Can I get you a drink of water?'

Helen gave one more feeble cough before taking her hand away. 'No, thank you, I'm fine now.'

'It's a bit dusty in here; that wouldn't help.'

A bit dusty? If Helen lifted one of the figurines up, she guessed it would leave a quarter-inch hole in the dust on the dresser.

'Come through to the living room.' Mrs Clough crossed the hallway to one of the doors leading from it. She struggled for a moment with the doorknob, rattling it to and fro. 'Everything is falling apart,' she murmured. Then with a final twist, she turned it.

It opened into another gloomy room. Heavy curtains at the bay windows hung askew, one part open, one fully shut, cutting out most of the natural light. Dirt went a long way towards dimming the rest.

Some effort had been made. A very half-hearted one. The front surface of one of the dressers had been dusted, leaving a thick layer towards the back. There was only one small sofa in the room. Dents in the pile of the carpet showed that other furniture had been removed. Possibly part of the downsizing the woman had mentioned. Helen felt a wave of sorrow for her. She had probably lived there all her life and was being forced to sell up because she could no longer cope. Probably hadn't been for a long time. 'Thank you for contacting me, Mrs Clough,' she said, trying to keep the visit on a business footing.

'Oh please, call me Jen,' the woman said, smiling and waving Helen to the sofa. 'Take a seat. I'll go and make us some tea, then we can talk about my book collection.'

Book collection? Helen wanted to raise a hand, tell the woman she wasn't a book dealer in search of rare old books. She was simply a bookseller. Second-hand books from preference. Ones that had lived. That had been read by others. Books that had been sinned against by having the corners of their pages turned down. Ones where readers had scribbled words in the margins – words of disagreement, or agreement – or had signed the book, with love, to some friend or relative.

Before she could speak, the woman had vanished back into the hallway. Helen heard the rattle of another doorknob, and then silence.

Her eyes were growing accustomed to the dim lighting. Looking around, in an even darker corner of the room, she could make out the shape of boxes. Several piles, three deep. 'Shit,' she muttered. Five boxes at the most would fit into her hatchback. It was going to take several journeys to shift that lot.

With no sign of Mrs Clough returning, Helen got to her feet and crossed to the boxes, hoping to have a look inside, but they were taped shut. She wrapped her arms around the first box and lifted it. Heavy, but manageable. She couldn't, however, imagine the petite old woman hefting them up. She guessed she'd had help.

Leaving the boxes, she wandered to the other side of the room to where framed photographs lined a mantelpiece. Whoever had half-cleaned the dresser had made no effort here at all. Dust and strings of cobweb looped from one frame to the other like eerie Christmas decorations.

Amongst the display of black and white photos and faded colour ones, two more recent ones stood out in garish contrast. Putting Mrs Clough in her mid-eighties, she guessed the young man and woman by her side were grandchildren, perhaps even great-grandchildren. She hoped they were kind to the old woman. Perhaps it was they who were helping her to downsize.

'Here you are.' Mrs Clough came into the room bearing a tray.

Expecting posh china cups and saucers, Helen was almost amused to see bright-red melamine mugs, a small carton of milk, and garibaldi biscuits in an unopened packet.

When they were both sitting with a mug in their hands, Mrs Clough sat back. 'Tell me about this shop of yours.'

It was the perfect question, and as she spoke, all Helen's paranoia and fears eased. Books, that was where she was happiest. 'It's called Appleby Books. My opening day is on Monday.' She told her about finding the ideal premises and having it refurbished.

When she'd finished, Mrs Clough smiled. 'It sounds like a magical place. I can tell you love books as much as I do. My grand-nephew has no love for them, and he's the one who's helping me to pack up. If I left it to him, he'd throw the lot in a skip.'

Someone with no love for books. There was only one word. 'He's a Philistine.'

Mrs Clough smiled. 'That he is. When I saw your advert, it was the answer to all my prayers.'

'I can't afford to pay you much,' Helen said quickly. 'I'm not a book dealer, just a simple book seller. If you have first editions, or anything like that, you'd need to find an expert. Someone who could afford to pay you well.'

Mrs Clough shook her head. 'I've been an avid reader all my life. They're simply books I've loved. I'll be pleased to see them find a new home. To know they'll be loved by others.' She looked around the room, her eyes losing focus. 'I've lived here for sixty years. All my married life. My husband passed away four years ago. I suppose I haven't been coping since. I did have a cleaner but she left last year and I never bothered to replace her. Things, as you can see, have got worse. Now I'm heading to an apartment.' She gave a rueful smile. 'Sheltered accommodation. To keep me safe.'

The sadness in her voice was clear. It was the end of her life as she'd known it.

'I'm so sorry.'

Mrs Clough reached a slim, bony hand out and laid it on Helen's arm. 'So am I, my dear, so am I.' Then as if deciding it was time to get down to business, she pointed towards the boxes. 'Some you may find too old, but many were bought in the last few years when I didn't leave the house much and enjoyed reading even more.' She put her barely touched mug down and leaned back as if the conversation had taken the last of her strength.

'If you'll tell me how much you want for them, I'll see if I can afford it. It might be that I can only buy a portion of them.' It was a business; she had to be practical.

'Oh, no, my dear, you don't understand. I don't want payment. I simply want them gone so that Jared can't toss them in the rubbish.'

Free books! Helen looked across at the mountain of boxes. Even if half were rubbish, or God forbid, encyclopaedias, she was bound to find something she could sell. 'Are you sure? And your family won't mind you simply giving them away?'

Mrs Clough's expression changed from friendly to forbidding with a speed that had Helen gulp. It was as if a switch had been pressed. 'I may be old. I may even be frail. But what I am not is feeble-minded, so if you're worrying that you're taking advantage of some demented old woman, think again.' She shuffled to the edge of the sofa then used the arm of it to push to her feet. 'My grand-nephew will be delighted to see the boxes gone. It'll save him the cost of the skip he was threatening to hire.'

She stood glowering down at Helen for a moment before, as suddenly as it had appeared, the angry expression vanished. 'Take the books, my dear. Make your new business a success. Booklovers are good people; I'm glad to help even in such a small way.'

Helen hoped Mrs Clough would live out the remainder of her life, safe in the belief that all booklovers were good people. Helen knew differently. She loved books, the magic of the words between the covers, the ability to be whipped away to a different time and place, or for a few hours to become a different person, but it didn't by any definition of the word make her a good person.

There was no way she could explain to the deluded, frail, old woman, that books were what kept Helen from being swallowed up by the darkness that life kept throwing her way. The truth was, it wasn't so much that she loved books, as that she needed them.

9

It took two hours to move the sixteen boxes from the house on Lansdown Road to the shop, and it was almost six o'clock before Helen arrived with the last of them. Exhausted as she was, the last thing she needed was to see a woman standing outside the shop, phone in her hand, thumb flying across the screen as she sent messages to goodness knows who.

They weren't sent to her. Helen checked her phone just in case, relieved to see only messages from her sister. She wasn't expecting a visit from this woman. She didn't want one either. Contrary to the friendly manner the parole officer always tried to exude, Moira Manson was not her friend.

Helen couldn't sit in her car all evening. 'Hi,' she said, as she climbed out, trying to sound friendly. 'I'm sorry, was I expecting you?' Helen was three months out of prison. For the first four weeks, Moira had checked in with her every week. That dropped to fortnightly in the second and third month. Now, she should only have to see the irritating woman once a month till the end of her licence in twenty-one months.

She'd seen her last two weeks before, so she shouldn't be

there that day. Shouldn't be at her shop at all. Helen had asked for the visits to take place at her home; she didn't want this woman contaminating her new life with dark colours from her past.

Moira finished tapping on her phone and smiled. 'It's not an official visit; I wanted to come to wish you every success with this amazing bookshop.'

'Thank you.' *Now go away.* 'If there's nothing else, I need to get these boxes unpacked.' She sounded rude. Dismissive. She didn't care. They were not friends. She hoped Moira would get the message and leave. Instead, to her annoyance, she nodded towards the packed car.

'Looks like you might need a hand with that lot. I'm stronger than I look.'

Before Helen could argue, before she could tell her that she didn't want help, didn't want her paws on her precious books, Moira had pulled open the back passenger door and was hauling out a box.

'Come on then, get the shop door open.'

Helen took a deep breath as she felt her teeth grate and her blood pressure rise. She'd be foolish to alienate a woman who had so much power over her for months to come. Nodding, she walked to the front door, inserted the key in the lock, and pushed it open.

'No alarm?' Moira said from behind her. 'That's a bit risky, isn't it?'

It was. Helen didn't need to be told. She'd planned to get one but had baulked at the cost and decided to put it off until she could afford it. She'd justified her decision by thinking, who would want to break into a second-hand bookshop? Nobody would be that desperate for a book to read. 'It's on my list of things to do,' she said, annoyed at having to explain.

'Okay, where do you want me to put this?'

Much as she wanted to get rid of her unwelcome guest, since she had pushed herself in, it seemed sensible to make use of her. 'Upstairs, if you don't mind.' Helen indicated the stairway, then returned to the car to pick up the next box.

'I'll get the next,' Moira said, meeting her on the way in.

Helen trudged up the stairs, dropped the box on top of another and turned to go back down, stopping as she heard footsteps approaching.

'There's just one left. I'll wait here for you,' Moira said, placing the box she held carefully on top of the pile.

Helen didn't want her to wait. She didn't want her there, full stop. But short of telling the supervisor to fuck off out of her shop – something she yearned to do but wasn't quite that stupid, or at least not yet – she pulled her lips into some semblance of a smile, turned without comment and took the steps down in twos.

When she returned, only minutes later, she was incensed to find Moira had pulled open the box she'd brought up and was rifling through the contents.

'Find anything interesting?'

Moira either didn't hear or, which was more likely, chose to ignore the heavy sarcasm in the words. 'Not in this one, nor in that one.' She indicated the box on top of the pile beside her with a jerk of her chin.

The cow had opened two! 'But then again, you don't know what interests me.' Helen shut the flaps of the box, giving Moira little choice but to withdraw her hands. 'I want to stock a wide variety, so I'm sure I can find a good home for all of these.'

'Some of them are quite old. Are you thinking of going into rare books?'

For Helen, books were to be read, not to be put in glass cases and handled with cotton gloves, treasured for their antiquity rather than their words. 'No, I've no knowledge or interest in that side of things at all.'

'Very wise to stick to what you know.' Moira looked around at the stacks of boxes. 'I can stay and give you a hand if you like. I'd like to think I'm a friend, not simply your community offender manager.'

Was it written down somewhere in a book called *How to be a Good COM* that she should treat the ex-con as a friend? Had she been completely fooled by Helen's forced cordial manner into thinking they'd developed a more personal relationship? Or was it simply that Helen was a very, very good actress? She always had been, but since Toby, she'd become Oscar-winning material. 'That's kind, thank you, but I'm going to call it a day and head home.'

'Okay.' Moira looked around the room. 'You've done a great job with this place. I read the details on the estate agent's website when it was for sale.'

Checking up on her. Helen had always been a private person. From necessity. It was galling to think this woman had a right to peer and pry into her life. Her smile became a painful rictus as she waited for Moira to finally leave.

Downstairs, there was more delay as she asked to see the garden. 'It looked like a big space on the website.'

Unable to think of a valid reason for not showing her. *Get out, please, go away and leave me some shred of privacy* didn't seem a rational thing to say, so Helen kept the increasingly painful smile in place and led the way to the rear of the building. Throwing open the back door, she waved a hand over the garden. 'It was an overgrown mess. I've chopped a lot down but haven't had the time to do more with it as yet.' She wasn't going to share her plans. These at least, she was able to keep secret.

Thankfully, Moira didn't suggest exploring the garden, merely casting an eye over it before returning to the front of the shop. 'Well, I'd better head. You've done a great job on this. Best of luck with it. I'll try and call back on your opening day. Monday, isn't it?'

It was. A day Helen had been looking forward to for so long. She refused to let this blasted woman spoil it. It was time, she decided, to spell things out. Politely, but firmly. 'That's not necessary, but thank you. To be honest, and I'm sure you'll understand, I would like to keep my new life separate from my old. To not allow mistakes I've made in the past colour my future. Do you understand?' *Please understand. Understand, go away and leave me in peace.*

'Mistakes you've made in the past?' Moira lifted her hand to cup her chin and tapped her lips with her forefinger. 'Hmmm,' she said, her gaze piercing Helen. 'It worries me slightly that you consider murdering someone as being a mistake.' She held the pose for a moment before dropping her hand and wagging her head. 'Let's put it down to the stress of starting your new business, shall we?'

And then she was gone, and Helen was left standing in the middle of her dream business with thoughts of murder dancing around her head. And she hated Moira for that. For bringing her back to a place she desperately wanted and needed to leave behind.

Helen wasn't a violent person. Killing Toby had been an aberration. A one off. Or maybe he'd been the final straw. But he'd also been a full stop. That life was over.

She'd no intention of killing again.

10

Helen waited until she saw the car pull away before she relaxed her grip on the doorway and turned to go back inside. She had shut the door, when she was startled by a face suddenly appearing in the glass panel. An old, rather wizened face that immediately reminded her of the old woman she'd met earlier. Perhaps that was why she opened the door again instead of pointing to the closed sign that hung halfway down.

'Am I too late?' In contrast to the frail physique, the voice was firm and slightly too loud. 'I'm completely out of reading material.'

How could Helen resist such a heartfelt plea? Instead of pointing out that, rather than being too late, the woman was a few days early, she stood back and beckoned her to come inside. 'You can have a look around, if you like, but I'm not officially open till Monday.'

'That's very kind,' the woman said, hurrying inside as if afraid Helen was going to change her mind. 'Is it your place?'

'It is.'

'I like the name, and the logo.'

Helen flushed with pleasure. 'It seemed like a good idea to make the most of my surname. Eventually, I'm hoping to have tote bags, mugs and other items printed with the logo too.'

The woman smiled with little enthusiasm and with a nod, wandered across to the half-filled shelves. Helen tried not to be offended. Not everyone was going to be interested in buying book-related items.

'I've not got much stock out yet, so you might not find what you're looking for. Perhaps,' she said, moving to join her, 'if you tell me what kind of books you like, I might be able to help.'

'That's very kind. My name is Joyce, by the way, Joyce Evans.'

'Nice to meet you, Mrs Evans.'

'Joyce will do.' She bent to look at the books on a lower shelf before straightening and turning back to Helen. 'I like more literary books.'

Unfortunately, the first few boxes Helen had opened were all genre fiction – mostly crime. 'I have some boxes upstairs that I haven't had a chance to open yet. Hang on, I'll grab a few books from them, see if anything appeals.' She hurried away before Joyce had a chance to reply. Suddenly, it seemed stupidly important to make this first sale.

The parole officer had, unbeknownst to her, made things easy for Helen. With two boxes already open, she simply grabbed several books from the top of each and returned to the ground floor in the hope that her unexpected first customer would still be there.

She was, flicking through the pages of a book with a curled-up lip. She put it down when Helen appeared and wiped one hand with the other as if she'd been contaminated. When Helen glanced at the title, she had to swallow the burst of laughter. She'd debated whether to bother putting *Fifty Shades of Grey* on the shelf or not, she wasn't sure she could give it away, but then who was she to judge other people's reading taste. It definitely wasn't likely to be this neat, dainty woman's cuppa.

'Here you go,' she said, putting the pile of books on the desk. 'You might find something here you'd like.' She spread them out. Books by Ernest Hemingway, Henry James, Kazuo Ishiguro and others. Mrs Clough had read widely and by the looks of things, her taste ran to more literary works. 'I hope these appeal more.'

'Some of my favourite writers,' Joyce said, her hand hovering over the books, picking them up, reading the blurb, putting them down.

Helen wasn't in a hurry. It was relaxing to watch someone who obviously loved reading. It soothed her thoughts, putting Moira Manson's visit to the back of her mind.

'I'll take these four.'

'Good choice,' Helen said, although she hadn't read any of the books the woman had chosen. 'Hemingway never lets you down, does he?'

'*A Farewell to Arms* is one of my favourite books. But these are short stories,' Joyce said, tapping the cover. 'I haven't read them.'

A horrifying thought hit Helen. 'I'm so sorry, I don't have any bags as yet.'

Joyce smiled as she reached into her pocket and pulled out a plastic carrier bag. 'I never go anywhere without one. On a pension, I can't afford to be paying out for bags every time I go to the supermarket.'

On a pension. It was coming to the part Helen knew she'd find difficult. The part where she had to remind herself it was a business, not a charity. She had been toying with an idea but hadn't worked out the nitty gritty of it yet. She did now, as the rather watery, pale-blue eyes fixed on her face. She picked up one of her business cards, wrote the day's date on the reverse along with the titles of the four books. 'The books are two pounds each,' she said. 'But I have a special offer, if you'd like to avail of it.' She handed the woman the business card. 'When someone buys four, which you're doing, if they bring them back within two weeks, in the same good condition, they can exchange them for four more with no charge. If you want to keep one or more of the books, you can exchange the ones you don't want to keep.' She held her breath as she waited to see if the offer was acceptable. It was a good one. To make money from it, she was depending on readers wanting to keep books they particularly liked, or to give them to others to read. If they came back to exchange one, they would be tempted to buy more. 'You'll need to bring the card back with you to activate the offer.'

'I think that's a very good offer indeed.'

Helen had a moment of panic as she watched her fumble inside her handbag. Until she figured it out, she couldn't offer credit card payment. She was about to apologise when Joyce pulled out a purse, opened it, took out a handful of two-pound coins and put four on the counter. 'There you go. Eight pounds.' She put her purse away, piled the books neatly into her carrier bag, then held her hand out to Helen. 'I'm guessing I'm your first customer. You'll do well, I'm sure of it.'

Helen shut and locked the door after her. She turned, jangling the four coins in her hand. This... this feeling was the one she wanted to hold on to. This was her future.

She had to make sure her past, and Moira Manson with it, stayed exactly where it was.

11

Helen pulled a ledger from under the desk and opened it. Her first sale. There should be some sort of a ceremony. She picked up a pen and wrote the eight pounds in neat figures. She had an accounting programme set up on her laptop. She had debated bringing it in but had decided, in the end, to use a written ledger. It went better with the old-fashioned vibe she hoped she'd captured. She planned on shutting the shop all day Sunday and Wednesday afternoons. Sometime in those two days, she'd input the figures from the ledger. That was the plan. But it wasn't writ in stone. It seemed safer to be a bit dynamic for the first few months, see how things went. Change when necessary.

She ran her hand over the smooth page, then shut the ledger and put it away in one of the drawers under the desk. The books were calling to her. So were the empty shelves. She was physically tired from the weeks of getting the shop ready to open, and from that morning's work hauling heavy boxes about, but it was the visit from her supervisor that had sapped her energy.

Deciding she'd done enough, she tidied a few things away. It was only then that she realised what she hadn't done with the books she'd sold to Mrs Evans: she hadn't stamped her logo on the inside. She had to remember to do that if they were returned.

The woman had seemed pleased with the book exchange offer. Helen needed to make it official. Maybe have a few flyers made up to promote it. But that was a job for another day. Probably in a week or two when she had everything else sorted.

Remembering to bring the remainder of the pizza with her, she locked up and headed home.

There, she grabbed a beer from the fridge, slumped on the sofa and switched on the TV. She'd never been a big drinker. It had been no hardship to do without during her years in prison, but there was something very satisfying about the taste of chilled beer straight from the bottle. The pizza too tasted just as good cold as it had earlier.

She hoped to be able to switch off, but the disaster movie she'd chosen, dramatic as it was, wasn't capturing her attention. There was still so much to do. She had lists, of course, and ticked things off as they were done. Nothing had been forgotten. It would all be good and would be a success. And she'd be happy.

She could be happy without pain. Physical or emotional. She'd turned a corner. Toby's death had held a mirror up, no, not a mirror, a magnifying glass, and she'd seen herself, the cold, hard truth of her and she'd hated what she was. She had seen, she had changed, and she would be happy.

She'd managed to convince herself of this by the time the pizza was gone, and the beer bottle empty.

But when she slept, the dream came. Not the brief, reduced flicker of red and the glint of sharp knives she'd almost become inured to. No, this time, it was Toby as he had been in their early days together, in the days when she thought he'd understood. In the days when she believed he loved her, and she him. And when he raised the belt and brought it down on her back, there was a gentleness in the act, an understanding. And Helen felt the pain, felt the pleasure, cried out as a deep, intense orgasm throbbed through her, waking as it ebbed, crying out, this time in disgust at herself.

Self-loathing was a vicious whip. The physical and mental pain of it far more damaging than the belt Toby had used on her or the words he'd whispered in her ear in the months before his death. *Sick weirdo. Depraved bitch. Pathetic slut.*

Perhaps Sarah had been right and it would have been better to have moved from a house that still carried the echoes of his words and her deed. Once the business was going smoothly, if she was still having problems it might be something to consider.

Toby's words echoing in her ears prevented Helen getting back to sleep. She lay there with her eyes shut and waited for morning to come. The antidote to self-loathing was to think of her precious shop and the plans she had.

Thinking of her customer from the evening before, she thought it mightn't be any harm to get some change, just in case. More people were using credit cards, but many of the older generation still preferred cash. If she was inundated with twenty-pound notes, she'd be in trouble. The optimism made her smile. The shop wasn't going to be a goldmine; she understood that. All she needed was to make enough to pay the bills, feed herself, buy the odd beer. Fashion wasn't her thing and she mostly bought what she needed in charity shops.

The credit card situation had to be sorted. She'd purchased a card reader but she hadn't looked at it as yet. Plus, she wanted to try it out, make sure she knew what she was doing before using it live on Monday.

By the time morning came, concentrating on the shop and her plans, she loathed herself a little less. It had been a bad night, that was all. It wasn't a step backwards. That period of her life was done.

After a quick breakfast, since there were no book collections planned, she walked to the shop. It was two days before the grand opening on Monday. She needed to get the remainder of the shelves on the main shop floor filled. If necessary, she'd bring a few books down from upstairs. The delivery of the paper bags was due too. Buying in bulk being much cheaper, she'd ordered four hundred. They'd go into the smallest upstairs bedroom that had been shelved for storage.

She was standing in the shop with a mug of coffee in her hand, frowning over which box to open first, when she heard a knock on the door and looked up to see Alex's face peering in. He waved when he saw her looking.

'Hi,' she said, opening the door. 'You want a coffee? It's not as good as yours, though.'

'No, I'm good, ta.' He wasn't smiling, which was unusual in itself, but he was also hesitating which, from the little she knew of him, also wasn't the norm.

'Is something wrong?'

He lifted a short, blunt-fingered hand and see-sawed it. 'Not sure. Last night, 'bout eleven, I was staring out the window when the security lights came on. If I hadn't been looking out, I probably wouldn't have seen the person who was at your door. As soon as the lights came on, they scarpered.'

Helen felt the first kick of fear. 'At my door?'

'Right up against it, as if they were trying to open it. Dressed in black, they were. Wearing a hoodie, the uniform of every bloody tea leaf as far as I can see.'

Fear, and now confusion. 'Tea leaf?'

'Thief, darlin', try to keep up.'

It would help if he didn't drift into Cockney rhyming slang. 'So you think some thief was trying to break in here?' She looked around the room. 'It's a second-hand bookshop. What's to steal?'

Alex held his hands up. 'Not a scooby-do. I'm just telling you what I saw.' He reached for the door and tapped it. 'Only a Yale lock. You need to beef up your security. You wouldn't believe what these tea leaves would consider valuable.'

He was making her head ache. Or maybe it was the thought that someone had been trying to break into her precious shop. She read the papers, watched the news, knew what mindless damage they could do. 'I can't believe someone would want to break in to steal books.'

He was looking at her as if she was an idiot. Perhaps she was.

'I suppose they were looking for money, or computers, or anything they could sell.'

'That'd be about it, darlin'.'

'But you haven't ever been broken into.' She'd asked when they'd first met, relieved to hear they hadn't. It had been one of the reasons she'd thought she could dispense with the ridiculously expensive alarm system. It had also been the reason she'd kept the old wooden door with the glass panel instead of replacing it with a uPVC one. It hadn't been in too bad a condition and a coat of paint had transformed it – and saved her hundreds of pounds.

'We haven't, but then we live over our place whereas your shop is obviously empty from when you leave.'

'Yes, of course, that'd make a difference.' She rubbed her cheeks with her two hands. 'I can get a locksmith to put a mortice lock on the door. That'd help, wouldn't it?' She wanted him to say, yes, that'd be ideal. Wanted someone to tell her that everything was going to be all right. When he said nothing, she sighed. 'I can't afford to get an alarm system installed. Not yet. I guess the next best thing is to do what you're doing. Live upstairs.' It wouldn't work long term; she hadn't renovated it to be living quarters. Anyway, the plan was to have it as a sales floor and eventually a space for hosting book clubs and author chats. It would be a short-term solution until she could afford an alarm system. No damn bastard was going to break into her shop.

'You're going to do what?' Her sister squealed down the line when she rang later to ask how it was all going.

'Move in upstairs until I can afford to buy an alarm.'

'That's ridiculous!'

It wasn't. It was the sensible solution. There was a toilet and a wash-handbasin upstairs, and a small kitchen downstairs. The cushions from her sofa at home would make a decent bed. 'It's a temporary measure.' If she told her sister what Alex had seen, it would worry her so she took the easy way out and said nothing.

'I thought you were okay for money.'

There was an element of criticism in the words that stung, as if Helen had somehow misled her. 'I am, but that doesn't mean I don't have to be careful.' There wasn't any point in telling her sister that her credit card was teetering near its max. 'Once I have money coming in, everything will be fine.'

'If you're sure.' Sarah didn't seem convinced.

'Positive, thank you. Now, more importantly, what time are you going to be here on Monday?' Sarah had volunteered to provide cupcakes for the opening day. Those and a glass of wine would, Helen hoped, entice customers through the door. The wine and glasses were courtesy of Alex and Zander. Not free, but at a hugely discounted rate. Sarah had suggested using plastic to save the washing but Helen wanted to fly her sustainable credentials from the start. No plastic cups, no plastic bags.

It took more time than she expected, and far more than she had to spare, to find a locksmith. Unfortunately, they couldn't come till the following morning. And annoyingly, it was going to cost a lot more than she'd expected.

'That's very expensive,' she said, pressing her mobile to her ear.

'Tomorrow's Sunday.' As if that explained it.

'Could you come before nine on Monday?'

'Before nine? That'd be out of hours, so it'd be the same price as Sunday.'

Helen's grip tightened further. 'So how much would it cost to do it on Tuesday?'

Almost half the price. Still more than she had hoped to pay, but a lot better. 'Right, can you come to do it on Tuesday then, please?'

'I need to take a deposit,' he said. 'We get our fair share of time wasters.'

'No problem.' She read out her credit card number, ignoring the squeal she was sure she heard as it fell over into red territory.

Until she had the new lock, she could wedge a chair under the door handle at night. It should serve to deter any intruders. With that problem sorted, she concentrated on getting books on shelves. She worked steadily, taking an inordinate amount of pleasure to see the rows build. The pile of rejects, books she wouldn't put on her shelves, was luckily small. A few were simply too worn to sell; a couple were the kind of erotica she didn't fancy stocking. That kind of clientele wasn't one she wanted to encourage.

At two, she took a break. Taking a mug of coffee with her, she went into the garden and sat to enjoy the sunshine. The day after tomorrow, her new life was going to begin. She deserved it. Shutting her eyes, she rested her head against the wall behind. Her past was a nasty ulcer that was never going to heal, the night's dream had proved that, so she should stop fooling herself.

All she could hope for was that it would scab over yet again and keep the lies she'd told hidden.

12

Instead of going back to work when she'd finished her coffee, Helen decided to go home and get everything she needed for what might be a protracted stay in the bookshop. If the launch was a success, if she managed to lure students through the door, and if people living nearby called in regularly, then she'd have the money to pay for an alarm and things could return to normal. There was a lot of uncertainty. She needed to stay strong for a month. Maybe two. It wasn't ideal, but she was good at making do. Luckily, with her home and business so close, she could pop home for a shower whenever she wanted. Her house had an alarm. Not a fancy monitored one, but one that blasted such a shrill noise that it would be sufficient to frighten the bravest of burglars away.

She had taken a few steps in the direction of home when she remembered the change she'd planned to get for Monday's deluge of customers waving twenty-pound notes. The thought made her smile again. The post office was a short walk in the opposite direction. If she walked quickly, she'd just about make it before it shut.

There was a queue as usual and she shuffled restlessly from foot to foot, wondering if she should bother. But then she was there, and minutes later she was speed walking home with twenty pounds in coins rattling in her pockets, her head spinning with thoughts of all she had yet to do.

At home, it took longer than she'd expected to load the car with everything she might need. She debated taking the TV but it was an old-fashioned, chunky model that would take up too much room in the car so she left it behind. By the time she'd brought out the cushions from the sofa, a suitcase packed with clothes and various other bits and pieces she thought she might need, the car was full.

With time ticking by far faster than she liked, she was in an irritable mood as she drove the short distance back to the shop and parked directly outside.

She'd started to open the car door when she stopped, her eyes fixed on the shop. Had she been stupid enough, or distracted enough, to have left without shutting the door properly after her? Surely not, yet ajar it was.

She'd only been gone an hour and a half. But she, more than most people, knew what horrors could occur in less time than that. Life ending, life altering ones. Was it happening again? In a daze, she opened the car door and stepped out. It crossed her mind that she should give Alex or Zander a shout to go inside with her. Just to be on the safe side. Or she could pull out her mobile and ring the police. And say what? That her shop door was open?

She pressed the fob to lock the car, then moved forward, slowly, hesitantly. Sun shining on the windows prevented her from seeing inside until she was closer. There didn't appear to be anyone there. Maybe she had simply left the door open. Could she really have been that stupid?

Yes, of course she could. Being stupid had got her sent to prison.

She stopped beside the door and peered through the gap. There was nobody to be seen. That meant nothing. If there was an intruder, they could be upstairs, in the back room or the kitchen. They could be picnicking in her damn back garden.

'Hello?' Her voice quavered. If there was someone there, if someone had broken in, did she really think they were going to reply? She checked the Yale lock. It wasn't broken, the wood around it intact. She remembered hearing that these type of locks could be easily opened with a credit card, but she'd always assumed that was a myth.

She had too much to do to be hovering, worrying if the bogeyman was there waiting or not. Pushing the door open, the jangle of the bell startled her. If there was someone loitering inside, they'd have heard it too. She stepped forward and stopped again with her head slightly tilted, listening, hoping that if there was an intruder, they weren't out of sight doing exactly the same thing. If they were, they were a lot more patient than she.

Leaving the door open behind her, she took a few more steps, her eyes flitting between the stairway and the entrance to the kitchen. She was so fixated on watching for an intruder that it was a couple of seconds before she noticed what had happened in her absence. When she did, when she realised what someone had done, she sank to her knees with a keening cry. All the books – all her carefully positioned books – had been swept from the shelves and lay higgledy-piggledy on the floor.

She buried her face in her hands, letting the tears come, hiding the mess from sight. It wasn't until her legs were numb that she got to her feet, pins and needles making her stagger. She searched her pockets for a tissue. When she couldn't find one, she pulled up the bottom of her T-shirt and wiped her eyes and nose.

Dry eyes didn't change what she was seeing. Hours of work she'd have to do again.

And she would. Anger had replaced the shock. Anger was better. It would get her through this, as it had got her through worse times. This time, she'd control it, though, wouldn't let it carry her too far. Not this time. She wasn't going back to prison.

Whoever had broken in had obviously left. It was time to have a look to see what further damage had been done. A quick glance into the kitchen told her nothing there had been disturbed. That left upstairs. The desire to call out again was as pointless as it was impossible to prevent, her 'Hello?' echoing in the empty space as she climbed the stairs, one careful step at a time.

She half-expected to see the boxes upended and the contents strewn across the floor, so was surprised, and relieved, to see they were untouched. The smallest bedroom had been converted into a storage room, shelved along one wall. The key was in the door but as yet there had been no need to lock it. It had, however, been opened. All that was stored there was a box of books too old, worn and tatty to be saleable. It was destined for the recycling centre at some stage. It had been toppled to the floor, the rejected books making a sad heap.

Helen scooped them back into the box and shoved it into a corner. Only as she walked down the stairs, and felt the coins rattle in her pocket, did she remember the four coins Mrs Evans had given her. She'd put them in an old tin tea caddy and left it in a desk drawer.

To her surprise, the tea caddy was still there, untouched. Exactly where she'd left it. What kind of burglar was it that wasn't interested in money? Even such a paltry sum.

Putting the thought to the back of her mind, she rested a hand on her forehead as she wondered where to begin. Thinking of her personal belongings packed into the car, she thought it was better to start there. With such gougers around, it made sense.

It took longer than it should have done. She stood for a long time at the shop door, staring through the glass panel to see if there was anyone suspicious on the street. The car was only a few feet away, but she couldn't bring herself to leave the door open in fear of someone bursting inside. The unloading was slow and laborious as a result.

She was on the last run, the car locked behind her, when Zander came out of the pizzeria, wielding a broom. Every day, on the dot of five, he came out and swept the pavement in front of the restaurant. 'Hello,' he called, giving her a wave.

'Hi.' Her smile must have been unconvincing because he immediately came over, an expression of concern creasing his face. 'You've been crying.'

She'd tried to stop but every time she saw the jumble of books spread over the floor, more tears came. She dropped the bags she was holding, pulled a tissue from her pocket, wiped her eyes and blew her nose. 'I had to go out for a while and unfortunately, I had a visitor while I was gone. They made a bit of a mess.'

'No!' He leaned the broom against the wall, then patted her arm clumsily. 'Have you called the police?'

She shook her head. 'There was nothing worth stealing and apart from knocking all the books from the shelves, they didn't do any damage. There's nothing the police can do, and I don't have time to waste dealing with them.' She didn't need the police to call around to tell her the obvious: that she needed both a new lock and an alarm. Anyway, she'd had her fill of police and prison officers.

She saw a knowing look appear in his eyes, and for the first time realised that the brothers knew about her past. She should have guessed of course. Her neighbours used the pizzeria, and although they were pleasant and always said hello when they saw her, she knew she'd caused tongues to wag with her return. 'I'd better get on,' she said, picking up the bags she'd dropped.

'Let me help you,' Zander said, taking one of the heavy carrier bags from her hand and waiting while she unlocked the shop door. 'Gawd, what a mess!' He dropped the bag on the floor beside the rest of her belongings and took in the jumble of books. 'I wish I could stay and help but we're just about to open, and Alex can't manage on his own.'

'Thanks, Zander, but I'll be fine. Alex probably told you I'm going to move in upstairs for a bit. Just till I can get better security.' She managed to drag up a smile. 'Probably as well, I've no excuse now for not getting the place sorted by Monday.'

'You need anything, you just come running in to us, okay?' He patted her arm again. 'Tell you what, I'll drop you in a pizza and coffee in a couple of hours, how's that?'

'That'd be great. But I'll pay for it, thanks.'

He shook his head. 'This time, it's on us.' He waved a hand and left.

She was sorry to see him go. Anger surged towards the unknown person who had broken in. Not only had they ruined hours of work, but they'd tainted the air of her shop and made her suddenly nervous of being alone. One thing was for certain: getting a proper lock on the door was now a priority.

She rang the company she'd contacted earlier. 'I've had a break-in; it seems I don't have the luxury of waiting till Tuesday. Is there any way you could fit a new lock tonight?'

'Sounds like it's an emergency. We always make room for those.'

It was more money than she had in her account. But the break-in had convinced her it was essential. Anyway, what was the point in having an overdraft if she wasn't going to use it?

True to their word, the locksmith arrived thirty minutes later. He raised an eyebrow at the books scattered across the floor but didn't comment. 'Have it done in a jiffy,' he said.

Less than an hour later, the door sported a solid and hopefully effective lock. Only when Helen had the key turned in it, did she feel safe enough to turn her back to the door and begin the task of restoring order to the shelves. Once it was done, her mood might improve.

She was almost finished, her back aching from the bending, when a tap on the front door startled her and she stumbled forward onto the few books that remained on the floor. She came down heavily onto her knees, wide eyes fixed on the face at the door, only then making out the round face as friend rather than foe.

A round, startled face.

Afraid he'd break through the door to rush to her aid, she lifted a hand and gave a wave to reassure him she was all right, then struggled to her feet. 'It's been one of those days,' she said when she'd unlocked the door and pulled it open.

Zander came through with a pizza box in one hand, a coffee balanced precariously on top. 'I thought I'd have to break the door down to ride to your rescue. You sure you're okay?'

Helen rubbed her knees and grimaced. 'I won't be wearing a mini skirt for a while.'

'I brought you your usual and a coffee, as promised.' He put them on the desk and turned to look at her. 'Glad to see you've got a decent lock now. Give you some reassurance.' He glanced down at the remaining books on the floor. 'You worked hard; you must be knackered.'

'I'm pretty exhausted all right.' She nodded to where the pizza sat, the aroma tantalising. 'Thanks for that.'

'I could get you some wine or a beer, if you fancied either. On the house.'

It was a tempting offer. 'That's really kind.' It was, they were good neighbours, nice guys; she wished she wasn't so ridiculously wary of them. 'I think I'll stick to coffee though; I still have quite a bit to do.'

'If you change your mind, you know where we are.' He left, waving his hand over his head. And she was alone again and, despite the new lock, still feeling anxious and edgy. Perhaps she should have accepted the offer of a beer. She considered going next door to get one and immediately rejected the idea. It would mean going outside where twilight and streetlights had changed the street she knew so well into something moody and unknown.

She'd been the victim of some thug taking advantage of her absence. That was all. It was nothing personal. She should try to forget about it. It's not as if there were a line of thugs hiding in the shadows waiting to break in. But there was the person Alex had seen the previous night; she shouldn't forget that.

Although the blinds were down on the windows, there wasn't one on the door, and conscious that someone could peer through the glass panel, she took the pizza and coffee upstairs. Two bucket chairs had been placed in the corner of the room with a small table between them. It was destined for future readers to sit and relax. It was also a perfect place to sit and eat.

She was on her third slice of pizza before the volume of the worries increased. It was nothing personal? Did she really believe that? Could she? That some opportunistic thug simply happened to come by during the couple of hours she was gone? How did they know there wasn't someone there? Upstairs, or in the kitchen?

Were they sure there wasn't because they'd been watching her?

Was the person who broke in the same person who'd been at her door the previous night?

The money in the tea caddy was the other puzzle. Okay, it was only eight pounds, but wouldn't a thief have taken it?

Unless it hadn't been money they'd been after at all.

Perhaps someone didn't want the ex-con to succeed. Didn't want a murderer in their midst. Her neighbours had been pleasant to her face, but what were they saying behind her back? Were they plotting to get rid of her?

She couldn't allow that to happen...

13

Helen's appetite evaporated as various thoughts ricocheted in her head. It was increasingly difficult to pin them down to probable or highly unlikely. The thought that she was becoming paranoid struck her again, and worried her even more. She finished her coffee, brought the remains of the pizza down to the kitchen and put it into the fridge.

Her mobile chirped with a message. Her sister, checking that everything was okay. It was tempting to ring her back, tell her that nothing was okay. Tell her about the shadowy figure outside the previous night, the break-in that day; that Helen was a nervous wreck, and desperately afraid everything was going to be a disaster. That maybe her sister had been right and returning to the area had been a bad idea; that she was scared someone was trying to make sure she wouldn't succeed.

But she was afraid her sister would reply with some version of I told you so, and Helen couldn't handle that.

In that second, she hated whoever had broken in with a passion that left her seething with frustrated anger.

For a few seconds, her thumb hovered over the key to call her sister but she couldn't do it, couldn't put herself in the helpless younger sister position again. Instead, she tapped out a quick message to say how well everything was going and that she'd see her bright and early Monday morning. She switched her phone off in case Sarah decided to ring because Helen wasn't sure she could speak without releasing the pent-up anxiety.

It took only a few minutes to finish reshelving the last of the books, then she set about putting away her belongings. She used the sofa cushions to make a bed in the corner of the upstairs space and spent several frustrating minutes trying to find where she'd put the bed linen and duvet. Her clothes were either left in the suitcase or placed on the shelves in the storage room.

She should be feeling good. Excited about this new venture. Everything was in place and she still had a full day to spare to figure out the credit-card reader and to arrange a window display to entice passers-by. She'd stuck coming-soon posters on the window a few weeks before. Devon's carpenter friend had done a brilliant job on extending the windowsill inside to provide her with a display area. She'd placed pillars of different heights along its length and had propped a plain white card on top of each with a simple ? in black ink. She'd hoped it would be tantalising; she wondered now if it had been a mistake. Perhaps she should have simply put books on them.

She was trying to keep her mind occupied so her thoughts wouldn't drift back to the earlier break-in. Several times, she found herself at the window, checking the street outside, looking up and down in both directions as far as she could. There were plenty of people to be seen – after all, it was a busy area – but most walked past with their eyes fixed on the path ahead. Only the occasional person gave her window more than a cursory glance.

Once the pizzeria shut at eleven, there was only the rare

pedestrian. Even the traffic quietened down. Helen tried to get into sleep mode. She brushed her teeth, cleaned her face and changed into pyjamas, but when she looked at the makeshift bed she knew she wasn't going to be able to sleep. Not yet.

It wasn't going to help, but she made herself a mug of coffee. She dragged one of the bucket chairs to the upstairs window and sat, sipping the coffee, her eyes sliding up and down the street almost of their own volition. She was being silly. The idea that it was something personal was paranoia. It had been some opportunistic scrag-end, that was all. She shouldn't let the little shit win twice by making her so anxious.

But she couldn't get that damn eight pounds out of her head. Why hadn't they taken it? It came back to the same thought she'd had earlier – because it wasn't money they'd been after. She let her thoughts loose to puzzle over that as she sipped her coffee. If it had never been about theft, if it was about making her feel uneasy, scared, worried. Then they... whoever they were... had succeeded.

But if she was right. If that was it, the million-dollar question was why?

Simply to get rid of her? She couldn't picture any of her elderly neighbours going to the trouble. Anyway, she thought they sort-of liked her notoriety. It gave them something to talk about.

Her fingers tightened on the handle of the mug, her expression hardening. Could it be Alex and Zander, her ever-so-helpful neighbours? No, she shook her head. They couldn't be that devious, that sick and twisted. Could they? She'd been suspicious when they'd said they hadn't been interested in buying her shop to expand their next-door pizzeria. Perhaps the bastards were playing a long and clever game. She'd spent money doing the place up. If the business failed, if she had to sell up now, she'd probably be grateful to take whatever she could get. A low offer from her kind neighbours.

But they had no idea what she was made of. What she'd been through to get where she was. They didn't know that she was never going to lose again.

14

Whether it was the surfeit of coffee or the anger that rolled through her in ever-increasing waves, it was almost daylight before Helen lay down on her bed in the corner. And then she couldn't sleep. The space was too open, uncurtained windows on both sides increasing her nervousness. She tried to laugh away her fears. Burglars didn't usually walk on stilts, and she doubted Spiderman was interested in her.

Her attempts at rationalising her fears failed. She struggled to her feet and dragged cushions, bed linen and duvet into the storage room. There was just enough floor space and when she turned the key in the lock, for the first time that night she felt safe and fell into a restless sleep. It might have been that the old trauma in her life would be replaced by new ones, perhaps by sinister bodies sneaking up on her, but that wasn't to be. It was Toby's blood-smeared body that appeared. So much blood, colouring her dream so vividly, she could almost taste it.

In this dream, he was dead; there was no repeat of the previous night's horror. She didn't wake steeped in self-loathing.

But she did cry out. It woke her and it was several minutes, with her heart thumping and thoughts spinning, before she could crawl from the bed. She went through the motions: a cursory wash in the small bathroom, pulling on the clothes she'd discarded in a heap on the floor.

She walked hesitantly down the stairs, partly from a weariness that weighed her down and made everything difficult, partly from the theory knocking inside her skull that blamed Alex and Zander for the previous day's break-in. If they hoped to get rid of her, what else might they plan to do to scare her away? With the new lock in place, they wouldn't be able to get through the front door so easily. The rear door, courtesy of the previous owner, was already fitted with a sturdy mortice lock. Nobody was getting in that way without her being aware.

Downstairs, she huffed a loud breath to see that everything was exactly as she'd left it the previous day, the space looking just as it was supposed to. She crossed to lift one slat of the wooden blinds to look at the world outside. The footpath was Sunday-morning quiet, the traffic reduced to the occasional car.

The row of pillars on the windowsill with their sad question-marked cards were waiting for her. But first, although she wasn't hungry, it seemed sensible to have some breakfast. A slice of cold pizza and coffee. A second coffee, sipped more slowly, helped make her feel a little more awake.

When she was done, she went back to the shop floor and pulled up the blinds. She peeled the Coming Soon poster from the window and rolled it up. It took a while to arrange the seven pillars. In the end, it was the simplest arrangement that looked best. The tallest pillar in the centre, decreasing in height both ways. On the tallest, she put something she'd organised weeks before – a ceramic apple, and a small stuffed bee holding a book that had taken her weeks to source. It wasn't identical to the one in her logo, but it was close enough.

She'd already chosen which books she was going to highlight on the other pillars. A mix of the best of the genre fiction she had, an obscure literary novel, a couple of classics, and finally a self-help book.

It was time to get on with doing the boring but important job of setting up the electronic cash register with its integrated credit-card reader. She'd researched what to get until she was totally confused, opting in the end for something that seemed to fulfil her needs. It turned out to be finicky rather than difficult and a practice run worked perfectly. She emptied the twenty pounds of coins into the cash drawer and shut it, leaving the key dangling in the lock. If, heaven forbid, she was burgled again, if she was that bloody unlucky, she'd prefer them to simply open the drawer and remove the money rather than smashing it.

And that was it. She was almost ready.

She switched her phone on and saw she'd missed a call from Sarah, but there was a message to say she'd see Helen the following morning. There was no reply to any of the messages she'd sent to the women she'd worked with for years. Women she'd considered friends. She shouldn't really be surprised. Not many people wanted to associate with an ex-con. It was silly to be disappointed. To suddenly feel lonely.

It was better to keep busy. Finishing off the little things. She brought down a large pile of paper bags and stacked them carefully on the shelf under the desk. This business was going to work. She was going to be a success and no Cockney duo was going to frighten her away.

As if by magic, when she looked up, there they were, both men standing outside, staring in.

Zander waved a hand up and down the window, then gave an emphatic thumbs up. Alex might have done the same but his arms were full of a large box she assumed either contained the promised glasses or the wine.

'You approve?' she asked, opening the door.

'Very nice,' Zander said. 'Simple, elegant, and eye-catching. You did good.'

Despite her suspicions, she was pleased to hear this praise.

Alex shifted the weight of the box he was holding. 'Where do you want me to put these glasses?'

'Here behind the desk, please.' She pointed to a corner. 'I can unpack them from there as I need them.'

'I'll go and get the wine,' Zander said, leaving them with a wave.

Alex put the box down, then walked around the shop floor, nodding as if he approved. 'It's looking good. You've done an amazing job getting it sorted. The place was in a right old state.'

Is that why they hadn't made an offer on it? Too much work requiring too much money? Had they been waiting for someone like her? Someone to come along, do all the hard work, then they'd manipulate the situation, take advantage, and grab it at a bargain price?

She watched him, his hard eyes taking everything in. They hadn't even had to ask her, she'd volunteered all the information about the renovation, what she'd done, what she hadn't, only too pleased to be talking about it with someone who seemed genuinely interested. Of course they'd been bloody-well interested!

Zander returned with the box of wine. 'It was only white you wanted, wasn't it?'

'Yes, thanks.' She waved towards the kitchen. 'If you'd take it through, that'd be great. I can put some in the fridge later.'

'What about soft drinks?'

'Sarah is bringing a couple of bottles when she comes in the morning, thanks.'

He walked over to the bookshelves, his eyes scanning the spines. 'Sarah?'

'Sarah Drew, my sister. She and her husband Devon helped me out getting this place sorted. Devon knows a lot of people so it was some of his mates who did the bulk of the essential work. You've probably bumped into them over the last few weeks.'

'Yeah, you mentioned you'd friends and family helping out. Kept the prices down, did it?' He walked the length of the room, peering through the archway to the space at the back. 'Still, it must have set you back a pretty penny on top of the purchase price.'

Was he actually asking her how much she'd spent on the refurbishment? Was he really that cheeky? She wanted to tell him she wasn't an idiot, that she was aware of what he was up to, but she needed to be careful. She knew how dodgy some guys could be. In fact, thanks to her years in prison, she knew how dodgy *everyone* could be. Anyway, she couldn't prove anything against Zander or Alex. It was simply enough to be wise to them.

'It did,' she said, with a smile that possibly looked as forced as it felt. 'Luckily, I don't have a problem with funds. Thanks to my mother, I'm in a financially secure situation.' She told the whopper of a lie with wide eyes and a smile. She waved a hand around the room. 'This is more in the way of a hobby. It doesn't matter if I don't make any money from it. In fact, I'd be better off. I can put my losses against tax.' She'd no idea what she was talking about; it was a line she'd picked up from a drama series she'd watched recently. If they thought she'd plenty of money and wasn't reliant on the business being a success, then maybe they'd stop trying to make her fail by scaring the wits out of her, by constantly unsettling her, by making her paranoid.

Or was that it? It was nothing to do with the brothers at all. She was just bloody-well paranoid. Or maybe just exhausted and stressed? She wasn't sure of anything any more.

Zander's forehead furrowed. 'I thought you weren't getting an alarm because you were short of cash?'

Had she said that? She couldn't remember. Probably though, it was just the kind of stupid thing she would say. She needed to learn to keep her big mouth shut. 'Oh, I think you must have misunderstood; I'm eager to get a particular high-spec alarm. They're not able to install it until the week after next.' One thing she had learnt over the years – say something with enough wide-eyed innocence and people believed you.

'He always gets the wrong end of the stick,' Alex said with a shake of his head.

They stayed a while longer, chatting about nothing. Helen wasn't listening. She nodded where necessary, laughed at Zander's slightly off-colour jokes, and all the while, she was cursing them for backing her into a corner. Because now, of course, she'd have to get that damn alarm.

She just had to hope the coming days would boost her finances.

It had to. More than ever, she wanted this business to succeed.

Those friends who'd deserted her, these men who might be trying to fool her, the little voice inside her head that whispered she was going to fail, she'd show them all.

15

After another restless night on the floor of the storage room, Helen finally gave up staring at the ceiling and got dressed. This was it. The first page of a new book. She should be feeling excitement, and maybe it was there, curled up under the sense of dread that something was going to go wrong. Heading down the stairs, she held her breath until she reached the bottom and discovered all was as it should be.

In fact, Monday had arrived with sparkling sunshine. It lit up the shop window and danced along the bookshelves. It was a good omen. She needed to put her worries and fears to one side and concentrate on this, the first day of her new life.

After a quick breakfast, she pottered about. A slight adjustment of books here and there, a repositioning of the stools and lamps. Nothing that needed to be done, she was simply desperate to keep her thoughts from sinking into gloom.

When she heard a rap on the door, she checked her watch. It was only eight forty-five. Sarah had insisted she couldn't get there till nine thirty. She'd obviously had a change of heart.

The blinds were still shut. If Helen had had sense, she'd have lifted a slat and peeked through to make sure it was her sister. But then if she'd had sense, she wouldn't have ended up in prison. Anyway, how could she possibly have expected to see the woman who stood on the other side of the door? Moira, dressed in her usual workday uniform of dark trousers and shirt, this last always fastened to the neck as if she was afraid someone would get the wrong impression if one button was left undone.

Moira, arriving to ruin her morning. She caught Helen looking and lifted a hand to wave, leaving her no option but to open the door.

'I know you don't officially open till nine,' Moira said. 'But I thought you wouldn't mind if I dropped in to wish you good luck with this amazing endeavour.'

Helen had no fanciful notions. She loved her shop but it was a second-hand bookshop, not an *amazing endeavour*. She resisted the temptation to say that in fact she minded very much that the supervisor had dropped in, and said, through painfully gritted teeth, 'That's very kind, thank you.'

It was too much to hope for, that that would be it. That her supervisor would now piss off and leave her alone.

'You've done an amazing job,' Moira said, indicating the space behind with a nod of her head.

There seemed to be no choice but to stand back and allow her in. 'It's all come together as I'd hoped.' As Helen had dreamed. All those months locked away with nothing but the dream for company. One she could lose herself in during the waking hours as if she was between the covers of a book.

Moira walked to the shelves. 'I'll have to buy something.' She turned back to Helen with a raised eyebrow. 'Am I your first customer?'

It was fifteen minutes before Helen officially opened; what did she expect? 'You are,' she said, before remembering Joyce

Evan's visit on Friday and the four books she'd sold to her. She was going to tell Moira, to remove the smug expression from her face at being the first customer, but the explanation would take more time than she wanted to spend with her.

As Helen half-expected, the supervisor drifted towards the shelves holding classic and literary novels, and from them, she moved to the section marked *educational*. But apart from running her fingers along the titles, she didn't remove any. She lingered for longer by the crime section, then sidestepped to the shelf dedicated to horror. She took a couple out, read the blurb on the back cover, and returned one after the other.

Helen moved to the space behind the desk and waited. She believed you could tell a lot about a person by the books they chose to read and was curious to see which the supervisor would eventually choose. Maybe she'd buy a few to give Helen a good start.

But when Moira finally approached the desk, she held one slim volume. 'I'll take this one,' she said, putting it down. 'I like a good scary read.'

'Me too,' Helen said. Although she didn't, it seemed the right thing to say. The book was by a writer she didn't know, the cover of the book and tagline indicating that not only was it going to be scary but likely to be graphically violent too. It wasn't for her to judge other people's reading taste, but she was surprised at what appealed to the buttoned-up, condescending supervisor. It told Helen that the woman had unexpected layers. It seemed she was right to be wary of her. 'That'll be a pound,' she said, slipping the book into a paper bag.

'A pound!' Moira laughed as if Helen had made a joke.

'I price to sell. You've chosen an obscure book by an unknown writer; I think a pound is fair.' A fair price for a book that Helen had considered tossing into the box destined for recycling.

'Well, thank you,' Moira said, picking up the package and putting it into her capacious shoulder bag. 'It was nice to be your first customer. Start your little business off.'

She said *little business* as if it was an insult and Helen felt her hackles rise. Luckily, the door opened and her sister burst through with a bag hanging from each hand. Her smile dimmed when she saw who was standing by the desk. 'Oh hi, I'm not interrupting an official visit, am I?'

'I'm here in an unofficial capacity,' Moira said. She patted her bag. 'Plus I had the honour of being Helen's first customer.' She jerked her arm forward to check her watch. 'Gosh, I'm going to be late if I don't hurry away.'

She said it with an air of criticism. As if it had been Helen's fault that she'd been delayed. As if she'd been invited to the opening instead of gate-crashing it.

'Thank goodness she's gone,' Sarah said, dropping both bags on the floor. 'I'm guessing you never got around to buying any food so I bought you a variety of things.' She touched the nearest bag with the toe of her boot. 'Put these away and I'll get the rest.'

Sarah was right, of course; Helen hadn't bought any food. She should be grateful. Shouldn't find it so bloody irritating to be managed, directed, pushed around. A belated acknowledgement that her sister was simply being kind made her sigh and do as she'd been bid. In the kitchen, she found a place for the eclectic mix of items her sister seemed to classify as essential. Helen didn't even like olives but she put the jar into a cupboard along with a packet of Weetabix, a childhood favourite she hadn't eaten for years.

She turned as her sister came through, a large box in one hand, two bags swinging from the other. 'You did well. How much do I owe you?'

'It's a business-warming gift, from me and Devon.' Sarah

proceeded to put everything else she'd bought into the cupboards. The box was left till last. 'And so are these.' She took the lid off.

Helen drew a breath, held a hand over her mouth, and battled tears away until Sarah grabbed her in a hug.

'It's all right to cry. You've had a tough few years, but you've come through to the other side and now the future is yours.'

Helen drew back and searched her pockets for a tissue. Once again, it was her sister to the rescue. She pulled a ream of paper from a kitchen roll and handed it to her.

'How did you do that?' Helen pointed to the rows of cupcakes; each were topped with the shop's logo on a round disc.

'You sent me the logo to see what I thought, remember? I searched the Internet and found a company who made edible cake toppers. They came in the post a couple of weeks ago. I made the cupcakes yesterday.'

Helen wiped her eyes and blew her nose again. 'They're amazing, thank you so much.'

'You're very welcome. I'm just pleased to see you happy after all you've been through.' Sarah opened the fridge. 'Wine cooling, cupcakes ready. So we're ready for the hoards, are we?'

'As ready as I can be.'

'Cash register and card reader sorted?'

'Yes.'

'Wine glasses?'

'Behind the desk.'

'Right, well we should take some out, maybe put them on the side of the desk. You're lucky it's long enough.' She reached into one of the shopping bags. 'I know you said soft drinks, but I went for sparkling water, okay?'

Just for once, it would have been nice if her sister had done as Helen had wanted. This was her big day, her fresh start. The choice should have been hers. But her sister had been so extremely generous, it was impossible to argue. 'Sparkling water is fine, thanks.'

'And rather than paper plates for the cupcakes, I thought we could simply use sheets of kitchen roll, what d'you think?'

Which Helen took to mean that Sarah hadn't bought the paper plates she'd promised to get. It didn't matter, and anyway, wasn't it more environmentally friendly? It didn't matter that Helen felt control of the day slipping from her grasp. Bizarrely, she wished she'd told Moira that she hadn't been the first customer, to have had some control even there. Sarah wasn't waiting for an answer, but Helen gave her one anyway. 'Sheets of kitchen roll. Yes, okay, that's a good idea.' It came out louder, harsher than expected and she saw Sarah look at her in surprise.

Luckily, the sound of the bell over the front door tinkled and put a halt to any more talk about arrangements.

Helen's eyes widened. 'Customers!'

'Well, don't just stand there, go and be bookseller extraordinaire.' Sarah tapped the box of cakes. 'I'll put these out on the tray I brought with me and bring them out in a tick.'

Helen bustled through the door, excitement finally making itself felt. There was one customer, a rather scruffily dressed young woman, standing in the middle of the shop floor.

'Hello,' Helen said, joining her. 'Welcome to Appleby Books.'

'This is so cool and just what we need around here.' She hitched the straps of the rucksack she carried, then waved towards the shelves. 'My name's Jess, by the way. Is it okay if I just mooch?'

'Mooch away. Through the archway, there's more. You'll find a couple of seats too, so feel free to sit and read.'

'I may never leave!'

Helen smiled. This was exactly the kind of young and enthusiastic customer she'd dreamt about coming through the door. 'If you get hungry, there'll be cupcakes in a few minutes, and as soon as I get organised, there's wine, or sparkling water if it's too early for alcohol.'

Jess laughed. A tinkling sound of pure amusement. 'It's never too early for alcohol in my opinion, but I have to go to class in a bit so I'd better stick to water, ta.'

Sarah came through just then with the tray of cakes. 'Here you go.' She put it down on the other end of the desk from the cash register.

'They look great,' Helen said, watching as her sister fiddled with the pile of folded paper towels she'd put on one corner of the tray. She'd been right about using them rather than paper plates. Of course she was right. Wasn't she always?

You can't come with us. You're too little. You're a nuisance.

Helen tensed as words drifted from her childhood to echo inside her skull. No, not today, she didn't need this today.

She could hear Sarah speaking, a hollow, booming sound as if it was coming through a tunnel.

The prison counsellor had advised Helen to let her past go. She'd been tempted to say that if it was that bloody easy, the counsellor would be quickly out of work. It wasn't easy, of course, because try as she might, her past – both the distant and the near – kept coming back to haunt her.

More customers had come in. Sarah was chatting to one. There were others taking books from the shelves, looking engrossed. Helen took a deep breath and shook those distant voices away. The present was what mattered. Maybe the counsellor had been right.

But as she looked around at the customers, at all the strange faces, that sense of dread returned.

16

The bookshop wasn't inundated with customers, but there was a steady flow during the day. By early afternoon, almost all of the cupcakes were gone, and Helen had opened two bottles of wine. Most of the first had been drunk by a very disreputable man who seemed to have come in solely for that purpose. Helen hadn't the heart to ask him to leave. Of the second, she and Sarah had had a glass and there was still half a bottle left. Most of the customers preferred water. Helen tried not to let that irritate her.

Alex and Zander popped in during the morning to wish her luck. They had a look around, chatted to some customers they knew, and despite claiming they didn't read, bought several books. 'It's going well,' Zander said, handing the pile to Helen, shaking his head to refuse a paper bag.

The card reader worked smoothly, printing out the receipt with a satisfactory whirr. 'It is, thank goodness,' she said, handing it to him.

Most of the customers were locals who she hoped would be return customers. Some were neighbours from Hungerford Street. She wasn't sure if they were curious about the shop, or keen to see their ex-con neighbour in action. Much better was the visit by several university students who promised to tell their friends. All bought at least one book. She pressed bookmarks on them, asking them to spread them around.

At one, she insisted Sarah take a break. 'Go, sit in the kitchen, have a coffee, make a sandwich with that nice bread and ham you brought.'

'Okay. I'll make us both one and we can take it in turns.'

Helen nodded, but she really didn't want to leave the shop, not even for food. She couldn't explain the continuing unease so she didn't try. Instead, she busied herself chatting to every customer. That was the key to success, she decided: to make it personal. Customers were chatting to each other too, a pleasant hum filling the shop.

'It's all going so well,' Sarah said, returning from her lunch.

It was exactly what Helen had been thinking but didn't want to say aloud for fear of tempting fate. A dart of irritation stabbed her that her sister had done so, and she looked around, almost fearfully, as if every customer was suddenly going to vanish in a puff of smoke, and all the books come tumbling off the shelves or self-combust.

'Go and get something to eat,' Sarah said, giving Helen's arm a nudge. 'You must be starving, I bet you had no breakfast.'

Had she? She couldn't remember. 'Right, if you're sure, I'll only be gone a few minutes.'

'For goodness' sake, take a break. Trust me. If any emergency occurs, I know where to find you.'

Helen glanced around. There were only two customers and she'd spoken to both. It was a good time to take a breather. 'Right, okay.' And still she hesitated. 'You're sure you'll manage the register and card reader?' Because it was better to focus her fear on something tangible, not the inexplicable disquiet she couldn't shake off.

Sarah folded her arms across her chest, gave a quick glance towards the ceiling as if asking for divine assistance, then sighed. 'It's not rocket science, Helen. I think I can manage.'

'Right,' she said again. She wanted to say more. To remind her sister that it was her business, her future, that she was no longer a child to be dismissed. But as ever, she said nothing. She sometimes wondered if Sarah was even aware of her lingering antipathy. She'd tried to tell her, once, after a few glasses of wine, but she'd bottled it when she saw Sarah's expression, the amused disbelief that Helen was harkening back to a period in their lives almost twenty years before. She guessed Sarah had the same mindset as the prison counsellor – that she needed to leave such things in the past where they belonged.

Sarah had left a sandwich on the counter covered in a clean tea towel. Neatly cut into quarters, it looked tempting and seemed sensible to eat it. Helen shook the kettle, judged there was sufficient water and switched it on. Once she'd a mug of coffee made, she listened at the door. If there were customers, they were quiet. She resisted the temptation to open the door to check that no catastrophe had occurred in the few minutes she'd been absent.

Instead, she took her coffee and sandwich into the garden. It was west-facing, and it was a sunny day, making it a perfect place to take a break. In the coming days, working alone as she'd be, she wouldn't have the luxury of getting outside, so despite her misgivings, she might as well make the most of it.

The sandwich was good and she demolished each triangle in a couple of bites. She was finishing the coffee and thinking about returning to the shop floor when she heard her name called. Sarah's voice. Raised in agitation.

The plate that had been on Helen's lap fell to the ground and

broke into three pieces as she stood. The door to the shop opened
and Sarah appeared. Behind her, stood two tall, burly, uniformed
policemen.

Helen's first thought was that this was what she'd been
waiting for all day. It hadn't been paranoia; it had been a
premonition.

Her second thought was that, somehow, they knew the truth
about Toby's death.

Her third, that this couldn't be happening now. Not when
everything was going her way.

The taller of the two officers slipped past Sarah. 'Helen
Appleby?'

*You're under arrest for lying under oath. For misleading the jury.
For not telling the truth about what happened that day. We're going to
lock you up and throw away the key for being a pathetic, lying,
depraved weirdo.* She could almost believe she heard Toby laughing. The way he'd done that day just before she decided she'd
had enough.

'Yes, I'm Helen Appleby.'

'I'm afraid I have some bad news for you.'

17

Helen's legs seemed to be liquifying. Afraid she was going to collapse, she took a step backwards to the chair, crushing the pieces of the broken plate under her foot. She sat heavily, her eyes never leaving the officer's face as she waited for his mouth to move, to say the words she'd probably always been waiting to hear: *you're under arrest.*

She was so sure it was what he was going to say, that when he spoke, she shook her head in confusion. 'What?'

It was Sarah who answered. 'Your house has been burgled.'

'Your alarm went off,' the officer explained. 'One of your neighbours was here this morning so she knew you weren't around. She had a look over the fence, saw broken glass on the ground and called it in.'

The other officer took up the tale. 'We weren't too far away so we arrived about fifteen minutes later, by which time your alarm had cut out. We found a glass panel in the back door had been smashed to gain access but the intruder had gone.'

When Helen said nothing, Sarah stepped around the two officers to be at her side. Putting an arm around her shoulder, she asked, 'Is there much damage?'

'A lot of stuff disturbed but there doesn't look to be any damage as such. Obviously, we have no idea what, if anything, is missing. We'll need you to come and ascertain that for us.'

She wasn't going to be arrested. Relief made Helen feel even weaker and she was grateful for Sarah's supporting arm. It took a few seconds to understand what they were asking of her. 'You want me to come now?'

They seemed surprised by her question. 'As soon as we know what's missing, we can make a report, then we'll be able to give you a reference number for your insurance company.' He frowned. 'You do have insurance, I hope.'

'Yes, yes of course.' She got to her feet with Sarah's arm weighing heavily on her shoulder. 'It's just that today is the opening day.' She registered their blank looks. 'My bookshop. It's the first day today.'

Sarah pulled her closer. 'I can take care of everything here till you get back. You need to go, get your home sorted. You'll need to contact someone to come out as an emergency to fit a new pane of glass in the door too.'

There didn't seem to be any choice. Once more, Helen was being managed by others.

The two officers led the way and Sarah, releasing Helen from her embrace, followed.

She watched them as they marched, single file through the door. None looked back to see if she was following. She could make her escape through the wooden gate at the end of the garden. It opened onto a small laneway. From there, she could make her way back onto the street, hop into her car and zoom away. Not face whatever chaos waited for her at home.

'Helen?' Sarah looked back through the doorway, her forehead corrugated in puzzlement. 'You all right?'

Yesterday, someone broke into my shop. Today, someone breaks into my house. So of course I'm feeling absolutely peachy. I'm not starting to feel absolutely fucking paranoid that someone is trying to scare me, to make sure I don't succeed. 'Just coming,' she said, moving slowly forward, suddenly afraid of going inside, afraid her earlier image was true, that there'd be no customers, and the books would have tumbled from the shelves, wisps of smoke coming from their covers where the words inside had been set on fire.

There were no customers, but apart from that, the shop looked just as it had before she'd gone to lunch.

'I won't be long,' she said to Sarah.

'Take whatever time you need. I'll hold the fort here.' Sarah pulled out her phone and checked the time. 'It's almost three. I'll shut at five anyway and drop the keys around to you.'

Helen wanted to cry in absolute frustration. They'd had this conversation already. She'd made it clear she wanted to stay open till six to catch people who were walking past on their way home from work. Sarah had sniffed in disagreement but said nothing. Now here she was, trying to take advantage of Helen's predicament to get her own way. 'No, don't worry, I'll be back before that. I've put open till six on all the leaflets I distributed and don't want to let customers down.'

She didn't wait for an answer, following the two policemen from the shop. They'd walked from her house. Helen debated driving, but the traffic was heavy, it'd be quicker to walk. She fell into step beside the officers. They didn't speak. Neither did she. She wondered if they knew about her. Her record. She wished now that she'd reported the break-in at the shop. It would have been reassuring to be told it was a coincidence. That she'd simply been unfortunate; that she was the victim of random events.

She'd liked to have discussed her theory that Alex and Zander had been to blame for the break-in at the shop, and might, at a huge stretch of her theory, have also been responsible for the one at her home. Were they that desperate to get their hands on her shop that they'd stoop that low?

Was their plan to have her so on edge that she'd give up?

Or had she simply chosen them as likely candidates because she needed some focus for her growing paranoia that someone was determined to make her fail?

They reached her home in silence. The end-of-terrace house had a side entrance. There was a gate. With a lock. It hadn't worked since she'd moved in eight years before.

'Might want to get that fixed,' one of the officers said, pointing to it. 'Many of these burglars are opportunistic. They try a gate and if it's open, they'll give it a go.'

Helen followed them around the back, heaving a sigh when she saw the broken glass strewn across the back patio.

The officer opened the door and pointed to the key still in the lock. 'I'm guessing you left it in place, yes?'

Of course she had. Because she was that bloody stupid.

'It made it even easier for him then; he simply reached through, unlocked it, and had the house to himself.'

'Him?' She looked at him wide-eyed. 'You know who it was?' Not Alex or Zander, she'd been unfair. Paranoid. Quick to blame. Wasn't she always? Blaming her mother, her father, her siblings, and finally Toby for the disaster she'd made of her life. What a mess she was. What a fucking mess.

But the officer shrugged and shook his head. 'No, I don't. It was a figure of speech. To be politically correct, I should probably have said they.'

It wasn't either the time or the place to discuss the issue of politically correct pronouns. It would have been so much better if they had known who'd broken in. Some local, well-known to the police, yob. She could have laughed off her stupid ideas then and put it down to bad luck rather than a personal vendetta. Vendetta – the word had hopped unbidden into her head. Yes, that was exactly what it was beginning to feel like.

Ignoring the officers, she stepped into the kitchen with her mind spinning as she came to terms with this new fear. A friend of Toby's perhaps, who was angry to see her released so soon? She couldn't remember any friend close enough to bear such a grudge. There had been his mother, of course. They hadn't been close, but she'd been there at the trial. Could it be her, seeking revenge for the loss of her son?

'Well, miss?' The officer was growing impatient.

Helen reined her thoughts in. There'd be time later to worry. She looked around the small kitchen. There were a couple of cupboards open, but nothing had been disturbed.

She wasn't so lucky in the living room. The built-in shelves to either side of the chimney breast were filled with a variety of things she'd collected or been gifted over the years. None had any value apart from sentimental. Most were lying on the floor. Some had been broken by the fall. Books had been swept from the bookshelf.

'They've taken the seats from your sofa, which is rather unusual.'

Helen turned to look at the officer. 'No, I took them to make a bed in the room above the shop.' She spread her hands out. 'I didn't report it but someone got into my shop on Saturday. They didn't take anything but they made a bit of a mess.'

The officer frowned. 'Why didn't you report it?'

'Because there was no sign of a break-in. I wasn't sure I hadn't left the door unlocked when I came away. It only had a Yale lock, and I had put the snib on so that I could bring stuff in from the car. I might have forgotten to take it off. Nothing was taken so there didn't seem any point in bothering you.' There was also no point in explaining that she hadn't called them because this was her new start, her second attempt at happy ever after, and she hadn't wanted it blighted by inviting the police into it. And now here they were anyway. 'There doesn't appear to be anything missing,' she said, looking around the room. 'My old TV was never going to tempt them.'

'They were probably looking for money, or small items they could flog. You have a laptop?'

'Yes, but I had it with me. Honestly, I don't have anything worth stealing.'

'Unfortunately, burglars don't know that.'

Upstairs, there was a similar level of disorder. Wardrobe and dresser drawers stood open. Her underwear was scattered across the floor. The pile of books by her bed had been picked up and dropped on top of the rumpled duvet.

One of the officers had remained downstairs; the other stood in the doorway as she assessed the damage. 'What about jewellery?' he said.

'My mother's engagement ring.' She lifted her hand to show him the diamond and ruby ring she wore. 'I rarely take it off.' She'd given it into Sarah's safekeeping while she was in prison. It had been the first thing she'd asked for on her release. 'Otherwise, I have a few earrings and that's it. I'm not really a jewellery person.' They were kept in a small box. She found it on the floor. The lid had come off and the contents flung onto the carpet. None of the earrings were missing. 'Perhaps I should be offended they didn't think they were valuable?'

Her attempt at humour failed. 'Are they?' the officer asked peering at the items she was picking up and returning to the container.

'No, they're not.'

'Then there's nothing missing?'

'Not here.' She checked the two spare bedrooms, one of which had been set up as an office. It was here that the burglar had wreaked the most destruction, perhaps frustrated by their lack of success elsewhere. There was a desk under the window. The four drawers each side of the footwell had been pulled out and emptied onto the floor. The freestanding bookcase had been dragged down with such violence that it had been twisted out of shape.

'How could they have done so much damage in so little time?' She picked up one of the folders that had fallen from the bookcase. 'How long had they had... fifteen maybe twenty minutes?'

'About that.' The officer reached for the bookcase. Pulling it upright, he manipulated it back into place. 'Can you tell if there's anything missing?'

Was he joking? She put the folder down and wiped a hand over her face. 'There was nothing here worth taking. Some training files from my civil service days that are years out of date and should have been binned a long time ago. Newspaper cuttings. Books. Stationery. No money. Not even a blasted postage stamp.' She knew this because she'd used the last one the previous week.

She pushed past the officer and headed into the final room. The wardrobe doors were hanging open, and suitcases she'd stored in the cupboards overhead had been pulled out and opened.

'Nothing missing?'

She wanted to scream at him. To tell him there was nothing missing because she had nothing of any value. But he was simply doing his job so she shook her head. 'Just my peace of mind,' she said.

Downstairs, both officers looked suddenly uncomfortable. 'Are you going to be okay?' one asked.

'We'll make a note of the break-in at your shop, to have it in our files too,' the other said.

She wasn't sure what the point of that was, but they were trying to be kind so she nodded. 'Thank you.' She pulled her mobile out. 'I'd better get someone to fix that panel.'

'Right, well, if you contact the station later, they'll give you a case number. For insurance purposes,' he added, when he saw her blank look.

'Oh right. Okay, thank you.' She had a fair idea her insurance excess was three hundred pounds, so unless fixing the door cost more than that, she wouldn't be making a claim. Her premiums were already crazy.

As soon as they were gone, she did an Internet search, found the nearest glazier and gave them a call. They answered immediately, gave her a quote she thought was acceptable and promised to be out within two hours.

'You can tell them to come around the back,' she said once she'd given them her credit card details. 'I won't be here but they'll see what needs to be done. If they could replace the glass panel and shut the door after them, that'd be fine.' She'd no worry about leaving the door unlocked. If she was so unfortunate as to attract a third opportunistic burglar in as many days, well, they'd soon see they were beaten to it. But despite the broken gate, and the key she'd left in the lock, she knew this hadn't been some opportunistic yob. She might be a little paranoid, but she wasn't stupid. This, like the break-in at the shop, had been personal.

She hung up and looked around the living room. The mess was going to take hours to put to rights. It was four thirty. There was no time to spare here when the shop was calling to her. Restoring order would have to wait. Probably for days.

Fifteen minutes later, she was back in the shop, pleased to see there were a few customers browsing the shelves.

'How'd it go?' Sarah asked.

'A broken panel in the back door, a bit of disorder inside, but nothing taken, so all's good.' She joined Sarah behind the desk. 'How's it been?'

'Fine. A few customers, and they all bought books too.' Sarah put an arm around Helen and drew her in for a hug. 'You sure it wasn't too bad? You hear such stories.'

'No, honestly, it's okay. It'll take me five minutes to get it back the way it was. My next-door neighbour kindly volunteered to wait for the glazier to come so I could return.' What a prolific and brilliant liar she was. But then she always had been. 'I'm sure you want to get home. Thanks so much for today, and those fabulous cupcakes.'

Sarah checked her watch. 'If you're sure you'll be okay, I will. I might beat the worst of the rush-hour traffic.'

Helen immediately felt guilty. She wondered if this was the reason for her sister's earlier comment about shutting at five. Sarah lived the other side of the city; it was always a nightmare to get across but rush hour added another level to the horror that was Bath traffic at the best of times. 'Go, I'll be fine.'

She was; she was also busy. Her idea that customers would visit on their way home from work paid off. There was a steady flow of people through the door and all bought at least one book, with some buying two or more. More wine was used in the last hour than she'd poured in the preceding eight. With only one cupcake remaining, there was a jovial argument between two customers as to who should have it, with a decision being made to split it in half. Helen did the honours and both left smiling with their half cake and several books.

Helen was serving another customer when she heard the doorbell tinkle and she looked over to see Zander coming through the door. He seemed surprised there were so many customers. Surprised her little bookshop was being so successful. If she'd any doubt that the break-ins were personal, it vanished when she saw his expression. And if she'd any doubt as to who was to blame, she brushed that away too.

She'd seen a monster before; she knew what one looked like.

18

Helen concentrated on the customer she was serving, bagging up the books he'd purchased and adding Appleby bookmarks. 'You've chosen well,' she said to him with a smile. 'These are three of my favourite books.' Actually, she'd only read one out of the three, and she'd hated it, but he wasn't to know that. She was a voracious reader, but it was impossible to have read everything.

Once he'd gone, Zander came over to the desk, a beaming smile fixed in place. Helen, reminding herself to keep her enemies close, greeted him with a broad grin that made her face ache.

'Looks like you're doing well,' he said. 'Congratulations.'

'I'm pretty pleased how it's going. People have been so nice.' She tapped the top of the register. 'Doing far better than I'd expected to.'

'Great news.' He nodded emphatically as if he really meant what he was saying. 'Always good to see success.' He leaned closer, dropping his voice to a conspiratorial whisper. 'I saw two policemen come in earlier. I hope there's been no trouble.'

If Helen was right, Zander knew exactly why the police had

been there. If she was wrong, it was none of his business. 'Police officers read books too,' she said, relieved when another customer came to the desk with two books in her hand. She gave the woman most of her attention, commenting on her choice of books, bagging them up, adding the bookmarks. But from the corner of her eye, she watched Zander's greedy little eyes as they scanned the place. Perhaps he was considering how many tables they could pack in. Or how much it would cost to knock down the party wall between her shop and their tiny, tiny restaurant next door. When the customer left, he hurried to rejoin her.

'I'd better get back to work,' he said with a glance at his watch. 'Congrats again, Helen.'

'Thanks so much for all your support.' The words almost choked her and when Zander had gone, she slumped over the desk, weary beyond belief.

'Long day?'

Helen jerked upright, quickly pasting an acceptable expression on her face. It became less forced as she met the brown eyes of the man who was standing with an armful of books. He was the final customer. She'd noticed him several minutes before, his long, lean body perched awkwardly on a stool in front of the classic novels, taking out book after book. There was a handsome face to go with the body, with extraordinarily expressive eyes.

'It's my first in business, so it's been...' she searched for the right word to describe the highs and lows of the day '...dramatic.'

'You have a lovely place.' He tapped the pile of books he'd placed on the desk. 'I have a particular fondness for classic novels so was pleased to find an old favourite and several I haven't read.'

She scanned the title of the top book. '*The Heart is a Lonely Hunter*. One of my favourites.' The truth this time, she'd read it several years before and had loved it. 'They made a good movie from it too, starring...'

When she came to a halt, unable to remember the name of the actor, he smiled. 'Alan Arkin. I've seen it.' He tapped the book again. 'I've read the book before too, a long time ago. When I saw it on your shelves, I fancied reading it again. My copy got lost somewhere over the years.'

'All the better for me,' she said with a smile, registering the four books. 'That'll be eight pounds, please.'

She picked up a bag and manoeuvred the books inside, conscious of the man's eyes on her. She slipped bookmarks in alongside and handed the package to him.

Taking it, he indicated the empty glasses with a tilt of his head. 'Have I missed the celebrations?'

Colour rushed into her cheeks. 'I'm sorry, no, I should have offered you a glass.' She reached behind her for the wine bottle, and into the box on the floor for a clean glass. 'Here you go.' She poured a generous amount and handed it to him.

His fingers, accidentally – deliberately? – brushed against hers, causing her to draw a sharp breath that she managed to pass off with a cough. She held her hand over her mouth and turned away, praying for her colour to fade before she needed to turn back. After Toby, she'd sworn off men, but that didn't stop her feeling attracted to a good-looking specimen.

He was holding the wine glass, staring at her with an expression half amused, half curious. 'You okay?' he asked.

'Just a tickle.' She reached for the glass she'd been using earlier. 'Maybe wine will help.' She poured herself a tiny drop.

'To your success,' he said, touching his glass gently to hers. He didn't take it away immediately. 'And to books and the worlds that live within them.'

It was so exactly the way that she regarded them that she had to smile. 'Not everyone looks at books that way.'

'My earliest memory is of my mother reading *Gulliver's Travels* to me.'

'A very adult novel for a young child.'

He shrugged. 'An adult reads it as a political satire or an allegory of the relationship between France and England at the time. A child, as I was, listened to the stories of shipwrecks, and a man being tied to the ground by little people.' He rested a hip on the desk and casually swung his leg to and fro. 'From that my mother moved on to *Alice in Wonderland*.'

'Shrinking people, talking rabbits and "off with her head"!'

'Exactly. So you see my imagination was stirred at a young age.'

Helen perched on the high stool behind. An interesting conversation with someone who was obviously a booklover was a pleasant end to what had been a difficult day. Almost subconsciously, she noticed the long fingers of his left hand curled around the glass and the absence of a gold band on his ring finger. It didn't matter. She reminded herself that her future was mapped out, and didn't include any romantic entanglements.

Love, for her, always entailed an amount of pain and she'd sworn she was done with that. Toby had ended that chapter of her life. It had been a full stop; she wasn't changing it to a comma.

'Are you living locally?' It wasn't prurient curiosity, she told herself; if he was a local, he might become a regular visitor and the more of those she had, the better for business.

'Not too far away. Newton St Loe. I pass this way to visit my grand-aunt.' He held out a hand. 'Name's Jared.'

19

Helen had taken his hand, had felt the long, strong fingers close around hers, before she heard the alarm bell ringing loudly and insistently in her head. *Grand-aunt? Jared?* It was too much of a co-incidence. 'You're Jen Clough's grand-nephew?'

'The very one,' he said, releasing her hand. 'I called to see her earlier; she told me all about you and your new venture.'

Helen searched his face for clues. Was he annoyed she'd taken the books, or pleased to be relieved of the trouble of getting rid of them? She'd thought from their chat that he was a fellow booklover, but according to what his grand-aunt had said, he had no love for books.

'I did offer to pay for them, but she insisted she didn't want money, that I was doing her a favour by taking them.' There was no change in his expression so she ventured more. 'She said you were talking about hiring a skip for them.'

That did get a reaction; he raised his eyes to the ceiling and huffed what could only be classed as a frustrated sigh. 'I am hiring a skip, in fact it's probably going to be several skips, because my beloved grand-aunt hasn't thrown anything out in years. I don't know if she told you, but she's moving into sheltered accommodation. Not too far away actually; she'll be able to keep in touch with neighbours. The apartment is huge, as these things go, but downsizing from a five bed, three-story house to an apartment, no matter how spacious, was always going to be a mammoth task.' He brushed fingers through his hair, making it stand on end. She'd thought he looked handsome; now he looked raffish... sexy... and reminded her suddenly of Toby when she'd first met him, when he'd been loving, kind and understanding, of Toby before he'd turned into a monster. She wanted to cry, run away and hide, and at the same time, grab this Toby look-alike and cover him in kisses.

Instead, she sat there with an inane smile fixed in place as she listened to Jared describing how much stuff his grand-aunt had accumulated in the decades she'd lived in her home.

'My sister was staying with her last month. Just for a few days. She lives in Switzerland and doesn't get home very often. She arranged for all those cardboard boxes but didn't get very far with packing them up. Unfortunately, I was away on business the following week and when I got back, I was horrified to find that Jen had done the rest herself.' He shook his head. 'You've met her; she gets breathless and worn out doing the slightest thing, yet she managed to do that.'

'You didn't want to keep any of them?' As a booklover, she found it difficult to understand someone who didn't want books.

'I live in a small cottage with limited space. I tend to only keep favourites that I know I'll reread someday.' He drained his glass and without asking, reached for the bottle and refilled it. 'You don't mind, do you?'

It was a bit late if she did. 'No, sorry, I should have offered.' What was she apologising for? This wasn't a date. It was a drink to celebrate the opening of her new bookshop. Apart from the rather disreputable gentleman that morning who'd drunk far more than his fair share, nobody had asked for a second glass. She should have been annoyed, and she was, but not with Jared. With herself for finding him fascinating.

He made himself more comfortable on the desk, shuffling around so he was facing her. 'I'm not displeased that you took all the books, but I'm slightly concerned.' He lifted the glass to his mouth and took a gulp of wine.

Concerned that his grand-aunt had given them away for nothing? 'I did offer to pay,' she said again. Was he going to accuse her of taking advantage of a frail, elderly woman? How stupid she'd been; she should have insisted she had something in writing.

Jared held up a hand. 'I'm not in the slightest bit bothered about you getting them for nothing. To be honest, you probably saved me money; there were so many, they'd have filled the skip.' He took another mouthful of wine, almost emptying the glass. 'What concerns me is that Jen packed so many of the boxes herself. God alone knows what she included. She has this habit of using letters, bank statements, all kinds of things as bookmarks.' He gave a gruff laugh. 'Once, she used a fifty-pound note, can you imagine! I had planned to flick through every book before packing it, just in case, but of course I missed the opportunity.'

Helen was going to say that using anything rather than bending the corner of a page was perfectly acceptable in her eyes, but she wasn't sure he'd approve of the flippancy. Anyway, it looked as if he'd more to say.

'I'm sure you can understand why I was slightly disconcerted to find she'd given them all away.'

Disconcerted. Not bloody furious.

'I suppose I can.'

'Good.' He drained his glass.

Before he reached for the bottle again, Helen picked it up. 'Would you like another?'

He shook his head. 'Better not, I'm driving.' Putting the empty glass down, he leaned towards her. The sudden movement startled her. She jerked backwards, and the stool, which had cost a fiver in a local charity shop and wasn't the sturdiest, keeled over, slamming her into the wall behind.

Jared was quickly on his feet, pulling her up. 'I'm so sorry, are you okay? I didn't mean to startle you.'

She brushed his hands away. 'I'm fine. It's just been a long day and I'm tired.'

'Right.' He stayed on his feet, looking at her with a worried frown. 'I'll get right to the point then, shall I?' He didn't appear to want an answer. Shoving his two hands into the pockets of his jeans, he said, 'I'm guessing you haven't had a chance to unpack the boxes yet. I'm hoping you'll allow me to go through them myself to make sure Jen hasn't left anything important in them.'

Was he serious? There was no point in lying and saying she'd already unpacked the books. He'd had a good snoop around, and now she knew what he'd been looking for. Books he'd have recognised from his grand-aunt's shelves. She felt suddenly let down, cheated even; it made it easier to answer bluntly. 'I'm sorry, that's impossible.'

He didn't seem offended; in fact, he smiled. 'I've found that nothing is impossible if we really want to do something.'

She wondered if his smarmy charm worked on most women, then had to admit it had been working on her. 'The problem is, Mr Clough, that I really don't want to let you spend what would be hours looking through the boxes.'

His smile didn't waver, but a glint appeared in his eyes. Helen was conscious of the light fading outside the window. She'd been so excited about making her dream come true that she hadn't considered the implications of running a business alone. The isolation. Of being vulnerable.

He was a tall man. Not broad, but muscles rippled under his T-shirt. And his hands looked strong. Those long fingers could squeeze the life from her with little effort. She was used to pain, welcomed it at times. Death was another thing altogether. Desperately, she sought for some kind of compromise. 'Since your grand-aunt was so kind to give me the books though, I'll tell you what I will do for you.' Each word seemed to fall from her mouth, dry and dusty. She reached for her glass and took a sip of wine. 'I'll go through the boxes over the next few days, flick through each book, and if there's anything between the pages that shouldn't be, I'll keep it safe. How does that work for you?'

His smile faded as she spoke, and when he answered, his voice was less friendly, less charming. 'It appears I have no choice in the matter.'

He didn't, but he could have been more graceful in defeat.

'If you like, I can post you anything I find—'

He held a hand up, halting her mid flow. 'I won't put you to that much bother. As I've already explained, I come this way to visit my grand-aunt every week, so it's no trouble to pop in for anything you may have discovered. Plus,' he waved a hand towards the shelves, 'it would give me a chance to get more books.' He tapped the bag holding the ones he'd purchased. 'I assume you buy them back, yes? As I said, I have little room to keep them.'

Relieved he wasn't insisting on searching through the boxes himself, she nodded. 'Yes, of course.' Buy, not exchange. That offer she intended to reserve for the elderly, retired, or those in need. People like this man, with his obvious air of entitlement, could pay. 'I give fifty p for each book I buy.'

He raised an eyebrow. 'Fifty p!' His smile returned, and his eyes softened. 'Quite the little business woman, aren't you?'

She guessed he wasn't referring to her five-foot three stature. 'I'm aiming to be a successful business owner. If you feel fifty p is too little, you can, of course, take the books elsewhere.' *Because you so obviously need the money, you miserable bastard.*

He was insensitive and condescending, but he wasn't stupid. 'Sorry,' he said, lifting his hand in defence. 'I've obviously offended you, and I didn't mean to. It's a bad habit to slip into stupid chauvinism when I'm feeling beaten by a woman.'

His apology eased her irritation. 'A bad habit that could get you into trouble in the twenty-first century.' She'd never met a man who had such an irritating ability to make her change her mind about him in rapid succession. 'And now, I'm going to have to ask you to leave. It's been a long day, and this little business woman still has a lot to do.'

'I'd offer my help, but I don't want to put my foot in it again.'

Did she look like a lonely, friendless person desperate for some random man to offer his services? He'd managed to offend and change her mind once again. Was it deliberate? A way to make himself more interesting, more of a challenge? 'That's very kind, but I have friends and family coming later to give me a hand.'

'Right, good. Okay then, I'll leave you and call in next week to pick up whatever you manage to find.'

'Fine,' she said, folding her arms tightly across her chest. She didn't want to shake his hand again. He unnerved her. Whether it was because he reminded her of Toby, or because he seemed a little bit too slippery, she wasn't sure. What she was sure of though, was that she didn't like the sensation.

With a smile, and another tap on the bag of books he held, he left the shop.

Helen stayed behind the desk and watched him go. She waited till he'd vanished from view before hurrying to the window to ensure he was really gone and not lingering outside. But despite peering up and down the street, there was no sign of him. Rather than settling her mind, it rattled it more. Where had he gone?

Had he gone next door for a meal or to get a takeaway? Maybe to speak to Alex and Zander? Did he know them? Was she going absolutely crazy?

The ring of her mobile startled her so much that she banged her nose on the window. The pain made her eyes water and her voice thick when she answered the call.

'Hi, it's me, how did the rest of the day go?'

'Good, Sarah, actually very good.' Helen held the phone away, reached into her pocket for a tissue and wiped her eyes and her nose. 'I was right, quite a few people came in on their way home from work. I've only just shut.'

'Really? It's six thirty; you must be exhausted.'

'It was hard to turn away customers who were buying books.' The lie came easily. She was reluctant to tell her about Jared, about feeling vulnerable there on her own.

'You're going to have to learn to be firmer or you'll wear yourself out.'

'Yes, I know,' Helen said.

She was going to say more, to say she wasn't an idiot, when a knock coming from the direction of the kitchen made her gasp.

It was loud enough to make its way down the line to Sarah's attentive ear. 'Helen, are you okay? What's wrong?'

'I thought I heard something?'

'Is the back door locked?'

'Yes, of course.' Was it? She'd come in with those police officers earlier, had she locked it behind her? She couldn't remember. 'Oh no, it's okay,' she said giving a fake laugh. 'It was only a book falling from one of the shelves where someone didn't put it back properly. Right, I'd better go, I've still a lot to do. Thanks again for your help, for all the food you bought me, and for those fabulous cupcakes.' She hung up, and stood there with the phone in her hand, listening for anything out of the way. Perhaps she'd imagined the knocking.

Shoving her mobile into her pocket, she locked the front door, carefully taking the key from the lock and putting it on the shelf under the desk. She passed the stairway, stopped at the door to the kitchen and pressed her ear to it. There was nothing to be heard. She had imagined the sound. But still she pushed the door open, slowly, warily, holding her breath until she saw the room was empty. The back door was shut, and she was relieved to find it was also locked tight.

Shaking her head at how easily she could be rattled, she returned to the shop floor. It was time to see how much money she'd made that day. It took a few minutes to get the narrow wooden blinds on the shop windows lowered without upsetting her display. Only when that was done did she feel happy opening the register to count the takings and check credit card receipts.

She'd done better than she'd expected. Engrossed in what she was doing, it was a few seconds before she became aware of a noise. Another knock, but this time it was repeated. Three, then silence, then three more.

Someone knocking on the back door? Nobody she knew would be using the entrance from the laneway through the rickety wooden gate at the bottom of the garden.

Once again, she approached the kitchen, her ear cocked to listen for a repeat of the sound. It hadn't come by the time she cautiously opened the door and peered around it into the dark room. She slid a hand along the wall and pressed the switch, her eyes fixed on the back door. Was there someone waiting on the other side? The Grim Reaper, scythe in one hand, the other raised, ready to knock again. The morbid thought made her shiver.

The door was a solid structure. No glass panel to peer through. The small kitchen window didn't add any clarity either. The rear garden was in darkness, so all she could see was herself staring back, looking scared.

It was an image she'd sworn she never wanted to see again. Reaching for the cord of the blind, she jerked it hard, causing it to fall with a noisy clatter.

Her reflection was gone, but the fear wasn't. Helen did what she'd done before, what she'd always done: she harnessed it and changed it into a fierce determination to succeed.

No irritating parole officer, no dodgy neighbours or odd customers, and definitely no strange sounds were going to ruin her new life.

20

Helen had one of the ready meals her sister had brought her for dinner and, because it was there, the last of the wine from the opened bottle. She dragged the stool in from the shop and ate at the kitchen counter. She ate for fuel, from necessity rather than desire. Her appetite, never good, hadn't been helped by two years of prison food where quantity had appeared more important than quality.

Neither did it help that after every mouthful, she felt the need to stop and listen, or that she ate from the container with one eye on the back door. With a spoon. Shovelling the food in and washing it down with sips of the wine.

'Shit!' She smacked her forehead with the flat of her hand. She knew there'd been something else she was to do that day. To ring the alarm company and organise for them to come to install an alarm. Until it was done, she'd have to keep camping out. She made a mental note to phone the following morning.

For now, she might as well make the most of her enforced stay.

The busy day had reduced the stock of books on the shelves.

She needed to fill the gaps from the boxes upstairs. Her thoughts shifted to Jared. What a strange, contradictory person he was. She'd brought about sixteen boxes from his grand-aunt's home. Did he really expect her to have gone through them all in a week?

What did he expect her to find? Fifty-pound notes? Private letters? Maybe a copy of her will? Was that it? she wondered, narrowing her eyes in thought. If Jen Clough were selling that massive house to downsize to an apartment, there was going to be a lot of money left over. She thought about the frail, little woman surrounded by the decades of her life, and sighed. How sad that it often came down to money in the end. Had Jared always been an attentive grand-nephew or had he become so because of expectations? Helen was sorry she hadn't asked the woman when she'd had the chance.

Tossing the almost-empty container towards the bin, she got to her feet. Those boxes weren't going to unpack themselves.

Leaving the lights on downstairs, because she was going to be going up and down, not because she was nervous of the dark, she headed upstairs.

It was a mammoth task and she was already weary after the dramas of the day but it had to be done. Hoping there was some logic to the way the boxes had been packed, she took down the piles, spreading them out in single rows and pulling the tape from each.

On first glance, the books appeared to have been packed in a higgledy-piggledy manner with contemporary and classic mixed together. It took a brief glance into a couple of boxes for it to become clear. They were packed alphabetically by author name. That lovely Jen Clough had obviously had very organised book-shelves, and whoever had packed the books, Jen or her grand-niece, had packed shelf after shelf together.

The logic didn't make Helen's job any easier, with classic

novels by P.G. Wodehouse sitting side by side with psychological thrillers by Anita Waller. These last she was grateful for. It was the crime genre that had suffered the greatest depletion that day. Putting these to one side, she continued lifting volume after volume. She flicked the pages of each book but so far nothing more exciting than a supermarket receipt had fluttered to the ground. She picked it up with a grin. Hopefully, she'd have a pile of them to give to Jared on his return.

On her last trip to the shop floor, she looked around, feeling a sense of pride in what she'd achieved. In spite of everything.

Switching out the lights, she stood a while in the silence, breathing quietly, allowing herself to feel a certain level of satisfaction in surviving all that had been thrown at her recently.

There were no strange sounds from the kitchen to intrude on her sense of well-being as she trudged back upstairs. After basic ablutions, she slipped under the sheet in her small, makeshift bedroom and rested her head on the pillow with a loud sigh. *What a day!* With all the thoughts dancing around her head... each of them wearing heavy wooden clogs too... she wasn't expecting to sleep. But the thoughts became more scrambled as events of the day pirouetted together. Jaden and rabbits, a giant Moira being tied up by miniature men. Thoughts crazy enough to make her smile, relax and sleep.

In a deep sleep, cocooned in the small storage room, she didn't hear the *knock knock knock* when it started again hours later.

21

Helen slept solidly for six hours, waking at five o'clock feeling refreshed. It gave her four hours before the shop opened. She lay thinking, wondering if she could risk going home to have a shower. It had come to this: a toss-up between security and hygiene. The thought made her chuckle and throw the sheet back. Washing with a flannel and soap would suffice. In fact, drowning the bathroom floor, she even managed to wash her hair. Only then did she realise she hadn't brought her hairdryer.

A rough rub with a towel dried it enough to tie back with the band she'd pulled from it the night before. Fresh chinos, and a T-shirt that was almost crease-free and she was ready to face another day.

Or almost ready.

She stood at the top of the stairway, looking down, apprehension rising despite her determination to let nothing get to her that day. Only when she reached the ground floor and looked around to find everything as she'd left it did she allow herself to relax. Just a little. The door to the kitchen was shut. She'd never found the source of that noise. It was probably the plumbing. Water rattling in the pipes. Nothing ominous.

Still she hesitated as her fingers closed over the handle, and it took a deep, steadying breath before she could bring herself to open the door. When she did, she pushed it open with more energy than required. It bounced off the wall behind and returned to hit her like something from an episode of *Laurel and Hardy*.

It would usually have made her laugh but not that morning. The normality of the small galley kitchen should have eased her concerns. Everything was exactly as she'd left it. And yet, she still felt uneasy. Not by the kitchen, but by the door to the back garden. The dark full-stop of it. As if beyond, there was another story.

She tried to laugh it away. This wasn't a chapter in a John Connolly book where paranormal events occurred with seamless regularity. Nor was the door an entrance to an alternative universe. It was simply the way into her messy back garden.

No hesitation this time, she flung it open and stood staring out, her shoulders slumping in relief to see the world just as it should be. What had she expected to see? That her garden had collapsed into the nine circles of hell? Where would she end up? Would she be blown around in the second circle of lust, fall deeper into the seventh circle of violence, or would she find a home in the ninth – the one for treachery.

'I've served my sentence,' she muttered.

Not for the crime you committed, though.

Was that it? Was there a part of her that believed she couldn't get absolution, couldn't find redemption, couldn't bloody-well move on into the future she desperately yearned for, because she'd never confessed to what she had done?

Because if she had, she'd have been tried for murder, not

manslaughter, and she'd have been sentenced to a lot longer than four years.

She slammed the door shut. On the garden. It wasn't that easy to shut away the curdling thoughts in her head. Work was the solution. And there was plenty of that to keep her busy. She skipped breakfast, making a coffee to bring upstairs with her. Minutes later, perched on a full box, she was delving into the one in front, quickly lost in the world of words, in the feel of the covers, the soft flutter of the pages. This was her happy place, her escape from the world and its woes.

By eight thirty, the box was only half empty but Helen had recovered both her sense of humour and her sense of calm. She'd been stressed about the opening day yesterday. The break-in at both the shop and her home had caused even more. It shouldn't be a surprise that she was imagining things and feeling a little discombobulated.

The word, one of her favourites, reminded her of something she'd planned to do, and it was with a spring in her step that she bounced down the stairs, a different woman to the one who'd trudged up only a couple of hours earlier.

In the shop, she searched on the shelves under the desk for the sketch pad and frame she'd put there days before. She pulled out a page and using a black marker, wrote on it: *Word of the Week. Discombobulated.*

It was almost time to open up. She pulled the blinds up, checked the display books looked tidy, then balanced the framed word in front of the middle pillar to catch the eye of the passers-by.

Unlocking the door, she opened it to check the bell worked. It was loud enough that if she had to go out back, or into the kitchen, she'd hear it. With five minutes to go before she was officially opened, she hurried back to the kitchen for a glass of water.

She sipped it as she stood behind the desk and waited for her first customer.

It wasn't till nine thirty that the door opened, Helen's smile pinned in place as the bell jangled seconds later.

She unpinned it when she recognised the woman who came through. Two mornings in a row. What had she done to deserve this? Oh yes, she'd killed someone. She had to laugh. It was that or cry.

'Moira, I wasn't expecting to see you again this morning.' *Or wanting to or needing to.* Only when the parole officer crossed the floor, stiletto heels click-clacking on the polished wood, did Helen realise she wasn't wearing her customary *I'm your best buddy* smile. On the contrary, she looked so unusually fierce that Helen wracked her head for whatever she might have done wrong.

'I'm here in my official capacity this morning, unfortunately.'

An unnecessary statement. Apart from the previous two visits, hadn't they all been official?

'I didn't think I was due a visit for a while.' She forced her tone to stay friendly. She'd asked that the meetings take place in her home, not in her business. It seemed that wish wasn't being granted. Her home... shit! She shut her eyes as she realised why Moira had a face like a pickled herring.

'You know the conditions governing your release on licence,' Moira said. 'You must ask permission to stay away from your registered address for two or more days.'

Helen lifted both hands palms out. 'I'm sorry. With all that's been going on, I forgot.'

'You forgot!'

As if that were her biggest crime. 'Someone broke into the shop on Friday.' She shrugged her shoulders. 'Or it may be that I left the door open, I don't know, but someone got in and did some damage. And late the night before, my neighbours saw someone suspicious at the door. So I decided it'd be better to stay for a few nights until I can get the alarm installed.' Damn, the alarm company, she'd planned to ring them first thing. She'd forgotten again.

'You've been released on licence; you have to live by the rules and regulations. Every breach is a black mark against your name.'

Black mark. It was worse than being back in school. 'I'm really sorry. It completely slipped my mind with all I had to do. As soon as the alarm is installed, I'll be moving back home.' She wanted to ask how Moira had found out but then it hit her. The police. They'd have logged the details of the break-in at her house and she was such a super-efficient bitch that she was sure to have seen them.

Moira balanced her briefcase on the desk, no lessening in the ferocity of her expression. 'I'll make allowances for you. *This time.*' She tilted her head towards the stairway. 'I'll need to see your living quarters here.'

Helen thought of the small storage room. The sofa cushions she was using for a bed. The basic washing facilities. 'It's only very temporary,' she said, leading the way upstairs after a glance towards the door in hope of a customer who might save her this final embarrassment. But the gods were having a laugh at her expense and it stayed firmly shut.

Upstairs, she opened the door to the storage room. 'As I said, it's basic.' She pointed to the open suitcase in one corner, her handbag slouching by the other. 'I brought everything I might need for a few days. It's not ideal, but as soon as the alarm is installed, I'll be going home.'

'And when will that be?' Moira's eyes swept over the small space, then crossed to the bathroom, her lips curling to see the lack of facilities.

Helen wanted to lie. To give her a definite date. But it wasn't a risk worth taking. 'I'm ringing them this morning.'

Moira turned to look at her with flint in her eyes. 'You mean it hasn't yet been arranged?'

Helen felt an inch tall. 'It will be today.'

'Right, well, when you have a date, I want to be informed, okay?'

Helen regretted killing Toby. Had done from the beginning, but never more so than she did right at that moment, facing this woman who had so much control over her life. She dropped her chin, trying to hide her suddenly water-logged eyes. Moira was reiterating the rules Helen was obliged to follow, as if she didn't already know them, as if the damn woman hadn't reminded her at every opportunity. She wasn't listening; she was staring through the tears at the woman's ridiculous footwear. It would be so easy to fall in them. So easy to take a tumble down the steep staircase behind her. All it would take was for Helen to give one hard shove.

She could do it. Anger was already bubbling as she listened to Moira going on and bloody on. Helen could release the anger, make it work for her as she'd done before.

The first murder had been hard.

This would be easy.

22

'Are you listening to me?'

Helen dragged her eyes away from Moira's ridiculously high heels and their proximity to the top of the staircase and nodded. 'I heard every word.'

'Right, well make sure you get the alarm sorted, and inform me of the date you'll be moving back home, okay?'

One push was all it would take.

'Yes.' The one word was all Helen could manage as she fought to dispel images of Moira lying twisted and broken at the bottom of the staircase. It was the tinkle of the bell from downstairs that dragged her back to reality. 'I'd better go and see to my customers.' She desperately wanted it to be one and not Alex or Zander from next door. Or the always smiling, irritatingly cheerful postwoman. A customer to show the annoying parole officer that she was running a viable business and didn't need to be spoken to as if she was a naughty five-year-old child.

And she was in luck. Not one customer, but two perusing the shelves.

Moira, though, wasn't leaving without having the last word. 'I expect to hear from you later today.'

Helen wasn't sure who got under her skin more. Ultra-official Moira with her snippy manner and high-handed tone of voice, or best-buddy Moira, all false smiles and fake camaraderie. She tried to put both out of her head and went to chat to her customers.

She wasn't expecting to be run off her feet, nor was she expecting the long periods when there were no customers at all, and she found herself twiddling her thumbs. All those boxes upstairs. If she brought one down, she could work on emptying it while she waited for someone to come through the door. It would have a dual effect: make her look busy and, as working with books always did, it would keep her calm.

It made sense, and a few minutes later, she was happily unpacking books. Jen Clough's alphabetical arrangement was slightly eccentric – biographies of Maureen O'Hara and Peter O'Toole in the same box as crime novels by Jenny O'Brien. She flicked through the pages of each, recovering a receipt from one, and a five-pound note from another. It was almost tempting to keep the money. The books had been given to her, so she could argue that it was legally hers. Legally, but not perhaps, morally. She snapped the note between her fingers. Was this some kind of test? Maybe it had been deliberately hidden to test her honesty? 'Oh hell,' she muttered and shoved the note into the A4 envelope she'd put aside for Jared. She really needed to stop overthinking things.

Late afternoon, she looked up to see Zander coming through the door.

'Came to see how you were doing,' he said.

'Good, thank you.'

He rested a hip against the desk and looked around. 'It's

looking so good. Hard to believe it's the same place that old geezer ran.'

Assuming that by *old geezer* he meant Reginald Taylor, the previous occupant, she smiled. 'I think by their nature, repair shops tend to be messy establishments.'

'Messy.' He snorted a laugh. 'He was a right pig of a man, and his premises was like a sty. Not surprising he went bust in the end.' He jerked his thumb towards the ceiling. 'He lived above the shop too. Permanently. Not temporary like you're doing.'

'Did you know him well?'

'Not really. We'd only moved in next door a few months before he died. But I was the one who found him.'

She'd known the sale of the shop had been an executor sale which indicated the previous owner was deceased, but she'd been too busy with her own plans to find out more. Had there been anything odd, the estate agent would have told her. Wouldn't he? Or was she being totally naïve?

'Found him? What do you mean?'

Zander folded his arms across his chest and looked at her through suddenly narrowed eyes. 'You didn't ask about the previous owner before you bought?'

Bristling at the implied criticism, Helen mirrored his stance. 'No, I didn't. I had other things on my mind.'

'Reggie used to shut the shop at five on a Saturday, then not reopen it till the Tuesday. He was a heavy drinker.' Zander mimed lifting a glass to his mouth. 'Seriously heavy, I mean. Rotgut stuff too. Cheap vodka, gin, and whisky. We'd see the empties piling up out back.'

Mildly curious, she asked, 'He died from liver cirrhosis, did he?'

'Probably would have done if he'd lived a bit longer.' Zander indicated the stairway with a tilt of his head. 'He fell down the stairs after drinking for hours.'

The end she was wishing on Moira not so many hours before. The thought made Helen gasp. 'What an awful way to die.'

'Worse,' Zander said. 'He didn't die immediately.' He rubbed the knuckles of his right hand. 'Alex is friendly with someone down at the station so we know he didn't die until a couple of days later. He'd broken his back in the fall, so couldn't move, but it seems he was trying to get help by knocking on the wooden stairway with his knuckles. They were a raw and bloody mess when I found him.' He grimaced and gave an exaggerated shudder. 'Awful to think of him lying there, knocking again and again in the hope that someone would hear him.'

Knocking. Helen struggled to keep her expression fixed in neutral while a tornado was spinning inside her skull. She didn't believe in ghosts. What she did, though, was read far too many Stephen King novels. She still clearly remembered her heart thumping when she read *The Shining.* But that was between the covers of a book. Words on a page. There were no ghosts in real life. The noise she'd heard the previous day had nothing to do with the late owner.

'Awful thought.' The words were squeezed through tight lips.

'Luckily, you're not a big drinker. Wouldn't want the same thing happening to you now, would we?'

Helen blinked and swallowed painfully. His tone of voice was neutral, but the words... Was he threatening her?

He dipped his head towards the stairway again. 'They made them much steeper when these houses were built, the treads narrower too because their feet were smaller. We had ours replaced when we refurbished.'

She opened her mouth to say she'd no money for that kind of change, then shut it again when she remembered she was supposed to have lots of cash. Lies and their tangled webs. They'd catch her out if she wasn't careful. She lifted her foot. 'I have small feet; they're fine for me.'

'They're still steep, though,' he said as if determined to have the last word on the matter. 'Right, I'd better get back. I'll take the wine glasses with me, save you the bother of coming around with them.'

The change of subject startled her. She'd forgotten all about the glasses. 'I haven't had a chance to wash them as yet. I can do that when I've closed up and drop them around, if that's okay?'

'Don't be daft. I'll throw them into our dishwasher, they'll be done in a jiffy.'

'If you're sure—'

'Absolutely. They're in the kitchen, are they?' He didn't wait for her answer, long strides taking him to the kitchen door; he'd opened it and had picked up the cardboard box from the floor before Helen had climbed over the books she was unpacking to join him.

'I didn't have time to tidy up after the crazy day I had yesterday,' she said, seeing him look around the small, untidy space. There were dirty glasses on the counter, a couple of used mugs in the sink. The container from her ready meal the previous night, the one she'd tossed towards the bin, had missed and sat looking dirty and forlorn on the floor.

'You need to be careful,' he said, resting the box he held on the counter. 'We had a problem with mice last year. The little beggars are hard to get rid of once they take a fancy to you. Your old books would be perfect nesting material for them too.' He picked up the dirty glasses and slotted them into free spaces. 'Right, that's them all done, what about the wine? We can take the full ones back, if you like, just charge you for what you used.'

That would have been the sensible option, short of money as

she was. 'No, that's okay, thanks, it was such a successful day that most of it was drunk. I think there's only a bottle left so I might as well hang on to it.' He didn't need to know there were eight bottles chilling in the fridge.

She opened the door for him and waved him off.

To her dismay, no customers came in between the hours of five and six that evening and the minutes crept by with almost painful slowness. She wanted to cry in frustration. Perhaps Sarah had been right and she should close at five. What had possessed Helen to start a business? It had been a crazy idea. She'd no experience, no business savvy. She should have gone back to her job in the civil service and hidden away from everyone and everything. Not put herself on show behind a desk where Joe Public could point a finger and judge the murderer. Not put herself on display, so that someone might look at her and think she hadn't paid enough for her crime and decide to take it all away.

When her sister rang seconds after six, Helen took a breath, put her best game face on and hoped it would translate into a positive sounding voice. 'Hi.'

'Hi, sis, have you had a busy day?'

'Not as crazy as yesterday, but yes, a steady influx of customers all day. Several in the last hour.' More lies. It looked like she was never going to be finished with them. 'I'm just heading in now to have another of those delicious ready meals you bought for me. I don't know if I thanked you for them; it was so kind.'

'That's what sisters are for. I'm glad it's all going well. I'm so proud of you.'

Helen swallowed the lump in her throat. The echo in her head of Sarah's voice saying *you're such a nuisance, such a baby*, was still there, but it was fading. Her sister was a good woman.

Maybe if Helen had more faith in herself and her decisions, Sarah wouldn't feel the need to organise and manage her.

They chatted for a while longer. Or rather Sarah chatted and Helen added an occasional *mmm, yes*, or *really* depending on the need. She didn't think her sister noticed she was a little distracted. She certainly wouldn't have been aware that Helen was thumping the side of her head with the heel of her hand, because she realised she hadn't done the one thing she needed to do that day. Ring the blasted alarm company. What was wrong with her? She needed to give herself a kick up the arse! No bloody wonder everyone felt the need to manage her!

As soon as Sarah hung up, Helen rang the number she'd saved on her phone, unsurprised when she was answered by a recorded message giving her the opening hours. She disconnected with a groan. Moira would be waiting for the promised call. There wasn't an option open to her. The situation called for another lie.

There was no point in putting it off. She walked to the window and stared out at the fading day before taking a deep breath and tapping the phone icon beside Moira's name. She waited, unable to believe her luck when she was greeted by the fake best-friend voice inviting her to leave a message. It made it so much easier to lie.

'Hi, Moira, I've been so busy with customers all day that I haven't had a chance to get back to you. Unfortunately, the alarm company doesn't have availability until next week. They did say in the event of a cancellation, they might be able to install it earlier. I'll keep you informed. Thanks, bye.' She hung up with a nervous giggle that lasted for too long. It might have kept going. They might have found her on the floor in the morning still giggling, if she hadn't heard a sound that silenced her, and put an end to the worries about what Moira might or might not think.

It was coming from behind her. A dull *knock, knock, knock*.
And she was suddenly afraid to turn around.

23

Helen had known fear before. They were old friends, and as such she thought she understood it. Over the years, she'd learnt to use the fear caused by the actions of others. To harness it for her own needs and desires. But this was different. It froze her in place, dried her mouth, caused her to breathe in short, jerky gulps and made it impossible to act.

As the light outside faded, the window began to reflect the interior of the shop. Blurred at first, taking form and shape as the minutes ticked by.

What did she expect to see appearing behind her? The broken, shattered body of Reginald Taylor lying at the bottom of the staircase? Did she really think the shop was haunted?

When no ghostly apparition formed, when the silence lingered, she turned ever so slowly and stared across the shop floor. She hadn't switched the lights on, and it was the streetlights outside that illuminated the space, throwing shades and shadows along the shelves, into the spaces between the books, darkening the corners to provide a hiding place.

She was being ridiculous.

It seemed sensible to lock the front door and draw the blinds. Shutting the scary things out, or locking them in. She wasn't sure of anything any more.

She was trembling as she switched the lights on. Stupidly, she'd skipped both breakfast and lunch. Her blood sugar was probably in her boots. No wonder she was so on edge, quick to paranoia, even quicker to imagine the worst.

Leaving the lights on behind her, she went into the kitchen, pulled out another of the ready meals, pierced the film with a knife, and slipped it into the microwave. She filled a glass with water and drank it as she waited for the food to heat, emptying the glass and filling it again. Hunger and dehydration: no wonder she was such a mess.

When the knocking came again, she spun around. The previous night, she'd thought it was coming from the kitchen. It was Zander, with his story of the previous owner's shocking death that had made her consider it was coming from the stairwell.

Zander.

Helen had already learnt that anger was an antidote to fear. It fizzed through her now. She gripped the knife she was still holding and drove it into the cupboard door with such force that it hung there in a dramatic testament to the emotion surging through her.

She'd wondered how far the two men would go to get what they wanted. Now it seemed clear. They were willing to do anything.

'Bastards,' she muttered, opening the microwave for her meal. Her appetite had vanished, but she needed to eat. Being weak and feeble wasn't going to help her win this fight.

Accepting that it was a fight was the first step. She could

brush away any nonsensical ideas of the shop being haunted and dismiss her worry that she was paranoid. They'd messed with her head, those twin bastards. Perhaps she should have told them that the last man who'd messed with her had ended up very, very dead.

24

Anger energised Helen. She shovelled the food into her mouth from the container and drank two more glasses of water. Then with a shake of her head at the state of the kitchen, she spent fifteen minutes cleaning it up, getting rid of the rubbish into the bin outside the back door.

It took only a few minutes to count the takings and put the bulk of it safely into her purse with the money from the previous day. The following afternoon, she planned to lodge it all in the bank. She updated the ledger, then after a final look around, switched out the lights and headed upstairs.

She worked steadily until a little after midnight. Focusing on getting books onto shelves, she emptied two boxes and added five till receipts to the envelope for Jared. If it killed her, she'd get through the rest of his grand-aunt's collection before Monday. And if she didn't, she'd lie and tell him that she had.

Anger might have been energising, but it wasn't conducive to sleep. When she finally lay down, she tossed and turned, got up to lock the door, lay down again, tossed and turned some more.

Usually, thoughts of books she loved would help her to drift off, but that night, no matter how much she tried to keep her mind on the covers, or the pages, or even the words, everything dripped with blood. She could almost feel the warm stickiness of it, smell its distinct stink as it dripped from Reginald Taylor's raw, bleeding knuckles and the stab wound she'd inflicted on Toby.

It seemed better to get up, get through more of the boxes. With the shelves downstairs full, she started filling the ones upstairs. Many of her customers were older so it made sense to use these for books that would appeal to younger clientele and students. It took a lot of rejigging, moving books she'd put downstairs to the upstairs shelves. It meant she could open this second space sooner than she'd expected.

By eight o'clock, the shelves upstairs weren't full but it was getting there and looked good enough for customers to come up if they wished. She pulled the remaining three boxes into a corner, stacking them neatly one on top of the other. Later, if she did a few more hours work, she could have them all unpacked. She was collecting more books that afternoon. Buying them though, not getting them for free, so she could afford to be selective.

She forced herself to eat breakfast. A bowl of cereal with milk that was edging past its best. She planned her day as she ate. That morning, she needed to ring the alarm company. In the afternoon, her first priority was to lodge the cash into the bank. Afterwards, a visit home, then some grocery shopping before driving to pick up the books.

Five minutes to the hour, she unlocked the door and pulled up the blinds. It left her free to ring the alarm company as soon as it hit nine. 'I need an alarm fitted,' she said when her call was answered. Simple, wasn't it? But no, of course it wasn't. They insisted they needed to come out and assess the building before they could quote.

'We can come out tomorrow, and discuss the options open to you, and all going well, we can install it on Friday.'

Friday! Sooner than she'd imagined. She could be sleeping at home in her comfortable bed by the weekend.

Although she was exhausted, she felt energised by all she'd achieved that morning and the evening before. Getting the alarm organised was the finishing touch.

It was a good morning too. Several customers came in and all bought books. Even better, the student who'd come in early on Monday came back with some of her friends.

'Hi,' Helen said. 'It's nice to see you back again. It's Jess, isn't it?'

'Yea, good memory. I was telling my housemates,' she waved to the three women who'd already gravitated towards the shelves, 'that you'd quite a mix of books to choose from.'

'Thank you.' Helen pointed to the stairway. 'Have a look upstairs too. I'm hoping to make it a more student-friendly section. It's not completely ready but you can have a look, if you like.'

A few minutes later, they came to the desk, each holding a pile of books. 'Can we leave these here while we have a look upstairs?'

'Yes, of course.' Helen cleared a space for the books they'd chosen. They were laughing and chatting as they went up the stairs, the sound filling the shop, lifting Helen's mood further. This was what she'd wanted. If students came in on a regular basis, if word about her bookshop spread, she'd do okay.

Even as she listened to the laughter coming from upstairs, she thought of the two men next door and a tide of fury washed away her good mood. Had they thought she'd be easy game, no match for wily Londoners?

A few years ago, they would have been right. But that was before Toby. That was before she discovered she could fight back. Before she discovered that death was a good place to end something, and an even better place to start.

She forced a smile when the four students came back down almost fifteen minutes later, her eyes widening when she saw they'd chosen even more books.

Helen needed to use three of her paper bags for the first student's. 'Sorry, I don't have any bigger bags,' she said handing them over. 'That's twelve pounds. Will it be cash or card?'

The student jerked her thumb to the woman standing behind. 'Cash, but Jess is paying.'

'Yea, she's paying for mine too.'

'And mine.'

Helen smiled uncertainly at the student who'd been so enthusiastic on Monday and who'd kindly brought her friends to the shop. They'd all seemed to be on good terms when they came in. All laughter and pleasant banter. But the dynamic had changed; something had shifted between them. Three of them were still smiling, but there was something off in the curve of their lips, something too knowing in their eyes. Helen was suddenly quite sure that she didn't like these women.

Jess wasn't smiling. She had her eyes on the books she held.

'Is that okay with you?' Helen asked. 'You're paying for everyone's books?' She did a quick tot up. 'That's going to be fifty-six pounds altogether.'

'Yea, that's fine.' Without raising her eyes, Jess handed her books over to be bagged. She reached into the pocket of her denim jacket, took out a roll of cash and peeled off three twenty-pound notes. 'There you go.'

Helen rang up the register and handed over the change. 'Thanks very much. I hope you'll all come back soon.' She didn't really. But this was business; she couldn't afford to be choosy, to like or dislike customers.

She watched them go. Three of them still laughing and jostling one another, Jess trailing behind looking as if the woes of the world had smacked her across the face. How old were they? Nineteen, maybe twenty. So confident. So sure of themselves. Helen couldn't remember being that certain of life. Not at nineteen, definitely not now when she seemed to be less sure of anything.

Only three more customers came in before she locked the door and pulled the blinds down on the dot of midday. It had been a good morning.

She had books to collect later that afternoon. Before that, first on her list of things to do was to bring the money to the bank. More of her customers had used cash than she'd expected. She filled in the ledger for that day, took seventy-two pounds from the register and looked underneath the desk for her handbag. She hunkered down, thinking she must have kicked it further under, and when it wasn't there, she straightened. She'd left it upstairs.

Later, she realised she must have known at that moment what had happened, some form of extrasensory perception, because she took the stairs slowly, lifting each foot as if she was treading on treacle, pushing upward as if she was climbing Everest, with that sixth sense screaming in her head that she wasn't going to like what she found when she got there.

Even when she saw the storage room door sitting open, when she knew she'd shut it, she refused to face what in her heart she knew. She picked up her handbag and reached inside for her purse and only then could she bring herself to acknowledge the truth. Those lovely students had robbed her. The books they'd bought, they'd paid for with her money.

And it was this betrayal – not the break-in at the shop or the one at her home, not the horrible men next door or the ever-annoying parole officer – that made her collapse on the makeshift bed and cry.

25

Crying wasn't going to get her anywhere. It certainly wasn't going to get her money back, so Helen did what she'd always done: picked herself up and got on with it. It was getting harder though, perhaps because it seemed to be one thing after the other, or maybe because she was tired, or because what those young women had done felt like such a dreadful betrayal. She was angry at them for having taken advantage of her kindness, and even angrier with herself for being so stupidly naïve.

The vague idea of going to the university to try to find them was dismissed as soon as thought. All she knew about them was that one was called Jess. The woman who'd come on Monday, who'd returned with her friends. Not the ringleader, though. She remembered her defeated demeanour as she was leaving. Perhaps she'd been coerced into stealing the money. Helen would like to have believed that, would like to have thought she wasn't such a mug.

She got to her feet, picked up her handbag, then dropped it again. There was no need to go to the bank. The takings from that morning would be needed to pay for the books she was picking up that afternoon, and for food. The pickup was arranged for three and was only a ten-minute drive away. She could go home, have a shower and check everything was okay there. She could unpack another box of books. Or she could continue to stand there feeling helpless and sad.

Deciding to focus on the shop, she went to the corner where she'd stacked up the remaining three boxes. It shouldn't have come as a surprise to find that the students had also been there. The boxes had been taken down, opened, one of them emptied on the floor in a mess of jumbled books.

'Bitches!' Her eyes filled again as she surveyed the tangle. They'd taken no care and some of the volumes had been damaged. Jess had struck her as being a book lover. How wrong she'd been.

Several had been damaged beyond saving. She brought them through to the storage room and dropped them into the box destined for recycling.

It took an hour to restore order. It would have taken less time if she hadn't been weighed down by the intense feeling of treachery and disappointment. Silly perhaps, but she was finding it hard not to take it personally.

Hard not to let everything that had happened in the last few days wear her down; to wonder if the fates were telling her that her future, like her past, was destined for heartache and pain.

'Fuck it,' she shouted suddenly. Those bitches had stolen her money; she'd be damned if she was going to allow them to take more than that. They'd taken advantage of her. They wouldn't do so again. A valuable lesson had been learnt. Painfully, perhaps. Nothing new there. She pushed the anger down, picked up her handbag from the storage room and headed downstairs.

When her mobile rang, she pulled it out and tried to inject

some businesslike dynamism into her voice. 'Appleby Books, Helen speaking, how can I help you?'

'Hi, it's Jared Clough. I thought I'd touch base, see if you've managed to get any further with my grand-aunt's books.'

The anger that she'd only dampened down flared again and searched for a target but she swallowed it down. It wasn't this annoying man's fault she'd been stupidly naïve. 'Not very far,' she said. 'And as yet, the most interesting thing I've found is a twenty-year-old till receipt.'

'Right, but you'll keep looking?'

'Yes.' Blunt, but she'd already promised; she wasn't in the mood to do so again. 'Now, I'm sorry, I really have to go.' She hung up without waiting for him to reply. *Irritating man!*

She'd already checked that the back door was secured, but she checked again, then left through the front door and locked it behind her. It was only a ten-minute walk to the convenience store and a little less than thirty minutes later, she was returning with a plastic bag hanging heavily from each hand. She was on the far side of the road and was relieved to see her shop appear in the distance as if somehow it might have vanished while she was gone. Stupid anxiety: it increased as she got closer, her footsteps slowing, faltering. She tried laughing away her fears, stopping when the sound that came out smacked of hysteria.

Moving to the side of the path, she put her bags down gently and took a deep breath. She could see the doorway of the shop. It looked exactly as she'd left it. Locked and secure.

Picking up her bags again, she carried on, her heart beating in time to her footsteps as she determinedly speeded her steps to face whatever it was that might be waiting for her.

She stopped when she got to the window. The display looked okay. Not exciting, just okay. Was the word of the week thing a bit silly? It was a bad idea to stop and look. Her reflection looked haunted, her cheeks hollow, bags under her eyes. She looked awful enough to scare away customers.

Stupidly relieved to find the door still secure, she put one of the carrier bags down while she searched in her bag for the keys. Inside, she shut and relocked the door behind her before heading to the kitchen. As was often the way, she'd bought more than she'd planned and struggled to fit everything into the fridge. She squeezed the last ready meal in sideways and shut the fridge in time to hear a dull thud. Holding her breath, she cocked her head, trying to decide where the hell it had come from.

She didn't want it to be from the stairwell where Reginald Taylor had grated the skin from his knuckles trying to call for help. But even as she squeezed her eyes shut in an attempt to get the image from her head, Toby's bloody body appeared in full glorious colour, and she relived that dreadful moment when she'd felt the cold handle of the very sharp knife in her hand. She still couldn't remember actually using it. Had there been much resistance or had it gone into his belly like a warm knife through butter? Probably the latter, because she clearly remembered the disbelieving expression on his face. She'd been startled too by how surprisingly warm and viscous his blood had been.

More than anything, she remembered watching him as he lay on the ground, his eyes wide, hands frantically trying to stem the deluge of blood that had burst from his split aorta, and her utter relief when the movement of his hands slowed, and he stopped blinking, his eyes staying wide and fixed on her face.

For several seconds, the knocking noise stopped and started. It didn't matter; Helen was lost in the past she'd tried so desperately to put behind her. There were days when she could, when the memory bounced around the periphery of her mind. Other days, it was the background of every thought. She found succour between the pages of a book, but if she'd hoped that owning a bookshop would be like an exaggerated version of one, she was wrong.

At least she was so far, but that might simply be down to the catalogue of misadventures the last few days. When Zander and Alex discovered the lady wasn't for moving, she hoped they'd give up. Leave her alone. Stop trying to frighten her.

She moved to the kitchen sink, turned on the hot water and squirted a puddle of washing-up liquid into the palm of one hand. Then she stood scrubbing her hands under water so hot, it made her eyes water with the pain. Minutes. Until her hands were red and raw.

It didn't work. It never did. She could still feel the stickiness of Toby's blood. Sometimes, on the worst days, she could smell it too.

She grabbed a towel and patted her hands dry. There were too many things to be done to be standing around wasting her energy on a man who'd caused her so much grief.

There was just about enough time to get home, have a shower, and make some small attempt at cleaning up the mess those bastards who'd broken into her home had made. Afterwards, she'd drive straight to the address in Widcombe and hopefully get some good books.

At home, she checked the work the glaziers had done on the back door, pleased to see they'd cleaned up all the broken glass too. She turned the key in the lock, taking it out and putting it in a drawer. That lesson had been learnt.

She examined the mess, the breakages, the stupid, mindless damage. It would be nice to get it back in order before she moved home on Friday but there weren't enough minutes left in that day. It'd get done. Eventually.

Her priority was to have a shower, wash her hair, blow dry it. Feel normal.

Twenty minutes later, her hair brushed back and tied in a ponytail, and dressed in a long-sleeved denim dress and boots, she felt better.

Checking her watch, she saw she had fifteen minutes to spare before she needed to leave for her three o'clock appointment. There was no point in letting them go to waste. In the kitchen, she pulled a refuse bag from a roll and headed to the living room. She stood at the door, unsure where to start, cursing the delinquents who'd done the damage using every derogatory word in her vocabulary.

They'd burst a cushion, its insides lying in a sad clump under the upended coffee table. The mindless destruction was soul-destroying. She scooped the cushion filling into the bag, dropping the broken pieces of a vase and broken glass from two photograph frames on top. Luckily, the two lamps hadn't been damaged and when they were back in place, the room started to look better. She'd need to vacuum to remove the residual debris but otherwise, it was almost back to normal.

She brushed dust from the front of her dress, cursing herself for having changed first, brushing it harder, her eyes filling with the utter frustration of everything in her life. 'I can't even do this properly,' she muttered, giving her dress a final shake.

She'd done enough. With the alarm on, she locked the house and headed to her car. It wasn't far as the crow flies to the house where she was to pick up the books, but there was the usual snarl of traffic so the journey took almost twenty minutes.

She pulled into the driveway of an ugly, squat house with a flat roof, and a garage door which took up an unnecessarily large amount of the frontage. Reminding herself not to judge a book by its cover, she got out and approached the unattractive uPVC front door and looked for the doorbell. There didn't appear to be one. Convinced now that this was going to be a gigantic waste of her precious time, she rapped her knuckles against a frosted glass panel and waited.

The door was opened almost immediately by a smiling woman with a mop of black hair. 'You must be Helen, come in, come in.' She stood back, lifted her arms and waved, causing the silky fabric of the multi-coloured kaftan she wore to flutter butterfly-like. 'Come through, I'll make us some tea.'

The inside of the house was a jaw-dropping contrast to the exterior. Everywhere there was colour. As they walked into a huge, open-plan kitchen-living room, with a view over a lushly planted garden, Helen's surprise must have been obvious because the woman laughed.

'People always react the same way when they come inside. It's incredibly ugly outside, isn't it?'

There was no point in lying. 'Mrs Rogers, it's probably one of the ugliest houses I've ever seen.' She smiled. 'It's quite a surprise then to come in and see this.' She waved a hand around the beautifully furnished and decorated room. 'It's stunning.'

'Thank you, and call me Dilly, please.' She nodded towards the table. 'Have a seat, I'll make some tea, or would you prefer coffee?'

'Tea would be fine, thank you.'

Helen wasn't surprised to see that the tea was served in dainty cups on mismatched saucers and was accompanied by a plate of chocolate biscuits.

'Help yourself,' Dilly said, nudging the plate. As if to give encouragement, she picked one up, dipped it into her tea and popped it whole into her mouth. 'Now, tell me about this shop of yours.'

The beautiful décor, lovely view across the garden, and obvious kindness in Dilly's eyes seemed to act like a balm for everything that had troubled Helen that week. All her muscles seemed to sigh and relax at the same time. If she'd taken a mouthful of tea, she'd have thought she'd been drugged, but she hadn't tasted it as yet. She did now and it was strong and delicious. There was work to be done back in the shop. She didn't have time for the luxury of sitting around, drinking tea and chatting. Yet, she did. She told the warm, encouraging woman about the shop, the break-ins, the students who'd stolen from her. And because she was such a good listener, she told her she'd been in prison.

'I served a couple of years,' she said, trying to make light of it, hoping she was giving the impression that she'd been inside for something relatively minor. Some white-collar crime, not something as awful as murder. 'I've been out a few months and I'm starting to get my life back on track.' She smiled. 'I don't usually offload on virtual strangers like this; you're a very good listener.'

'You looked like you needed to talk.' Dilly reached for the teapot and refilled their cups. 'You looked stressed coming in. I think offloading, as you put it, helped get things into perspective a bit.'

Helen's sister said similar things. That she should talk about everything, get her problems out in the open. But when she did talk to Sarah, she often didn't listen – or ignored what Helen said in favour of what she herself believed was right. Dilly, on the other hand, really listened. 'Yes, it has, thank you.' And it was true; it had helped a bit.

'I think you're doing an amazing thing, opening a new business after what you've been through.' Dilly put her cup down, pushed her chair back and got to her feet. 'I suppose I'd better show you the books. There's quite a lot of them, but you can have a look, see which would be of interest.' She led the way to a small room at the front of the house. 'Anna calls this the library,' she said, opening the door.

'Wow!' Helen's reaction was instinctive. The room may have been tiny, but every wall was fitted with floor-to-ceiling shelves. And every shelf was tightly packed with books.

'Anna is a prolific reader.' Dilly pointed to rows of folders stacked on one of the shelves. 'She also kept the notes for every university subject she's studied, every post-graduate course she's ever done. And she's done many. She wants to keep these, but not the books.'

Helen's gaze flicked along the spines. Stephen King, of course, but also plenty of fairly recent thrillers by John Connolly, Keri Beevis, J. A. Baker, Michelle Kidd and Diane Saxon. More by Jenny O'Brien and Anita Waller too. Even some historical fiction by Pam Lecky. There was enough there to fill the remaining shelves in her shop. If she could get them at a good price.

She turned to Dilly. 'Your daughter doesn't mind you selling them?'

'Not my daughter, my wife, soon to be my ex-wife.'

Colour flooded Helen's cheeks. 'I'm sorry, I jumped to a silly conclusion.'

'Don't worry. Easily done. Anna and I were together for fifteen years, but in the last couple of years, we grew apart. Still friends but our lives are going in different directions. She's moved to Wales. To a cottage where she's going to paint, she says.' Dilly sounded sceptical. With a shake of her head, she waved a hand around the room. 'She said I could have all the books, that she only wants her folders. I'm packing them up and sending them on to her next week.'

'And you want all the books gone.' All memories of the woman she'd once loved. Maybe not such an amicable separation after all. 'I have some boxes in the car; I'll fetch them and make a start.' She looked along the shelves. There were probably hundreds of suitable books. 'Most would be perfect for me, but it'll come down to price really. I'm only starting out, as you know, so funds are a bit limited.'

Dilly seemed unperturbed. 'Get your boxes, I'll make more tea and we can talk money.'

The room was empty when Helen returned. She was eyeing the books she definitely wanted when the door opened and Dilly came through with the tea. In mugs this time. Helen took the one offered to her and nodded towards the shelves. 'There's so much here that I'd like. I'm offering fifty pence a book, but I'm afraid that means I'm only going to be able to afford to take about a hundred.'

Dilly used her mug to point to the empty boxes. 'You won't fit a hundred in those two.'

'I should have asked how many you had when you rang.' Helen should have been more professional, more organised. Not so bloody stupid. She felt a curl of anger lash out, making her mentally squirm. 'I could always come back.' Now she sounded pathetic too.

'Of course you can, my dear; don't worry about that.' Dilly drained her mug. 'Let's see how many we can fit in these two. The money isn't really of concern to me, you know.' Her smile faded as she looked around the room. 'In the last couple of years, Anna would spend hours in here, curled up in a chair, reading. I think I resented the books for all the time she spent with them and now that she's left, I resent them even more, and want them gone.' She looked at Helen, a rueful expression on her face. 'Does that sound silly?'

'I've been in love. I've done silly.' She wondered what her parole officer would think if she heard Helen reducing her crime to *silly*. 'My depth of silliness landed me in prison, so you've a long way to go before you reach my level.'

'Ah,' Dilly said without surprise. 'That explains the sadness I can see in your eyes. Do you want to talk about it?'

It wasn't prurient curiosity. Helen saw genuine kindness in the eyes that were fixed on her face. 'It's not something I like to talk about, but thank you, you're very kind.' She crossed to the bookshelf. 'I should make a start. Are you okay with fifty pounds for a hundred books?'

'I intend to give any money I make to charity. So how about we reach an agreement? You take everything, even books you think you mightn't have a use for, and give me the fifty you have, and someday, when your finances have improved, you can give some money to a charity of your choice.' She tilted her head. 'Deal?'

It was such an extraordinarily generous offer that Helen was dumbstruck.

'It'll go some way towards restoring your faith in women.'

'I don't know what to say.' Helen looked at the shelves of books. There were so many bestsellers here, it was an absolute goldmine.

'Say yes. Honestly, as far as I'm concerned, it's a good deal. Despite how I feel about them, I wouldn't be happy simply throwing them away.'

'Right then, it's a deal. I promise, I'll keep an account of how much I should be paying you and as soon as my finances improve, I'll donate that sum to a good charity.'

'Okay, well let's get packing.'

With both working together, it didn't take long. Helen concentrated on packing the more recent crime and psychological thrillers, books she knew she had immediate shelf space for.

It didn't take long for the two boxes to be filled. 'I have lots of empty ones back in the shop,' Helen said, kicking herself again for not having brought more. 'I don't shut until six tomorrow, but if it suits, I can come back then.' She looked around the room. 'It might take a few trips to get them all. My car isn't that big.'

Dilly shrugged. 'Take as much time as you need. I've nothing planned for the rest of this week, or the weekend, for that matter. I'm assuming you don't open on Sunday so you could always finish then.'

'If you're sure I'm not imposing.' Helen's fingers played along the tops of the books in front of her as a trickle of guilt dampened her pleasure. 'Are you sure you don't want to try selling them elsewhere? I feel I'm taking advantage.'

Dilly reached a hand out to pat Helen on the shoulder. 'Honestly, I think this is going to work out for both of us. You'll get the books you want, and I'll get rid of an unpleasant memory. And don't forget, the money was going to charity.'

It would have been rude, and stupid, to argue. 'I'll be back tomorrow evening, probably around six thirty,' Helen said when the boxes were stowed away in her car.

'I'll be here.' Dilly gave her a wave as she backed out of the driveway.

What a nice woman, Helen thought.

She was concentrating on reversing onto the narrow road so she didn't see Dilly's smile fade or the expression of sheer hatred that replaced it.

26

Helen was buzzing with a renewed sense of purpose on her journey back to the shop. What an amazing woman Dilly was. How easy she was to talk to, how well she listened. Helen didn't feel judged or managed. Instead, she felt valued, appreciated.

What a lifeline she'd thrown her too. She might put a higher price on some of the books she'd taken with her. They were in pristine condition. Maybe worth two-fifty or even three pounds. At last, something was going her way.

The spirit of optimism continued until she pulled up outside the shop. She recognised the car in front even before the driver's door opened and Moira Manson climbed out in that elegant, cat-like way she had.

Fear shot through Helen with such ferocity, she gasped. Had she forgotten to contact her about the alarm? She thought she had, but maybe she'd imagined ringing and leaving a message. She'd have liked to have had time to check her phone to make sure, but it was too late; the parole officer was striding towards her with her professional, grim expression in place. Irritating as she found it, Helen would have preferred to have seen her *we're best mates* one. It wouldn't land her back in prison; the professional one might.

Was Moira going to tell her that she'd broken the conditions of her licence and would have to return to prison to serve the rest of her sentence? Helen couldn't go back, couldn't face two more years locked away. If she lived between the covers of a book, she could drive away, go home, pack a suitcase and disappear. But this was real life. And in that building behind the parole officer sat her future. The Appleby Books sign in the primary colours she'd delighted in choosing. The window display with the framed word of the week. She'd already decided on the following week's one. It was, thanks to Dilly, going to be *serendipitous*. But now, looking through her car window, seeing that hateful woman waiting for her to get out, she thought she'd put *flagitious* and if anyone asked what it meant, she'd tell them about a wickedly shameful woman who was haunting her.

If she was recalled to prison however, she'd leave a great big *fuck* in the frame.

Since she wasn't going to drive away, it seemed she had no option but to get out and face her nemesis. Composing her expression as best as she could into positive lines – a smile, wide eyes, frown lines smoothed away – she opened the car door and stepped out. 'Hi, Moira. Goodness, I'm being spoilt by visits from you these days.' As if she was the person Helen most wanted to see. As if they really were best mates.

Leaving the boxes in the car, she unlocked the shop door. 'Come on in. I'm going to have a coffee; would you like one?' If she kept talking, if she kept pretending everything was okay, maybe it would be. She kept babbling words that probably made little sense as she walked through to the kitchen to put on the kettle. 'Or there's tea if you'd prefer.'

'Neither, thank you.'

The words were spoken in the parole officer's best official manner. Helen's hand trembled and sent grains of coffee skittering across the countertop. She ignored them, poured the water when it boiled, took her time, tried to appear calm. The parole officer was immediately behind her, saying nothing. Helen turned with the mug held to her mouth. Not sipping the coffee but using it to hide the tremor in her lower lip that she couldn't seem to stop.

'I have to admit to being a little perturbed,' Moira said at last.

Helen pressed the mug tighter to her lip, feeling the soft tissue crush against her teeth. Pain centred you. She'd always known that. Anyway, the woman's pomposity had pricked the bubble of fear that had enveloped her. *A little perturbed?*

'Why's that then?' She took a sip of her coffee, then held it clasped in both hands against her chest.

'You were supposed to ring me yesterday to fill me in on the alarm situation, and when you'd be returning to your registered address. Instead, it wasn't until six thirty that you deigned to ring, leaving a very lackadaisical message.'

Helen couldn't remember exactly what she'd said. Had she been too casual, too flippant? Hadn't she been sufficiently humble and grateful? The mug of coffee was burning her hands. The temptation to throw it over the woman was almost unbearable. She'd wait to see what she had to say. If she was sending her back to prison, it'd be worth it to add *assault with a deadly weapon* into the mix. The thought almost made her laugh and she had to concentrate to keep her voice steady. 'I'm sorry if you thought that. I didn't get confirmation from the company myself till six. Probably, I should have rung you then straight away but I wanted to lock up first. You know, for safety.'

'It wasn't only the timing; it was also the tone of your voice.

You don't seem to appreciate the seriousness of breaching any of the conditions of your licence. By rights, I should have you recalled to finish your sentence in prison.'

The handle of the cutlery drawer was biting into Helen's back. If she turned and slid it open, she could pull out the big carving knife she knew lay along one side. It wasn't as sharp as the one she'd had. The one that had been taken by the police and never returned. But it was sharp enough. It would do the job. It would go into Moira as easily as that sharper knife had gone into Toby's beer-softened belly. Helen reached behind, her fingers curling around the handle of the drawer.

'But I won't. Not this time.'

Relief weakened Helen's legs. She sagged back, her hand falling away from the handle. From the almost irresistible temptation. 'Thank you.'

'Don't make me regret it.' Moira's expression relaxed a little.

'I won't.' But what Helen needed to do was spin yet another lie. 'Actually, I was going to ring you tomorrow because the alarm company contacted me to say they'd had a cancellation. They're coming in the morning to do an assessment. Unless there's a problem, I'll have the alarm installed on Friday and should be able to return home.'

'That is good news. Now, if you don't mind, I'll just pop up and use your facilities.' A smile appeared. 'And I will have a coffee before I go, if that offer still stands.'

The transition from pompous officialdom to the skin-crawling *we're buddies* was unsettling. 'Yes, of course, coming right up.' Helen turned so suddenly that coffee sloshed from the almost-full mug she was holding, a wave of it splashing across her denim dress. She wanted to swear, grind her teeth, scream, but she waited until she heard the footsteps ascending the staircase before she muttered a quiet 'shit' under her breath. She reached for a towel to dab the stain and mop up the puddle of liquid from the floor.

The kettle was re-boiled, the coffee made and cooling before Moira returned.

'My apologies,' she said, waving her mobile. 'Honestly, I can never get away from this job.' She looked surprised when Helen handed her the mug. 'Coffee?' She shook her head as if confused. 'Oh yes, of course, I did ask for one, didn't I? Silly me.' She took a couple of quick sips. 'Before I forget, I really enjoyed that book I bought; would you have another similar?'

Helen remembered the graphically violent one that Moira had chosen. 'I'm sure we do; would you like to go out and have a look?'

Moira shook her head. 'I'll drink my coffee; just pick one for me. I trust your taste.'

Helen tried to look pleased by the compliment. 'I'll see what I can find; back in a tick.' She didn't bother taking time over the choice, picking the first horror novel off the shelf. Returning to the kitchen, she handed it to Moira. 'I think this might suit.'

'Excellent, thank you.' Moira didn't even look at the cover, putting it into her bag and taking out her purse. 'A pound, is it?'

Helen didn't know; she hadn't looked. 'Yes, that's fine.'

'Okay, now I must dash.' Then, as if she'd suddenly remembered why she'd come, Moira added, in her most official tone, 'And please, no more slip-ups. I expect to hear from you on Friday to say you'll be returning to your registered address that night. Okay?' As if Helen was an idiot.

'Yes, that's clear. As soon as the alarm is up and running, I'll be happy to return to my home.' She wanted to add that it hadn't been easy, sleeping in that tiny storage room, coping with minimal facilities, but she could see by the expression on the parole officer's face that her thoughts were elsewhere. Maybe it had been a boyfriend on the phone and they'd had a lover's tiff. She'd like to believe that. That all wasn't perfect and sunny in the woman's life.

She really hoped someone was making Moira's life as miserable as she was making Helen's.

27

At nine the following morning, Helen opened the shop and looked around the shelves in satisfaction. The books she'd brought from Dilly's more than filled any gaps so she'd arranged a separate display on a table she'd brought down from upstairs. She'd debated asking three pounds each for them but decided two-fifty was a more realistic price to tempt customers.

At five minutes past the hour, the alarm-company rep came through the door. A thin, wiry man with a cheerful smile and keen eyes, it didn't take him long to assess the premises and come up with an efficient plan for the shop's security.

She was persuaded to pay a little extra for a smart system that would link to an app on her phone but shook her head emphatically when asked if she wanted a monitored system. It reminded her too much of prison. And anyway, she guessed it would cost more than she could afford.

As it was, it cost more than she'd expected. Yet, she had to have it. She handed over her credit card, hoping it wouldn't start to laugh when he processed it, only marginally relieved when he handed it back with a nod. 'All done,' he said.

It was indeed; paying for it would take her well into her overdraft with the subsequent cost implied. She needed to sell a lot of books in the next couple of days if she'd any chance of keeping her bank happy. Once again, she thought of those students and the money they'd stolen and felt acid burn in her belly.

The alarm would be installed the following day. She was tempted to ring Moira to let her know, to get the conversation over with, but she'd had her fill of the woman and decided to reward herself with a Moira-free day.

By midday, she'd had several customers, all of whom gravitated towards her new display so that the books on it were soon gone. Since it seemed to work, she arranged more books on the table to see if the magic would continue. Whether it was witchcraft, or the almost-new books, she wasn't sure, but by closing time, she'd had her best day since opening.

She was smiling as she crossed to lock the door, once again lost in dreams of the bookshop being a complete success, so was totally unprepared for the face that appeared at the window and let out a yelp of alarm. Her fingers groped for the snib of the Yale lock while her other hand scrambled to pull the keys from her jeans' pocket.

'Please, let me come in. I need to explain.'

'You have to be kidding me!' The keys had caught in the lining of Helen's pocket and she heard the material tear as she jerked them free. She was swearing loudly as she jabbed the key into the lock and turned it. 'Go away before I call the police. No, on second thoughts, stay there.' She pulled her mobile from her other pocket. 'I'll call them and they can arrest you for robbery.'

'Please!' A hand appeared on the glass, fingers splayed. 'Let me explain.'

Helen reached for the blind cord and yanked it, the blind falling with a clatter, shutting the face away.

'Please!'

There was so much pathos in that one word, Helen found herself weakening. Wasn't she proof that second chances could work? Or was she? That doubt irritated as much as the repeated 'please' she could still hear coming through the window. How long was the thieving cow going to stand out there?

'I made a mistake.'

As Helen had done years before. Believing in Toby, or killing him. Reducing what had happened to a chicken-and-egg scenario. She doubted if Moira would be impressed with that either.

Unlocking the door seemed preferable to having the same debate in her head that she'd had over and over for more than two years.

'You have one minute,' she said, holding the door open with one hand, her other on the frame to block the entrance.

'Can't I come in?'

'Last time you came in, you stole money from me; why would I let you in again?'

She waited for an answer, watching as the young woman shuffled her feet and adjusted the straps of the rucksack she was carrying.

When she spoke, her voice was thin, hesitant, barely audible, as if regret had weighed the words down. 'It wasn't planned. Honestly. I shared a flat with those girls and mentioned this place to them. You were so enthusiastic when I was in on Monday, so keen for the place to be a success, so I thought I was doing good by bringing them in. And it was all going fine till we went upstairs.'

Where Helen had sent them, thrilled to have real-life university students replace the ones in her imagination. 'Oh, for goodness' sake, you'd better come in since this appears to be a convoluted tale.' Helen stood back, waved her in and pointed to a spot on the floor. 'Stand there, don't move till I lock up, then you can finish.'

It crossed her mind that locking herself into the shop with a woman she knew couldn't be trusted was a careless move, but there was something about the pathetic, weary stance of the woman that told her she meant no harm. Or no further harm at any rate. Helen had to remind herself that she and her gang of thieves had stolen from her. And they'd made her cry; she wasn't sure she could forgive them for that either.

But there was something about this young woman that stirred her sympathy. Helen remembered how she'd looked when she followed her friends from the shop the previous day. She'd looked defeated.

'It's Jess, isn't it? Or was that a lie too?'

'No, it's not,' she said, nodding her head. 'Jess Milgate.'

'Show me your student identification.'

Jess looked up, startled.

'Don't be so surprised. You've already proven you can't be trusted. You might have plucked that name out of the sky for all I know.'

Jess nodded again as if seeing the justice in this. She reached into her back pocket, pulled out her phone and a second later was holding it out to Helen. 'There, you see, I'm not lying.'

Helen took the phone, looked at the screen and back to Jess's face before returning it. 'Right, so you are who you say. Good to know if I decide to call the police.' Jess didn't know that it was the last thing Helen would want to do. They'd want to know why she hadn't reported it. What could she say? That she wanted to avoid any interaction with the police because she was afraid they'd see through her lies? She wouldn't even have reported the break-in at her home; that's how desperate she was to keep them at a distance. She ran a hand across her forehead. 'I was going to have a coffee. You want one while you tell me the rest of your sorry story?'

'Yes. Thank you.' Jess shuffled the rucksack again.

It looked heavy. Surely she didn't need to take that much stuff to college every day. 'Why don't you put that down before you collapse under the weight of it.' Helen raised an eyebrow. 'Don't worry, it'll be safe here.' She pointed towards the kitchen. 'Through that way.' It might have been crazy to let Jess in, but Helen wasn't stupid enough to turn her back on her. Yesterday, she'd been making coffee for her parole officer, today she was making it for a thief; how life could change in twenty-four hours. But then she'd already discovered that, hadn't she?

When they were both standing with a mug of coffee in their hands, she nodded for Jess to continue. 'I'm looking forward to hearing your justification for theft.'

'I wasn't seeking to justify; I wanted to explain.'

'Fair enough, explain then.' Would she believe her? Helen of all people knew how easy it was to spin a web of lies around the truth, although sometimes, increasingly often, she couldn't separate the strands of one from the other.

'Until recently, I'd been living with my boyfriend in his apartment. We split up just over a month ago. I needed to find somewhere in a hurry—'

'He was violent?'

'No!' Jess sounded horrified at the thought. 'He's a really nice guy; we just weren't good together. He'd have been happy for me to stay, but it was awkward and I was finding it hard to concentrate on my studies. I saw an advert for a house share and went to see it. It seemed okay. Good price. My own room. Three housemates all going to the same university so we had something in common.' She blew gently onto her coffee but instead of drinking, put it down. 'I don't know why I said yes; I don't actually like coffee.'

'I don't *actually* care.' Helen was growing irritated. Why had she allowed this stupid woman inside?

As if understanding she was on borrowed time, Jess jumped into her story. 'They were fine to begin with. Or maybe it was more a case that I wanted them to be. I'm in my final year, you see; I have to do well.'

'Could we have a shortened version of this story?' Helen said, using sarcasm to bat away the tide of sympathy. 'I've had a long day; I want to have my dinner and relax without more melodrama.'

Jess reached into her pocket for a tissue and blew her nose. 'Okay, shortened version it is. Those three are prize cows. Nasty, manipulative, completely uninterested in their studies. I didn't realise they were also dishonest until we came here.' She pointed to the ceiling. 'I was interested in the books. They were more interested in snooping around. When Lizzie came over holding a roll of cash, I knew she'd lifted it and told her to put it back. She laughed, then divided the money up between us. When I refused to take it, she shoved it into my pocket.' Jess held her hands up. 'I didn't know what to do. I knew if I said anything to you, they'd just leg it out the door without buying anything at all. At least I was able to give you some of the money back.'

Helen grunted in disbelief. 'You bought books using money you stole from me; how is that giving it back?'

'If we'd left without buying anything, wouldn't that have been worse?'

'True, I suppose.' Helen couldn't help laughing at the rather warped logic. 'I'm to be thankful for your generosity, is that it?'

'No!' Jess sighed. 'I'm not very good at this, am I? Far better off with my head in a book. Social interaction really isn't my thing.'

Something the young woman had said earlier suddenly struck Helen. 'You said you'd shared a flat with them. Past tense.'

'I had to leave in a bit of a rush—'

Helen tensed. 'You killed them?'

'No!' Jess looked at her in horror. 'Why would you say such a thing! What is it with you and violence, eh? Anyway, would you look at me.' She waved a hand down her body. 'Do you seriously think I could have taken on all three and won? Even if I'd wanted to, which I didn't. I'm a pacifist. And I have to admit, you're showing a strange tendency towards violence that's as unexpected as it is unsettling.'

If she only knew the half of it. Helen thought Jess was waiting for some sort of explanation though, as if she was owed. She wasn't, but it made it easier to offer her something. 'I read a lot of psychological thrillers. People do the strangest of things in them.'

'Sounds to me like you should think about switching genres.' Jess pointed back towards the shop. 'I have something for you.' She darted off, returning with the rucksack clutched in her arms. Balancing it against the wall, she opened buckles on one of the pockets. 'This is why I had to leave in a hurry,' she said as she pulled a crushed handful of notes from the pocket. 'I didn't have much time so had to grab what I could before they discovered what I was up to.' She shoved the money at Helen. 'It's not all but it's a good bit of it.'

Helen took the mess of five-, ten- and twenty-pound notes and began to smooth them out. As Jess said, it wasn't all that had been taken but it was most. 'Thank you.'

'I was only doing what was right. I'm so sorry I didn't stand up to them yesterday.' She gave a rueful grin. 'I'll be more careful who I choose to house share with in future.' She fastened the buckles and hefted the rucksack onto her back. 'I'd better get going.'

'Where?' What was Helen doing asking such a ridiculous question? This slightly strange woman wasn't her responsibility. Okay, she'd returned some of the money, but she'd stolen it in the first place.

'I'll find somewhere.'

'You didn't do such a good job of that last time. Where are you going to find somewhere at nearly seven o'clock?'

'I'm going to go back to the university. Someone will have a floor I can doss down on.'

Anger jolted through Helen. She'd have preferred if Jess had let her stupid friends, or whatever they were, keep the damn money rather than put her in the situation where she felt a level of responsibility for her predicament. 'Don't you have family you could stay with?'

'They live in Sheffield.' Jess adjusted the straps on her shoulders and smiled. 'Honestly, it's okay, don't worry, I'll find somewhere.'

Don't worry! As if she was absolving Helen of any responsibility. What did she care if Jess was taken advantage of by some nefarious character? What a ludicrous situation. Despite her explanation, she had robbed Helen and wasn't her responsibility. She barely knew her. That she obviously loved books wasn't a good enough reason to feel sorry for her. Helen should push her out of the shop and forget about her.

'No.' She said the word with such ferocity that Jess took a step backward and looked nervously towards the door as if wondering if she should make a run for it.

It amused Helen, but perhaps Jess was right to be nervous. She was a thief, but Helen, after all, was a murderer.

28

Helen held a hand up. 'Sorry, that came out a bit harshly.'

Jess's eyes flicked between the doorway and Helen's face as if unsure whether to stay or go. They finally settled on Helen. 'A bit,' she said.

'Ridiculous as it may be,' Helen said, more calmly. 'I feel partially responsible for you having to abandon your house share, so I really can't think of you roaming the streets trying to find somewhere to sleep.'

'I wasn't going to roam the streets, as such,' Jess said mildly.

'It doesn't matter. I have somewhere you can stay. Hang on a sec.' She went out to the shop. Leaning down to pull her handbag from under the desk, she dug out her house keys and returned to the kitchen. 'Take this,' she said, sliding one key off the ring. 'It's a spare, so don't worry. You know where Hungerford Road is?' When this was met with a head-shake, she pointed towards the front of the shop. 'Out the door, turn right, cross the road and it's the first turn left. Number 44A. Only about six houses down on the left. It's in a bit of a mess. I was burgled on Monday and haven't had a chance to put it all to rights as yet. But there's a spare bedroom upstairs at the back. You'll find sheets, etc. in the laundry cupboard.'

Jess stared, obviously bemused. 'You're letting me stay in your home? After what I did?'

'I know, I must need my head examined.' Helen didn't say that it was the determination in the *it's my final year, I have to do well*, that had appealed to her, that had made her want to help. Fighting for a future was something she could relate to. She held the key out. 'Take it. Stay until you can find something suitable. You'll be on your own there tonight, I'm sleeping here till I have the alarm fitted tomorrow then I'll be moving back.'

Jess took the key, looking at it as if she wasn't sure she could believe her luck. 'I don't know what to say.' She slipped it into her pocket. 'Maybe I could pay you back for your kindness somehow. Help in the shop at the weekends when I have time.'

Maybe that wouldn't be a bad idea. All those books Helen was getting from Dilly... 'Shit!' She checked the time. Seven fifteen. 'I was supposed to collect books this evening. Damn it.'

'Can I help?'

Helen shook her head. She needed to think more about what she was getting herself into before she made any more promises or accepted assistance.

'Just go. I need to get sorted and head off.' She gave Jess a shove to get her moving. At the front door, she held it open. 'This is a short-term arrangement. As soon as you can, find somewhere to live, okay?' She didn't wait for an answer, shutting the door as soon as Jess had passed through before turning and running up the stairs to collect an armful of flattened boxes. She'd make them up once she got to Dilly's place.

Once she was in the car, she pulled out her mobile. The call was answered almost immediately. 'Hi, Dilly, so sorry, I've been delayed. I'm in the car now, heading your way. I should be there in about ten minutes. Is that okay?'

'That's not a problem. See you when you get here.'

Helen hung up with a sigh of relief. It would have been the last straw if she'd lost such a fabulous collection of books because of Jess's visit.

As she pulled into the driveway, Dilly opened the front door and gave a friendly wave.

'I'm really sorry for being so late,' Helen said, getting out and dragging the boxes from the back seat.

'It's not a problem, honestly. Here, let me take those for you.'

'I have a roll of tape somewhere.' Helen found it where it had rolled under the passenger seat. When she stood and turned, she was surprised to see Dilly had already gone inside the house. Shutting and locking the car, she hurried to follow her into the library. 'I'll have them made up in a jiffy,' she said, pointing to the boxes with the tape. 'I brought five, but I don't need to fill them all tonight if you'd prefer not.'

Dilly patted her on the shoulder. 'Stop fretting, honestly, it's no problem. I'd no plans for this evening. Now, while you're getting those boxes sorted, shall I go and make us a cuppa?'

Helen would have preferred to get on with the task in hand but it seemed churlish to refuse. 'That'd be lovely, thank you.' She started on the boxes, unfolding them, taping across the bottoms.

For speed, she didn't bother looking through the books, simply starting at one end of a shelf and packing them into the box. She had one almost filled before she heard footsteps behind her. 'I'm doing well,' she said, dropping a handful of books on top before turning to smile at her host.

'Sit, have your tea, then we'll work together.'

Maybe Dilly was lonely. Spending time in conversation with her was little return for all the books Helen was getting. She sat and sipped the tea. 'I put all of the books I took yesterday onto the shelves when I got back and a lot of them were sold today.'

'It's nice to know Anna's books are doing something useful.'

Helen had been glancing along the shelves yet to be emptied, but she turned at the sharp tone of Dilly's words. But when she looked at her, she seemed as affable as usual. Maybe she regretted giving the books away so cheaply. 'I can afford to pay you more for them now. Remember I told you about those women who stole from me yesterday?'

'The university students?'

'Yes. Well one of them returned today and gave me most of the money back. It was unexpected.' She didn't tell Dilly the rest of the story: that she'd given the woman a key to her house. She'd have thought she was crazy. And Helen would have had to agree with her. What had possessed her?

'That's wonderful. Went some way towards restoring your faith in humanity, I suppose.' Dilly shook her head. 'I'm happy to stick to our bargain. When you're on your feet, you can give money to a charity of your choice.' She leaned closer and smiled. 'I can see you've had some hard times; it's good to help put them behind you.'

The kindness brought tears to Helen's eyes. 'They're not quite behind me. I told you I'd been in prison, but I'm not free of that yet. I'm out on licence, so I have to follow certain conditions or I could be recalled. I have a community offender manager.' Helen gave a harsh laugh. 'Commonly referred to as a parole officer, but the lovely Moira Manson likes the proper title. Her visits are supposed to be monthly at this stage.' Helen's sigh was loud. 'This week, I've seen her almost every damn day. I moved into the shop when it was broken into. I should have asked permission, and didn't, so she wasn't happy.'

'You could be sent back to prison to serve out the rest of your sentence, is that it?'

'Yes.' Helen shook her head. 'I'm sorry, you don't want to hear all this gloom and doom.'

'It's good to talk. I often wonder, had Anna talked to me rather than hiding in here and burying herself in these damn books, if we'd still be together.'

'Break-ups are almost always sad.'

'Tell me about your last one,' Dilly said. 'It might help me with mine. You know the old saying: misery loves company.'

'There've been a few over the years,' Helen said smoothly.

'But the last one, what was that like?'

Her insistence was slightly irritating. Luckily, Helen was good at lying. The art was to use the truth and slant it whatever direction you needed it to go. 'The end of my last relationship was probably the easiest. He left and we never spoke again.' It was a bizarre version of the truth. There was no point in adding that Toby still spoke in her dreams, that she still heard him sometimes in the quiet of the day. That the names he called her still rattled around her head. *Disgusting weirdo. Depraved slut. Pathetic piece of work.*

'Gosh. How long had you been together?'

'Six months.' Not long, but long enough for Helen to have thought that this was it. That he loved her enough to accept her for who she was.

'Did he ghost you?'

Helen blinked, her mouth opening and shutting like a defective elevator door. Did Toby haunt her? Every day. How could he not?

'I've read about it,' Dilly said, seemingly oblivious to Helen's rigid silence and faulty mouth. 'Men who stop ringing or texting and seem to vanish. It's supposed to be very passive-aggressive and immature. Sounds like you had a lucky escape.'

Ghosting! She pressed her lips together to stop them trembling. 'No, no it wasn't like that,' she said finally. 'We were living together. In my house. One day, he just left.'

'Oh dear. With no explanation. Had you any indication it was going to happen?'

'No, none.'

'And this was before you went to prison, yes?'

'Yes.' Helen hoped the bluntness of the one-word response would give Dilly a hint that she didn't want to talk any longer. In case there was any doubt, she gulped down the tea and put the mug on the table. 'I'd better get back to the books.'

'I'll help,' Dilly said, finishing her tea. 'We can chat as we work.'

'Great.' Helen picked up a small pile of books and slotted them into the top of the box she'd been filling. 'That's this one done.' She slapped some packing tape over the top of the box to keep it shut and reached for the next. 'I'm planning on having the upstairs finished by the weekend. You'll have to come over and see it sometime.' She kept up a continuous stream of inconsequential chatter about her plans for the shop: the logoed items she'd planned to have made, the special offers she was considering. Anything to stop Dilly instigating another conversation about her past.

Helen packed quickly, determined to get as much done as possible, unsure if she was going to return. Dilly was probably lonely, but she was also intensely curious, and there were some things that Helen was never going to be happy to talk about. 'That's that,' she said, taping the top of the final box. 'We've made good progress.' She looked around the room, estimating that one more journey would complete the business. It would be foolish not to return. If Dilly insisted on asking about why she'd gone to prison, she could make up some acceptable white-collar crime to appease her curiosity.

She dropped the final box onto the passenger seat, wrapped the seatbelt around it for safety and stood back. 'One more trip should do it,' she said to Dilly, who was standing in the open doorway of the house. 'Is it okay for me to come again tomorrow? I promise I'll try not to be late this time.'

'Of course.' Dilly closed the distance between them and enveloped Helen in a hug. 'I enjoy your visits. You're easy to talk to. I'll be sorry when you're done.'

Helen returned the embrace. She'd been right. Dilly was lonely. It was only Helen's tendency to see everything as a personal attack that made her think Dilly's questions were too intrusive. She was simply a sad, lonely woman, trying to get over a break-up. A generous, kind woman who was reaching out for company and support. In contrast, what a miserable bitch Helen was. 'When I'm done, I'll come back to visit, I promise. And you'll have to come and see the shop.'

She felt the arms around her tighten for a second before she was released.

'But you will come tomorrow?'

'Of course, definitely.' Helen sat into the driver's seat. 'I should be here by six thirty at the latest.' A final wave and she pulled the door shut.

She drove away, wondering again at how lucky she'd been to have met Dilly, with no idea that the sweet old woman was plotting her downfall.

29

By the time Helen had unloaded the car, she was too exhausted to do more. It was only when she was lying in her bed, with sleep already creeping over her, that she realised she was feeling good. Almost happy. This last came as a surprise. It had been a long time since she'd been able to say that. She owed Dilly a lot.

When she woke some hours later, it was with a suddenness that startled her. For a moment, she was in that twilight place between dream world and reality. In the dream, she'd been running away from people whose faces had only one feature ~ a huge, jagged-toothed mouth that emitted a continuous, shrill scream. With her eyes open, the sound faded, replaced by the heavy silence of the night. Silent now, but hadn't there been something? Hadn't that shrill scream in her dream been disrupted by a thud? One loud enough to pop the image of the open-mouthed monsters.

She sat up, lips pressed together, listening. Her hand reached for her mobile to check the time. Three o'clock. Not enough sleep to do more than take the edge of her tiredness. She flopped back onto the pillow, wondering if she could get back to sleep, knowing she wouldn't until she checked downstairs to make sure that thud wasn't something ominous.

Anxiety finally forced her from the bed. Simmering fear made her switch on every light upstairs and clomp around on the wooden floor to scare the bogeyman away.

She was shaking her head and had forced a wavering smile at her childishness when she finally went down the stairs. Very slowly. Stopping every couple of steps to listen again. Only when all the lights in the shop were on and everything looked as it always did, with the front door still solidly locked, could she relax. The thud, if there really had been one and it wasn't simply an extra sound effect in her dream, probably came from outside.

Unfortunately, she was now wide awake. If she lay down, she'd simply toss and turn and think of all she needed to do. It was better to get something to eat, make a start on the work, and aim for an early night instead.

Leaving the lights on behind her, she headed into the kitchen, a craving for hot toast dripping with butter making her mouth water. She ate hurriedly, desperate to get on with the work.

The satisfaction of lifting a book, stamping it with her Appleby logo and finding a home for it on a shelf – she hoped it would never grow tired. By six, she'd filled every empty shelf downstairs.

There were still three of Mrs Clough's boxes to be sorted. That was going to be a slower job, the books older and harder to place. But she was on a roll; she'd make a coffee and get started.

She was humming as she filled the kettle, jigging to the tune as she reached for the jar of coffee and a mug. It was going to be a good day. The alarm would be installed. She'd be able to return to her home, sleep in her bed. She resolutely put Jess from her mind. Today was going to be a worry-free day.

With a shake of her head at the dirty mugs and teaspoons in

the sink, she pulled open the drawer and took out a clean spoon. The drawer was shut, her fingers still resting on the handle, when something struck her and she pulled it open again.

Unlike her kitchen drawers at home, which seemed to accumulate bits and bobs at a ridiculous rate, this one was neat and tidy. A plastic cutlery tray with a couple of knives, forks and dessert spoons all neatly laid out. A few teaspoons to last till she did the washing up.

There was nothing else in the drawer.

But there should have been.

She lifted the tray up to look under it, then dropped it with a noisy clatter. Since the burglary at home, she'd changed her habits. The keys to the back doors were no longer left in situ for any opportunistic bastard's convenience. The key for this back door should be here, in this drawer.

She turned to glare at the door, as if somehow it was at fault. But if she'd hoped to see the key sticking out of its hidey-hole halfway down the door, she was disappointed.

'Damn it!' She wrenched open the drawer again and this time rifled among the cutlery, growing increasingly frustrated. Finally, she pulled the tray out and emptied the contents onto the counter. No key. Leaving the mess, she opened the cupboards. Maybe she'd put the damn thing somewhere else. The kitchen was small, utilitarian, with little storage for what was supposed to be used only for coffee breaks and lunch, so it didn't take long to discover the key wasn't anywhere. Where the hell had she put it?

Crossing to the back door, she peered at the lock as if it was going to magically appear and slapped the door with the flat of her hand. It wasn't the end of the world if she couldn't open it. The key would turn up. She'd probably taken it with her and put it down somewhere in the shop or upstairs. With a grunt of frustration, she pulled on the handle to rattle it, stumbling backwards as the door opened inward.

She put a hand on the counter to steady herself as it swung lazily to a halt. And that's when she saw it. The key she'd been searching for. In the lock, on the outside. Where it shouldn't be. There was no reason to lock the door from the outside. So how the hell did the key end up there?

Tugging it out, she pushed the door closed. It shut with a noise she recognised. It had seemed louder in the quiet of the night but she knew it was the same sound she'd heard hours before. Someone had been in her shop. But why? Apart from five pounds in coins she'd left in the register, what little money she had was in her purse, in her handbag, upstairs. The storage room door had been shut; there was no way anyone could have entered without waking her.

She walked back into the shop and looked around. As before, she didn't notice anything out of place. The money was still in the till. Everything was just as she'd left it the previous night. But someone had been there. They'd let themselves in with the key. Maybe they'd walked around to see what she'd done. Then they'd left. Not quietly though. And they'd left the key in the lock instead of taking it with them. Whoever it was, they'd wanted her to know they'd been there.

To scare her. To set her on edge.

They'd succeeded.

Back in the kitchen, she locked the door and put the key into her pocket, moving like an automaton as she tried to keep all the swirling thoughts from overwhelming her. She put the plastic tray back into the drawer and, slowly, with far more care than the cheap cutlery deserved, put each piece back in place. Then she washed the dirty spoons and mugs that were in the sink and dried them with equal care. The slow routine calmed her a little and when she was done, she climbed the stairs to do what she knew would offer more balm. Work. There was no point doing nothing and allowing worrying thoughts to breed and multiply in her head.

Three boxes remained from the supply Mrs Clough had given her. She opened the first with little enthusiasm but within minutes, the feel and smell of the books had soothed her thoughts. Most were old, literary rather than genre, a few Hemingway and Faulkner. She looked around the shelves on this floor. They'd fit well up here. Both were authors beloved of university English degree courses.

She flicked through the pages of each and added another supermarket receipt to the collection for Jared.

When she'd been holding a book for several minutes without moving, she sighed. It was time to face what had been worrying her. How many people had been in her kitchen since she'd last opened the back door.

Which of them would have lifted the key?

And most importantly, why?

30

The first question was the easiest to answer. Only three people had been in the kitchen at any time over the previous couple of days. Zander, her parole officer, and Jess. Annoying as she was, Helen guessed she could discount Moira.

Either of the other two could have found the key. There was only one drawer in the room; she'd made it easy for them.

Was it simply the next step in Zander and Alex's plan to force her out?

Or had it been taken the previous day by Jess? When Helen had gone to get her keys, she'd been alone in the kitchen. It would have been easy for her.

But why?

Helen sat back on her haunches, tapping the book she held gently against her chin. She'd swallowed Jess's story. The whole convoluted rigmarole of it. If she'd read it in a book... in one of the psychological thrillers she preferred... she'd have considered it to be very far-fetched. How gullible she'd been. How stupid to have offered Jess a room in her house. She'd given a woman she barely knew a key to come and go as she pleased.

Serve Helen right to go home and find she'd emptied it of everything.

And yet, it didn't strike true. Helen wasn't materialistic; there was little of any value in her home. The furniture cheap and tired.

She stood and shook the pins and needles from her legs. What did she know for a fact? That sometime in the last couple of days, someone had taken the key from the drawer and had let themselves into the shop that morning. And had chosen to make it obvious by leaving the key in the lock outside.

Whoever it was, they didn't seem interested in harming her. She supposed she should be grateful.

If it was done to frighten her – she'd already considered that someone disapproved of her presence in the area. But wouldn't they have made it obvious? Perhaps daubed MURDERER across her shop window in garish capitals or something more in-your-face like that? She thought about Toby's mother. Helen's legal team had pointed her out in the courtroom. A small, grey woman who sat with her eyes cast down. Helen couldn't imagine her creeping around the shop.

No, she decided, this was something sneakier, something more insidious. And once more, her finger was pointing at the two crafty Londoners, Zander and Alex.

Helen looked at the pile of books she'd taken from the box brought from Jen Clough's house. Was she on the wrong track altogether? Jared had been so insistent that she looked through all the books she'd acquired from his grand-aunt. Had even rung to ask if she was still looking. Maybe there was something valuable hidden between the pages of one of them. Not a treasure map – she wasn't stepping into the realm of the totally ridiculous – but something he was desperate to get his hands on. He'd been quite anxious to look through them himself, hadn't he? So far, all she'd found were a couple of five-pound notes, and several supermarket receipts. Maybe she should look closer at them. *At supermarket receipts?* Helen snorted. It seemed she was pretty close to that realm of the absolutely crazy. That's what tiredness and stress were doing to her.

Her mobile buzzed. Picking it up, she sighed to see her sister's name before pressing to accept the call. 'Hi.'

'Hello, tell me, how's it going? Almost the end of your first week.'

'It's going really well, thank goodness.' It was the truth, wasn't it? The business was doing well; it was her life that was collapsing like the houses she used to make with playing cards when she was a child. Houses she built, knocked down and built again to fill in the lonely hours. 'I was lucky and got a great supply of books that are selling well. So, yes, it's been a great start.'

'That's good news. And you're managing by yourself? I hope you're not skipping lunch; you've never put back on the weight you lost in you-know-where.'

Sarah's refusal to say the word *prison* sometimes amused Helen. That day, it added to her irritation. 'Prison food, as I'm sure I told you, left a lot to be desired. But don't worry, I'm managing fine.'

'I thought I'd call over tomorrow. Maybe give you a hand with anything that's left to do.'

'That'd be great, Sarah, thank you. There's still stuff needing to be sorted.'

'Great. Okay, I'll come mid-morning and bring us lunch.'

'That sounds perfect. I'll look forward to it.' Helen hung up. Her sister was good to her. It was important she remembered that, especially when Sarah was being managing and controlling. It made up for neglecting Helen when they were children.

She was tired, and when she was, it was easier for the old

hurts to come barrelling back. 'Stupid,' she muttered. Checking her watch, she saw it was almost nine. She'd make the coffee she'd missed earlier, then open up.

Leaving the drink on the desk, she crossed to pull up the blinds and unlock the door. The window display still looked good. It might be a good idea to change it that day. Put some of the newer books out for the weekend trade. When the door opened, she pasted a smile in place. It wavered and faded when she saw who it was.

'Jess, I wasn't expecting to see you this morning.'

'I wanted to stop and thank you again for allowing me to stay.' She played nervously with the straps of her rucksack.

Helen noticed that it looked far lighter than when she'd been carrying it the day before. She was obviously planning to stay in the house another night. It was time to make things clear. 'I'll be home myself tonight. You do realise this is a short-term arrangement, don't you?'

Jess's head bobbed up and down. 'I'm going to talk to a few people today and hope to get something suitable.' She jerked her thumb over her shoulder. 'I hope you don't mind but I've left some things in your house.' She played with the straps again. 'It was a bit heavy to take everything with me. When I get fixed up with somewhere, I'll pop back for the rest, then drop the key in to you.'

'Right.' Helen crossed to the desk, picked up her mug, took a sip and put it down again. 'You didn't come back last night, did you?' She felt stupid asking the question. If Jess had come back, if she had taken the key and crept in during the night for some nefarious reason, she was hardly going to admit to it, was she? Helen was being paranoid again. Suspecting everyone. What possible reason could this young woman have for doing such a thing? It had to have been Zander or Alex.

'Last night?' Jess frowned. 'No.'

Of course she hadn't. Helen shook her head. 'Forget it.'

Jess's frown deepened. 'Why? Did something happen last night?' She looked around, her eyes wide. 'You weren't broken into again, were you?'

'Ha, ha.' The fake laugh hung between them for a moment. 'No, don't be silly. Not even I could be that unlucky.'

'Not even you?' Jess swung her rucksack to the floor as if settling down for a long stay. 'Do you consider yourself to be unlucky then?'

It was Helen's turn to frown, suddenly suspicious. 'What is it you're doing in university?' She'd put Jess at twenty, maybe twenty-one, but when she lifted her head and met Helen's eyes, she realised she was older. Maybe in her late twenties.

'I'm doing a PhD in psychology.'

Helen, who'd assumed it would be something in the arts, or in fashion, was taken aback. 'You're training to be a psychologist?'

Jess smiled. 'I've a bit to go as yet, but that's the plan. The way people tick fascinates me.'

The day was just getting worse. Helen tried to look impressed, tried to look as if she didn't give a fuck that this woman might be analysing her. The woman that she'd stupidly invited into the home where Helen had murdered someone and lied about it.

'So, what happened last night?'

'What? Ha, ha.' There it was again, that ridiculous fake laugh. 'No, it's nothing, forget it.' Helen picked up her coffee again, but didn't drink. 'Was there something you wanted?'

Jess picked up her rucksack and swung it onto her back. 'No, I just wanted to call in and thank you again for being so kind to me.' She adjusted the straps on her shoulder. 'It's obvious that something happened last night. You look exhausted and sad. If you don't want to share with me, share with someone you trust.'

Helen smiled, as if to say Jess was talking nonsense. She kept it pinned in place till Jess left the shop and vanished from view. Even then it stayed. A meaningless rictus. She shouldn't have mentioned what had happened. Shouldn't have given someone – a psychologist, for pity's sake – a reason to look sideways at her.

As if she was going crazy.

31

Helen was still standing with that weird, forced grin on her face when a van pulled up outside bearing the logo of the security company. She'd almost forgotten about the damn alarm. The coffee in the mug was cold; she drained it anyway, hoping the caffeine would give her the kick she needed.

By midday, the alarm was installed and the app on her phone easy to use.

There was a continuous stream of customers through the door and if she hadn't been so exhausted, she'd have been pleased with how the business was going.

Lunch consisted of two slices of bread hurriedly spread with butter and eaten at the desk. And coffee, of course. It was the only way she was able to get through the long day.

The clock was ticking towards six when the last person she wanted to see crossed in front of the window. It would have been nice to have believed it was a coincidence, that Moira wasn't coming to see her, but Helen knew the truth. And she knew why. She was supposed to have contacted her parole officer to tell her the alarm had been installed and that she'd be going back to her home address that evening. She'd stupidly, stupidly forgotten.

'I was just about to ring you,' she said as the door opened and Moira came through. As a pre-emptive strike, it was a half-hearted attempt but the best she could do. She added a smile, hoping it looked relatively normal.

'Really?' Moira didn't sound convinced.

'Business has been crazy.' She pointed towards gaps in the line of books on the nearest shelf. 'As you can see. That was full this morning.' The almost-new books she'd brought from Dilly's were proving to be a big success. She needed to get rid of Moira so she could go to pick up the last load. 'But the good news is that the alarm is in and running perfectly.' She pulled out her mobile and brought up the app. 'I can set or disarm it using this, so if I accidentally forget, I can set it from home.'

'And it's monitored?'

'Well, no, it's not.' Helen put the phone away. 'Monitored alarms worked out far more expensive than I could afford. But I'll know if it goes off, and be here in a few minutes—'

'And you'll chase the burglar away.' Moira sniffed. 'You'd have been better off paying the bit extra and having it monitored professionally.'

'The business is doing okay, but it's not a goldmine; I have to be mindful of expenditure.'

Moira's expression was clearly critical. 'It's your business, of course, and your decision.' She rested her handbag on the desk. 'It's been a long day; could I trouble you for a coffee?'

Helen wanted to say no, that she had an important collection to do, but as she always did, Moira made her feel small, intimidated. It wasn't what she said, or even the way she looked at Helen as if she was beneath her socially, intellectually, every bloody way there was; it was the way she regarded her as if she was of no account whatsoever. Or was this another case of Helen being paranoid?

'Yes, no problem.'

'I'll have a look through the books while you're getting it.'

As if Helen was her bloody servant. 'Right, I'll go make you a cup.' She checked the time as she moved. Six ten. She put the kettle on to boil, then took out her mobile.

'Dilly, hi,' she said when the call was answered. 'Listen, I'm sorry, something's come up again and I'm going to be a little delayed. Is it still okay if I call to pick up the last of the books?'

'That's perfectly all right. I have no plans.'

'Thanks, you're a star. I'll see you in a bit.'

She made a mug of coffee, adding extra milk to hurry the drinking of it.

Back in the shop, she was surprised to find Moira on the business side of the desk.

'Just looking for a bag for these,' she said without embarrassment. She pulled one out and tapped the few books she'd set on the desk. 'Three, so that's six pounds, yes?' She put three two-pound coins on the desk.

They were some of the newer books, the ones Helen had decided to sell at £2.50. The price was written clearly in pencil on the top right-hand corner of the first page. She wanted to be firm and businesslike, say clearly that the price was seven-fifty, instead of nodding and smiling as if the bitch was doing her such a great favour in buying them.

'Here's your coffee.' *Drink it and go away.*

'Thanks.' Moira took it, sipped and nodded. 'Just the way I like it. I needed this; I've had one of those days.'

Helen swallowed a groan. Moira had reverted to her *we're friends* mood. It meant she wasn't going to rush away. Dilly had been so kind, so patient; she couldn't arrive very late two nights in a row. 'Listen,' she said, interrupting Moira mid-sentence in a monologue about some case she was having problems with. No details, of course. Not that it would have mattered; Helen was barely listening. Moira didn't appear to have noticed. Helen wasn't sure she'd have cared anyway. It was as if she simply needed to speak and it was irrelevant if her audience was deaf to her words. 'Listen,' Helen said again, more softly this time. 'I'm sorry, but I really need to go. I have a collection to do and I don't like to be late.' *Again*, but she didn't add that bit.

Moira lifted the mug to her lips and took a sip. 'I could wait and give you a hand to bring the boxes in when you get back, if you like. I'm not doing anything else this evening.'

'That's so kind of you,' Helen said, frantically scrambling for an excuse. 'But I'm not sure if I'm going to come back here; I might go straight home.' She ran a hand through her hair. 'I'm desperate for a shower, to wash my hair. To be back in my own house again.' Then afraid Moira was going to argue that she couldn't leave boxes in her car overnight without tempting fate, she added, 'There aren't many books to collect anyway; they'll stay in the boot till I come back here tomorrow.' She was babbling. Making excuses when she shouldn't have to and didn't need to. It should have been possible to simply say, *Thanks, but no thanks*. The thought of almost two more years dealing with this woman made her want to cry.

Moira raised an eyebrow and kept it raised until Helen fell silent. 'Looks like I have no choice but to drink up and go then, doesn't it?'

The words *I'm sorry*, were on the tip of Helen's tongue but she resisted the almost unbearable need to say them. Again. Apologise again for daring to want to live her life, run her business, do what she bloody-well wanted. *Small punishment for killing someone.* She brushed that irritating inner voice aside too.

It was another few minutes before Moira finished her coffee. She put the mug down on the desk with a smile in Helen's direction. 'Thank you. Now, I'd better let you get on.' She picked up her briefcase and the paper bag holding the books she'd bought and left.

Helen released her clenched fists and stretched her fingers.

Regrets, she believed, were generally a waste of time, but if there was one thing that she did regret, it was not taking the opportunity when it had presented itself to push that cow down the stairs.

32

It was almost seven before Helen pulled up outside Dilly's home half-expecting the door to open as it had done the previous night. It didn't, and without the cheerful face to greet her in the door-way, the house looked even grimmer than ever.

Helen climbed from the car, reached in for the flattened card-board boxes and the roll of tape and headed to the front door. She pressed the doorbell, heard it jingle within and waited. When a couple of minutes passed with no answer, she pressed the bell again. It was a little later than she'd said; perhaps Dilly had somewhere else to be. Or maybe she was pissed off at being kept waiting. If Helen lost this last load of books thanks to Moira, it would be the perfect ending to a shitty day.

Another minute, and Helen was convinced she'd missed her chance. She'd picked up the boxes, ready to leave, when suddenly the door opened.

'Helen. Come in.'

It wasn't the friendly greeting Helen was used to. Nor was Dilly wearing her usual amiable expression. Perhaps this second day being late was the last straw for her.

'I'm so sorry. I intended being on time but my parole officer turned up out of the blue. If you remember, I told you she keeps popping up unexpectedly.' If she was hoping for some recognition of the fact, an element of sympathy even, she was disappointed. In fact, Dilly's expression grew more disdainful, even irritated. Helen, who'd come to expect a kinder reception from her, wanted to cry in frustration, wanted to say it wasn't her fault. But of course, it was. Her fault for having killed Toby. 'Okay, perhaps I should go away. Maybe reschedule for another day. Or perhaps you'd prefer me not to come back.'

'You're here now; you might as well come in.'

It wasn't the most gracious of invitations. Helen would have liked to have climbed onto her high horse, shook her head and said, *No thanks, I won't bother*, but it dawned on her in that moment that she was running a business and no longer had the luxury to take offence at slights.

'I do apologise for being late,' she said again, manoeuvring through with the boxes under her arm.

'Just make sure this is your last visit.' Dilly nodded towards the final shelves. 'There isn't that much left. Now, if you'll excuse me, I have things to do. See yourself out when you're done.'

Helen stared after her. What was it with people these days? Moira and her irritating habit of fluctuating between Madam Most-Official and Ms Bessie Mate, and now Dilly throwing a Jekyll and Hyde. With a sigh, Helen tore a strip from the roll of tape and made up the first box. She'd brought three: more than enough to fit what was left.

Trying to put both Moira and Dilly from her head, she started to take the books from the shelves, slotting them neatly into the box. It didn't take long. No cups of tea or intrusive chats interrupted the work.

She was taping the top of the first box shut, when Dilly returned.

'I suppose you're heading back to put all these on your shelves now, are you?'

Helen felt the first twinge of irritation. It had been Dilly's idea to give her the books so cheaply, now she sounded critical that Helen was making the most of them. She was on her knees. It seemed to be where she was most of the time these days. A suitably penitent position. She tapped the top of the box and got to her feet. 'I can leave them if you'd prefer. If you've changed your mind.'

Dilly gave an almost imperceptible shake of her head, then held out her hand. 'If you give me the tape, I'll finish closing the boxes while you start to take them out.'

Helen handed the roll over. 'Right, thank you.' She hesitated, then decided to try another apology. 'I know you're annoyed with me for being late a second night in a row, but I really had no choice, and I'm genuinely sorry.'

Dilly twirled the roll without meeting Helen's eyes. 'I think it's best if we just get this job done and leave it at that.'

Not taking offence was one thing, but lying down to be stamped on was another. 'Fine.' She bent to lift the first of the boxes. By the time she got back, minutes later, the other two boxes were taped shut and Dilly was nowhere to be seen.

Helen carried the final two boxes out to the car, then stood in the hallway of the house and called out. 'Thanks, Dilly. You've been very kind, and I'm sorry I let you down.'

There was no answer. With a sigh, she left, shutting the door gently behind her.

On the drive back to the shop, she mulled over the dramatic change in Dilly's manner from genial and supportive to angry and dismissive. She had told Helen not to worry about being late, so what had caused the sudden shift in her attitude?

Back at the shop, feeling disappointed and frustrated in equal measures, she opened up, switched off the alarm, then dragged the boxes from the car and took them upstairs. She had planned to unpack them first, but the almost sneering remark Dilly had made about them going straight onto the shelves changed Helen's mind. She'd finish Mrs Clough's instead; it would give her the opportunity to be honest with Jared when he returned.

But she was done for that day. She wasn't doing anything else apart from bringing her personal belongings home. It took almost an hour. Several trips up and down the stairs. Locking and unlocking the front door. Her final act upstairs was to drag the remaining boxes into the storage room.

She'd put the alarm on, locked the door and sat into the car before she remembered the food in the fridge. It was tempting to forget about it, but she was hungry, and she knew there was nothing at home.

'Shit!' She'd forgotten all about Jess. The young woman hadn't returned with the key while Helen had been there, nor had the key been shoved through the letter box while she was at Dilly's. Did that mean Jess had been unable to find somewhere else to live, so Helen would have to face her when she got home? Bone-weary as she was, she didn't want to have to deal with her.

It was almost tempting to reverse the last hour's work and stay in the shop that night. She would have done too, if it weren't for fear that her nemesis would find out she hadn't moved back home. Moira was such a sneaky snake that Helen wouldn't put it past her to pop around to Hungerford Road to check.

Climbing from the car once more, she unlocked the door, turned off the alarm, and crossed to the kitchen. She took out the remaining ready meals and other things Sarah had bought for her, and was standing with the fridge door open, when over its hum, she heard a knock, followed by a few more in quick succession.

Between Moira and Dilly, Helen had had a shit evening. It was almost tempting to go next door and have it out with Alex and Zander. Tell them they were barking well up the wrong tree if they thought they could frighten her away. She would have done, if the tears she'd been holding for hours hadn't started to flow in a continuous stream down her face.

She grabbed a roll of kitchen paper, pulled some sheets from it, rubbed her eyes and blew her nose. The knocking stopped. She waited to see if it would start again, and when it didn't, she picked up the bag of food and left the kitchen. It wasn't until she reached the front door that she realised she'd shut her eyes as she passed by the staircase. It made her laugh. Did she really think she'd see the ghost of poor Reginald Taylor lying there, his knuckles bloody from banging on the wood?

No ghost inside, and thankfully no Moira hovering outside.

There must have been a part of her that had hoped Jess wouldn't be there when she got home. Because when she pulled up in front of her house a few minutes later, and she saw the light glowing from the front room, she groaned and banged her head back against the head rest several times.

What had possessed her to give the younger woman a key to her home? Was she playing the good Samaritan? Or had she thought that by reaching out to Jess, she might help her to avoid the mistakes Helen had made? She rested her head back and shut her eyes. She was still too anxious, too eager to please, and despite her attempts to look towards the future, still too quick to dwell on the past. She could sit there all night, trying to decide why she'd done so many things in her life, or she could get out of the car and face the consequences of yet another action of hers. At least this one, she hoped, wouldn't land her in prison.

She turned the key in the lock and pushed the front door open. Usually, she'd be greeted by a comfortable silence. That evening, there was music. Something soft and melodic. There was also the distinct aroma of something cooking. She hesitated, pulled between the need to unload her belongings from the car and to find out what was going on.

Curiosity won.

The back room of the house had been extended and refurbished by a previous owner. It was one of the reasons Helen had fallen in love with it the first time she'd seen it. The only thing she'd had to do to make it perfect was to paint the white walls a pale yellow. It wasn't a big room, but it had been well-designed so held everything she needed in the small kitchen, leaving room for a table and chairs. Near the large picture window, she'd put a small, rather battered, but extremely comfortable chair she'd picked up at a car boot sale. It was her favourite curling-up place to lose herself in a book.

When she opened the door, quietly, as if worried about what she was going to find, she wasn't too surprised to see Jess curled up in it, a book in her hand. Obviously a good one that she was completely lost in, making her oblivious to everything else. It gave Helen a chance to take stock – to hear the faint whirr of the fan oven, see the table set for two and the candles waiting to be lit.

An apology for the theft, a thank you for offering Jess a bed for the night, or a bribe to allow her to stay?

Helen cleared her throat, amused when Jess still didn't take her head from the book. Reaching behind, she pushed the door shut. The slam echoed in the room and finally drew Jess's startled eyes.

She dropped the book on the chair as she jumped to her feet. 'Sorry, I was lost.'

'You're still here.' It was stating the bleedin' obvious, but Helen couldn't think of anything else to say in that moment when she was remembering how nice it was to come home to someone. It was the first time she was able to think of the good moments with Toby. The early days when they were still dancing around one another, finding their way, teasing out what made each other happy, what each of them needed.

When did it start going wrong? The police, the counsellor, her sister had asked this question. Helen had insisted she didn't know, but she did; it had started back then, when she and Toby had discovered exactly what each of them had needed... what *she* had needed.

'Helen, are you okay?'

From Jess's concerned expression, Helen guessed she'd been lost in her thoughts for longer than she should. 'Yes, thanks, I'm just surprised by...' she waved a hand around the room '...all of this.'

'You forgave me, offered me a place to stay. I wanted to thank you.'

'You seem to have forgotten the temporary nature of my offer,' Helen said, refusing to be swayed by what Jess had done. 'I thought you were going to find somewhere else to stay. Isn't that what you said when you called into the shop this morning?'

'Yes.' Jess sighed. 'I did find somewhere but I can't move in until Monday. I hoped you'd let me stay till then.'

Helen gave another wave around the room. 'So this, it's a bribe?'

'No, because you can still say no, and I'll leave.' Jess brushed past her to the cooker and switched the oven off. 'I made a lasagne.' She grabbed a towel, opened the door, and removed the dish. 'I wanted to thank you for giving me a second chance.'

A delicious aroma was drifting from the lasagne. Helen blamed that for weakening her resolve. 'I suppose you could stay till Monday.' She jerked her thumb to the door behind her. 'I'll just unload the car first.'

'I'll give you a hand; it'll make things quicker.' Jess put the dish down and popped two plates into the oven.

Helen carried two of the sofa cushions in, Jess trailing behind with the third under one arm, a holdall dangling from her other hand. 'I did some tidying up while I was waiting.'

She'd vacuumed the floor, put stuff away. It was almost back to how it was before the break-in. Helen dropped the cushions in place. 'That was kind of you.'

'I did a bit upstairs too. Mostly just picking up the stuff that was tossed on the floor. I put it on piles on the table so you can go through it and put it away yourself.'

Suddenly it didn't matter whether Jess was acting from gratitude or self-interest. 'Thank you. I was dreading having to face it all.'

Working together, it only took a few minutes to unload the rest of Helen's belongings. 'If you don't mind drinking white wine with the lasagne, I could open this.' She waved the bottle of wine she'd taken from one of the bags.

'Sounds good to me.' Jess pointed to the table. 'Why don't you sit and open it while I dish up.'

There didn't seem any point in arguing that it was her home, so Helen sat and did what she'd been told. The wine was still chilled and the first mouthful slipped down nicely. They said alcohol wasn't the right way to deal with stress, but it sure as hell helped drown the memory of both Moira and Dilly's odd behaviour. There was a box of matches sitting beside the candle in the centre of the table. It seemed a shame not to light it.

'Here you go.' Jess put a plate in front of Helen, then sat with her own. 'It might need more salt.'

'It smells great.' Helen dug her fork in. 'And tastes good too.'

They ate without speaking, the candle flickering between them, the music still playing. Country and western music, the current song a sad ballad about losing your man. 'You like this kind of music?'

'Yes.' Jess tilted her head, a forkful of food held halfway to her mouth. 'Don't you? I can change it for something else.'

Helen shook her head. 'It's fine.'

'The songs quite often tell stories. I like that about country music.' Jess moved the fork closer, but before she took it into her mouth, she said, 'So tell me your story. Tell me about this man you killed.'

33

Helen's first reaction was to feel cheated. She'd been lured into trusting this woman. Anger came then. At herself for being so stupidly fucking gullible that all it would take to make her give way was a mediocre lasagne and some tidying up. Anger at Jess for misleading her, for reading her private papers. Because of course that's where she must have read about Toby. She wasn't a fucking mind reader.

That she was swearing so much, even in her head, told Helen how badly she was taking this. How cheated she felt. First by Dilly, now by Jess. What a dreadful judge of character she was. Had her experience with Toby taught her nothing? She dropped her fork on the plate and pushed it away. 'Seriously, you think cooking dinner and doing a bit of cleaning up allows you to question me about my personal life? Details of which you'd only have known if you'd read through my private correspondence. Something that is beneath contempt.'

Jess swallowed the mouthful of lasagne, then reached for her wine glass. Taking a swig, she put it down. 'I didn't read your letters. I didn't need to. All I needed to do was to run an Internet search on your name. It told me everything I needed to know about you.'

Of course, Helen's life was on the Internet, all the details of who she'd been, what she'd done. Jess hadn't needed to read Helen's letters. It didn't lessen her anger towards the woman, or her feeling of betrayal. 'Why would you need to know anything about me? You're only staying here for a few days; we're not going into partnership.'

Jess cut another piece of lasagne with the edge of her fork. 'I told you I was going to be more careful who I shared with in future. You showed an unusual tendency towards violence. I may have been an idiot in deciding to share a flat with those stupid women, but I wasn't so much of an idiot that I'd share accommodation with someone who might become violent. I did a search, and it told me about your trial. The man you killed.'

'And you thought it was perfectly acceptable to ask me about him, did you?' Because it wasn't, was it? Helen had been in prison two years; things hadn't changed that much, surely. Had it become acceptable to be this intrusive?

Jess shrugged. 'I thought you might like to talk about it. You seem so buttoned up at times. It's really not good for you.'

Buttoned up! Helen didn't know whether to be amused or offended. 'I've had a lot to deal with recently. The break-in here and at the shop, the—' She stopped herself before she mentioned the noises, unwilling to sound totally flaky. She didn't owe Jess an explanation.

'I was surprised you were given a prison sentence at all. Seems to me you were the victim of coercive control and domestic abuse and were only defending yourself. It was just bad luck that he died.'

Helen wondered what Moira would say to this summary. That Toby's death was simply 'bad luck'. She should have shut down this conversation; instead, she found herself explaining. 'I'd bought the knife the previous day. It was a good quality one and expensive. It was also very sharp. I didn't want to put it loose into the cutlery drawer and hadn't decided where to store it, which is why it was sitting on the counter. The prosecution claimed it showed premeditation.'

'I'd call it a lucky coincidence myself.'

There was no guile in Jess's expression, or the tone of her voice. She believed Helen's story. And why not? At this stage, she almost believed it herself. That the knife simply happened to be within her reach when Toby, with that look of disgust in his eyes, had approached her with the belt taut between his hands. She'd reached blindly behind, her hand sliding over the cold, granite counter in search for something to protect herself with. She remembered her fingers curling around the handle of the knife, the tinny sound as the point of the blade scraped along the granite. There was a gap in her memory then, a void between that screechy, tinny sound, and the heavy thud as Toby fell to the floor. She couldn't remember actually driving that blade home. Because surely she wasn't capable of that level of violence.

Of course, she knew what she'd done. The evidence was bleeding out on the floor by her feet, the knife still in her hand, blood dripping from the edge of the stainless-steel blade and running down the handle onto her hand. It clung there, warm and viscous, as blood pumped, then oozed, then trickled from the hole she'd sliced in Toby's stomach.

'I really don't want to talk about this any more.'

'Okay.' Jess seemed totally unperturbed by Helen's sharp tone. 'Tell me about the plans you have for the shop instead then.'

Helen blinked away the images of Toby and stared at Jess for a few seconds. She knew nothing about this odd woman, who it now appeared knew a lot about her. Reaching for her wine glass, she took a careful sip before putting it down. There was no harm in telling her about the plans for the shop. It was soothing to talk about it, so she did. 'It's a dream come true for me,' she said finally. 'I have to make it work.'

Perhaps she should have left out this last sentence. It made her sound weak and pathetic, and she wasn't either any more. She refused to be. 'I'm *going* to make it work,' she said.

'I know you will.' Jess lifted her glass. 'Let's make a toast to Appleby Books and its success.'

Why not? Helen lifted hers. 'To Appleby Books and its success.'

With their glasses touching, Jess said, 'I meant what I said about wanting to help.'

'I don't need any help, thank you.' It was blunt, rude even, but Helen had had enough of people for that day.

Jess slid her hand across the table to where Helen's hand rested, lifted her index finger and gently tapped the back of her hand. Making a connection. 'Go on, say yes. I'm free tomorrow. It'd be like payment for the accommodation. What d'you think?'

Helen wanted to repeat her refusal, to insist she didn't need her assistance. That she was perfectly well able to manage. After all, Sarah was coming to lend a hand sometime the following day. But it was the first Saturday in business and it might be busy. If Jess did come, she could unpack and shelve the books Helen had collected from Dilly, leaving Sarah to unpack the last of Mrs Clough's. She could trust her sister to flick through the books and remove anything she found.

'Okay, yes, I'll accept your offer.'

Jess beamed. 'You won't regret it. I'm a good worker. And I know books; you won't have to worry I'll put them on the wrong shelf.'

That was so far down Helen's list of worries that it made her laugh. 'I'm sure you won't.' She finished the wine in her glass, shaking her head when Jess lifted the bottle in invitation. 'No, I don't have a great head for alcohol. Anyway, I'm shattered; I'm going to tidy up and head to bed.'

'No, I'll clear everything away. You go ahead; you look knackered.'

There didn't seem to be any point in arguing, especially since that one glass of wine had pushed Helen from being shattered towards utterly exhausted.

She didn't bother with the shower she'd been longing for; instead, she peeled off her clothes, pulled on a cotton T-shirt and crawled between the sheets. It was nice to be back in her own home, sleeping in her comfortable bed. And oddly, despite her reservations about Jess, there was something comforting about having another presence in the house.

34

When Helen woke, her first thought was that she must be back in prison because she could hear voices. Lots of them. It had all been a dream. The shop, the break-ins, the odd noises and strange people. It was a relief. Once again, she was safely locked away; she'd be told what to do and be protected from the vagaries of life.

She kept her eyes shut, even as reality pushed its way into her head. She wasn't in prison; the voices, the murmuring in the background, it was coming from the radio in the kitchen. Jess, making herself at home.

A week ago, Helen had been fizzing with excitement about opening the shop. Her new business, a fresh start, and a dream come true. She'd been planning for such a long time, she thought she knew how tough running a business would be, but what she hadn't envisaged were all the other variables that would impact on her life. The break-ins had been bad enough, but it was the strange noises, and even stranger people she was having to deal with that were dampening her enthusiasm.

Several minutes passed before she forced herself to throw

back the duvet, and it was another few seconds before she could drag herself from the bed and into the shower. She'd read somewhere once that having a shower could increase or even restore positive energy. It was as good a reason as any to stay in it a long time. She wasn't sure she was feeling more positive, but she did feel a little calmer as she dressed.

Downstairs, when she opened the door into the kitchen, Jess was curled up in the chair by the window, a book held open in one hand. She looked up when the door opened, looking slightly startled as if surprised by Helen's appearance. It made her feel like an intruder in her own home.

The feeling was heightened when she saw that a place had been set for her at the table. The mug, bowl, plate and cutlery all neatly lined up. As if she was staying in a B&B.

'I'll make you some coffee,' Jess said, shutting her book and jumping to her feet.

'No.' The word, almost shouted, brought Jess to a halt, eyes wide. Helen held a hand up, half in apology, half to keep Jess where she was. 'I was very tired last night, and it was kind of you to look after me, but really I prefer to help myself.'

'I'm not much of a morning person either, especially before I've had some coffee.'

Now she was making excuses for her! Helen gritted her teeth and turned away to fill the kettle. She took a perverted kind of pleasure in making tea rather than coffee, conscious of Jess's eyes on her as she opened the tea caddy, took out the teabag and dropped it into the mug she took from the cupboard. Not the one Jess had left on the table. Helen almost smiled at how childish she was being. Jess had an amazing ability to rub her up the wrong way.

Ignoring her, she popped some bread into the toaster and sipped her tea while waiting for it to be ready.

'Are we going to walk to the shop?'

We. The last time Helen had been a *we*, it hadn't ended well. Perhaps she should warn Jess. The thought made her chuckle. It turned into a full belly laugh when she caught sight of Jess's expression – part apprehension, part curiosity, mostly wariness. It seemed a warning was unnecessary. 'Relax, I'm not going crazy; I just had an amusing thought.' She took her toast and tea to the table, and sat. 'We'll walk.'

* * *

They left twenty minutes later. It was mid-October; there was a chill in the air that made Helen button up the thin jacket she'd pulled on over her T-shirt. Jess, she noticed, was more sensibly dressed in a cosy-looking parka. There was also a definite chill between the two women since Helen's earlier rejection of the breakfast set-up.

She told herself she didn't care. That she'd been right to make a stand. But guilt jabbed her when she noticed Jess looking like a whipped puppy. She was merely trying to be kind. Why had Helen made such a fuss about it?

'I appreciate you volunteering to help today,' she said, as they walked towards the shop.

Jess's expression immediately lightened. 'I'm glad to have the opportunity to repay you for all your kindness. Plus,' she added with a smile, 'I'll enjoy working in the shop.'

Chatting about books restored a friendly relationship between them as they walked, comfortable enough for Helen to say, as she unlocked the door, 'It's always a relief to get here and find everything is as I left it.'

'Hasn't it been?' Jess sounded puzzled.

The break-in, the books tossed from the shelves. 'I mean owning a bookshop still feels a bit like a dream.'

'Oh right, yeah, it must do.'

'Come and I'll show you where I'd like you to start.' Upstairs, Helen pointed out the boxes she'd brought back from Dilly's. 'They're mostly contemporary fiction so you shouldn't have any problem finding the right shelf for them downstairs.' She handed her the stamp. 'Just press the logo onto the top right corner of the first page.'

Downstairs, Helen prepared the shop for the day ahead. Blinds up, door unlocked, a fresh display on the table. Within minutes, Jess was down with an armful of books, moving from shelf to shelf, slotting them into place. 'Some great books,' she said, then ran back upstairs.

Helen was standing behind the desk looking at the pages on the ledger when she heard footsteps on the stairs again. Descending more slowly this time. Helen looked over, expecting to see Jess's arms laden with books. They weren't. She was frowning and holding something in her hand.

35

'I found this,' Jess said, opening her fingers to show an ornate medallion on a fine gold chain.

'You found it?' Helen took it and held it up to the light. She wasn't big into jewellery, and she thought the piece was remarkably ugly, but there was little doubt in her mind that the stones set into the gold were diamonds. 'Where?'

'I took another few books from the box, and it fell from between them.'

Helen stared at the medallion. Ugly it may be, but it was heavy, and obviously valuable. How had it ended up in the box? Perhaps it had been on the shelf and had got caught up in the books. It seemed unlikely that she wouldn't have noticed, but then she had been distracted by Dilly's odd manner so perhaps...

'I'll contact the woman who sold me the books and let her know I have it safe.' She smiled at Jess. 'Thank you.' She didn't need to say the words. That Jess could have kept the medallion. It would have fetched hundreds of pounds for the weight of the gold alone.

'I'll get back to the books then; hopefully, there'll be no more surprises.'

Helen had Dilly's phone number; she could ring her, let her know she'd found the medallion. Or perhaps it would be better to call around with it, use the opportunity to ask Dilly why she'd been a bit off with Helen the previous evening. Because now that she was seeing it through calmer eyes, there'd been something decidedly odd about her behaviour. And there were enough puzzles in her life without adding more.

She put the medallion in the pocket of her jeans, then pushed it to the back of her mind and smiled as customers came through the door. There was a steady stream and most purchased at least one book. They were happy to chat too and all promised to return.

'It's nice to have a bookshop to visit,' one elderly lady commented, putting two books on the desk. 'Even if it is a second-hand one.' She sniffed. 'It's all about sustainability these days, isn't it?'

She said *sustainability* as if it was a bad thing. Helen hid her smile and slipped the two books into a paper bag. 'When I dreamed of opening a bookshop,' she explained, 'it was always a second-hand one. I like the idea of books being read, and read again, of them being loved and passed on for someone else to enjoy.'

'Pre-loved then rather than second-hand.' The woman smiled. 'Yes, that I can understand.' She gave a little wave and left.

Sarah arrived at ten. 'It's looking good,' she whispered in Helen's ear as she gave her a hug. 'And busy! I'm so pleased for you.'

'Thank you, and for coming to give me a hand too. My first Saturday in business, it was impossible to know how it would go.' She nodded towards the stairway. 'There's a university student helping us out. Her name's Jess.' She'd never told Sarah about the money being stolen; she was pleased now that she hadn't. 'She came in the first day and has been back a couple of times since, so we've got friendly. In fact, she's staying with me for a few days.'

Sarah stood back; an eyebrow raised. 'Staying with you? That's moving a bit fast, isn't it?'

Helen was amused by her sister's reaction, the obvious suspicion in her eyes. 'Don't jump to the wrong conclusion. I meant friendly in a non-sexual context.'

'Well, after two years in a women's prison,' Sarah said, obviously choosing her words with care, 'you might have decided it was preferable to swing that way rather than meeting someone like Toby again.'

'I might, but I haven't, and anyway, I don't think my choice comes down to becoming a lesbian or meeting Toby Mark 2.'

'I didn't mean any offence,' Sarah said, looking decidedly embarrassed.

'And none taken.' Helen gave her sister a gentle punch on her arm. 'Go on up, introduce yourself to Jess; you'll like her. I've left the three boxes in the corner for you to do, if you don't mind.' She explained about Jared's request and took the A4 envelope from the shelf under the desk to hand to her. 'Anything you find, shove it in here. Mostly it's grocery receipts, but there's been a couple of five-pound notes too.'

'How odd.'

'Better than turning down the corner of a page. Some of the books are quite old, so see where you think they might fit. Ask Jess if you're stuck; she's as much of a bibliophile as I am.'

Several minutes later, into the quiet of the shop, a peal of laughter rolled down the stairway. It made Helen smile. It seemed her two helpers were getting on well together. She should have warned Jess not to mention how their relationship had started, that she hadn't told Sarah. It seemed though, she'd enough sense to keep quiet about their dodgy beginnings.

Once the boxes were empty, Helen would put up a sign saying there were more books upstairs. Then she'd start contacting book clubs, see if she could persuade them to meet up there. She wasn't sure if authors would want to give talks since she wouldn't be in a position to buy their books. It was something she'd have to think about. She knew the authors T. G. Reid and Lizzie Lane lived in Bath; it wouldn't do any harm to contact them, see if they'd be interested. They could bring along their own books to sell. That might work out well.

Recent events had dented both her enthusiasm and her excitement, but she was a resilient woman, she'd had to be, and both were slowly reappearing.

Sarah and Jess appeared like clockwork toys every now and then with armfuls of books that were neatly shelved before they vanished again.

Late morning, Jess came down with only a couple in her hand. 'That's it,' she said, slotting the books into a gap. 'I'll give Sarah a hand with the others, but I thought I'd stop for something to eat first.' She nodded towards the door. 'They do pizza by the slice next door, so I thought I'd get one for my lunch. Sarah said no, she's brought sandwiches, but do you fancy one?'

Guessing her sister would have brought sandwiches for her too, Helen shook her head. 'No, thanks, I'm good. But if you're done, you can head off; you don't have to hang around.'

'I like being here,' Jess said simply, before she ambled through the door in search of pizza.

It was almost twenty minutes before she returned and when she did, her hands were empty.

'No pizza?'

'I ate it there. Met the owners; what a howl they are, eh?'

Helen would have preferred if Jess had come back saying she'd met Alex and Zander and found them a bit creepy. A bit dodgy. If she had, perhaps Helen could have shared her suspicion of them. Talked about the strange sounds she'd heard: the ones she was certain they were making in order to drive her out. She'd really like to have told Jess about the previous owner, and his sad, hideous death on the stairway. Instead, she forced her lips into a smile and said, 'They are that all right.'

Sarah came down as Jess was recounting something funny either Alex or Zander had said to her. She was laughing as she told it and dragged Sarah into the conversation. Both were still laughing as the door opened and two police officers came through.

They were the same two who'd informed Helen of the break-in at her home. Thinking they'd come to give her an update, she greeted them with a smile. 'Hi, what news? Have you caught someone?' She looked to the taller officer, PC Reid, who had seemed the more talkative of the two.

'I'm afraid we're not here about the break-in at your home,' he said quietly. Then glancing around the shop, seeing a couple of customers turning to look, he nodded towards the back. 'Could we talk somewhere more private?'

Sarah stepped closer, put an arm around Helen's shoulder and stared at the officer. 'Is something wrong?'

The constable met her eyes and gave an almost imperceptible nod. 'If we could go somewhere more private, it'd be best.'

'I'll keep an eye on the shop, if you want to go into the kitchen,' Jess said.

'Right, that'd be perfect,' Sarah said, taking charge. 'Shout if you have any problems. We won't be long.' This last was directed at the two officers as she led the unresisting Helen past the stairway and into the kitchen.

The second officer shut the door when they were all through. It was a small space, forcing them to stand too close together for anyone's comfort, especially Helen's, whose eyes flitted from one officer to the other as she tried to guess from their faces how bad this was going to be. 'What is it?'

'I'm afraid we've had a complaint,' PC Reid said. 'That yesterday evening, while collecting books you bought from a customer, you took a valuable item of jewellery.'

'What?' Sarah almost yelped the word. 'Helen isn't a thief.'

Helen reached a hand out to rest it on the wall. Was this it? The final straw. Dilly had reported her to the police. Dilly who, thanks to Helen, knew exactly what it would mean if she was found guilty of theft. Did she genuinely think that Helen had repaid her kindness by stealing from her? But that wouldn't have explained the woman's strange manner the previous evening. Unless she believed Helen had taken it on one of her earlier visits. 'It's Dilly Henderson, isn't it? When did she say it was stolen?'

'She said she'd had it yesterday, and when she went to put it on this morning, it wasn't where she'd left it. And as there'd been nobody else in her home...'

He left the sentence hanging, but they all knew how it would finish. The only person Dilly had let into her home had been the ex-con Helen Appleby. She was confused. If Dilly thought Helen had taken it yesterday evening, then it didn't explain her strange behaviour from the moment she'd arrived. She didn't know what was going on, but she knew she had to clear herself of theft. 'I think I can explain. Hang on...' she pointed to the door behind the officers '...I need to get Jess to come in and then you'll understand.' She turned to her sister. 'Would you go out, take over from her, and ask her to come in. I'll explain everything to you later, I promise. And don't worry, it's all going to be okay.'

With obvious reluctance, and giving each of the officers a defiant glare, Sarah left, shutting the door behind her with a bang.

Helen said nothing until the door opened again and Jess's puzzled face appeared in the gap. 'Come in. Don't worry, you're not in any trouble.'

'Good to know.' She slipped between the two officers to Helen's side. 'So what gives?'

'Would you tell us what you found this morning while you were unpacking the books I brought back with me last night.'

'You mean the medallion?'

'Yes.'

Jess shrugged. 'I'd taken a few books from the box and when I reached in for more, I found a piece of jewellery stuck between the next two. A medallion on a chain. I immediately brought it down to Helen, who said she'd contact the woman... Dilly I think her name was... and return it to her.'

'Which I'd planned to do when we shut this evening.' Helen reached into her pocket and pulled out the medallion. 'I kept it on me as being the safest place. It looks valuable.' Pre-empting the next question, she continued. 'I've no idea how it got into the box. I packed the books myself, but I was tired, perhaps distracted. It might have been on the shelf and was knocked into a box and I didn't notice. I didn't steal it. If I had, I don't think I'd have left it in the box for Jess to have found, do you?'

PC Reid didn't appear to have a comment to make; instead, he took the medallion from Helen's hand and looked at it. 'Looks like an antique.'

'A bloody ugly piece if you ask me.' She reached out and tapped the diamonds. 'But I'm guessing they're real so it's probably worth a tidy sum.'

'Yes, it probably is.' He looked Jess over with a measuring glance. 'And you are?'

'Jess Milgate.'

Helen could hear the nerves in the younger woman's voice and took over. 'Jess was one of my first customers and we bonded over our love of books. She's a student at Bath Spa university and volunteered to help me out today.'

'And you found this inside the boxes you were unpacking?'

Jess nodded. 'There were three. Each were taped shut. I think you did that to make it easier to transport them, yes?' She looked to Helen for confirmation.

'Yes. Plus, if it's raining, I don't want the books getting wet while I cart them in or out.'

PC Reid's eyes narrowed. 'So the boxes were taped up before you left Mrs Henderson's house, and weren't opened until this morning by Miss Milgate.'

'That's correct.'

'At which stage, you found this nestling between the books.' He tossed the medallion in his hand. It made a clinking noise that drew all their eyes.

'Not quite.' Jess's voice was more assured now that she realised she wasn't in any trouble. 'I'd taken out several books before I found it so it was probably two or three books deep.'

'Hard to think it accidentally fell inside, isn't it?'

It was. In fact, the more Helen thought of it, the more she discounted the idea. The ugly medallion would have been obvious. Had it fallen, she'd have heard it, seen it. But if that wasn't the way it happened, there was only one other explanation. Dilly had put it there. It had been she who'd insisted she'd tape up the remaining boxes while Helen started to take them out. She'd had ample opportunity.

Opportunity, but what the hell had been her motive?

36

A soon as the two police officers left, Sarah bustled back into the kitchen. 'What the hell was that all about?'

Jess didn't need to be told. 'I'll mind the shop.' She shut the door behind her.

It would have been nice to have gone out into the garden. Perhaps to sit on the grass under the apple tree with a good book. Escape into a different world. One where everything wasn't one great big fucking puzzle. But Helen didn't have that luxury. Instead, she smoothed a hand over her forehead and filled her sister in on what the police had said.

'So that's it then, is it?' Sarah said when she'd finished. 'They'll give her the medallion thing back, and that'll be it?'

Life should be that easy, but in Helen's experience, it rarely was. 'Despite the item being returned, Dilly could still cause trouble for me.' She held a hand up to stop the words she could see waiting on Sarah's tongue. 'Yes, I know, it's all ridiculous, and the officers said it wouldn't go anywhere, but it still might impact on my licence.'

Sarah reached out and grabbed Helen's arm. 'No!' she said,

horrified. 'You didn't steal it, and she has it back now anyway. Perhaps you should explain to her the negative impact it might have on you.'

'She knows.' Helen heaved a sigh. 'Because I told her.' Pulling away from the grip Sarah had on her arm, Helen took the key from her pocket and crossed to the back door. 'I need a bit of fresh air.'

Outside, she pulled the chair out of the shade into the weak sunlight that filtered through the branches of the apple tree. 'I should really check that Jess is okay,' she said, sitting heavily, the feet of the chair sinking into the rain-softened soil underneath.

'Jess is fine, she's a sensible woman; she'll come and get you if there's any problems.' Sarah lifted the other chair and placed it beside Helen's. 'There's something iffy about this medallion thing, isn't there?'

'The first couple of times I called to pick up books from her, Dilly was really friendly. There was always tea, she insisted we sat down for a chat. She asked a lot of questions, most of which I was happy to answer, but she was a little pushy about things I prefer to keep private. I thought she was a bit lonely so didn't mind giving her my time. Plus, she'd sold me the books at an absolute bargain price, so I felt it was the least I could do.' Helen rested her head back and looked at the sky through the leaves of the tree. Some were already turning brown. Soon the branches would be empty and she'd be able to see the sky more clearly. Unlike this situation, which was getting more muddled. How naïve she was, how fucking stupid to think that Toby's death had been a full stop. An end to the woman she'd been. That she could start again and do better second time around. It wasn't working out that way.

'Last night,' she said, 'it was like Dilly was a different person. She was rude, dismissive, almost hostile.'

'Maybe it was a different person. A twin.'

Helen gave up staring at the sky in hope of enlightenment and looked at her sister. 'We both need to stop reading so many psychological thrillers; we're in danger of becoming paranoid and seeing mysteries where there aren't any.'

'Okay, maybe the twin idea is a bit far-fetched, but you have to admit, it's stretching credulity more than a bit to think that the medallion thing simply upped and jumped into the box all by itself.'

'I was a bit distracted, but no, I'd have noticed if I'd picked it up by accident or it had somehow fallen in.' She told Sarah about Dilly's insistence that Helen carry the boxes out while she taped up the remaining ones. 'She must have put it inside.'

'That's it!' Sarah almost squealed with excitement at finding a logical solution. 'She was bending over, it fell into the box, and she taped it shut without noticing.'

That would have been a perfect explanation except Helen had seen the chain. It wasn't broken, so it couldn't simply have fallen off. No, Dilly had deliberately placed it inside. Helen wracked her brain in an attempt to come up with an explanation for why she'd have done such a thing. She'd gone over as much of their conversations as she could remember. She hadn't said anything terrible, had she? Nothing wrong? Apart from opening up about her fears and worries. Had that been it? Had she been too much *woe is me*, so Dilly decided to show her what real misery was like? Send her back to prison, make her lose the business she obviously loved. Far-fetched, perhaps, but what other reason could there be?

It was easier to allow Sarah to believe she'd solved the conundrum than to listen to her casting around for alternatives. 'Yes, you're right, that's probably what happened,' Helen said. 'When the police tell her where it was found, she'll likely remember she was wearing it when she was taping up the boxes.'

'I bet she rings later, grovelling an apology. The old bat.' Sarah got to her feet. 'Now that's sorted, I'll get back to those books. So far. I've added three more receipts to your collection. There's only one box left so I shouldn't be much longer.'

'Great.' Helen tried to sound pleased but her head was still struggling with what Dilly had done. She wouldn't be happy until she'd spoken to her and found out why she'd done such a horrendous thing. 'Right, I suppose I'd better get back to work too.'

Jess was speaking to a trio of middle-aged women when Helen returned to the shop, and another couple of customers were perusing the shelves. According to the ledger, which Jess had filled out in neat, tiny writing, they'd sold ten books in the last thirty minutes. Saturday was proving to be even more successful than she'd hoped. She should be thrilled, excited, but every time the door opened, her heart dropped in expectation of seeing Moira, her features set into grim lines as she prepared to pounce on her and drag her back into a cell. Helen knew she was being overly melodramatic. Moira probably didn't even work on a Saturday, but it didn't stop her from worrying.

She recognised the next woman who came through the door, but it was a happy recognition. Her very first customer. 'Hello, I'm so pleased you've come back.'

The elderly woman reached into a huge tote bag and awkwardly removed four books. 'You made me a very good offer,' she said, putting them on the desk. 'I thoroughly enjoyed these, especially the Hemingway one.' She tapped the cover of the book, almost affectionately. 'I'm not usually keen on short stories, but these were something else.' She searched in her pocket for the business card Helen had given her the previous Saturday. 'And here's the card to prove I'm bringing back the same books.'

There was really no need to check, but Helen did all the same. 'That's perfect,' she said. 'Feel free to choose four more books.'

She pointed to the stairway. 'There are more upstairs if you don't find what you want on the shelves here.'

'Thank you.' The woman looked around, smiling in anticipation. 'I'm going to grab one of those little stools and work my way around. The danger will be that I find too many I want to read.' She said this last almost to herself as she toddled across to a stool and dragged it to the first shelf.

Another customer came to the desk to claim Helen's attention. 'I'll take these,' she said, handing over a pile of books. 'I couldn't choose so decided to treat myself to all five in the end.'

'I like that I sell treats that aren't calorific or in any other way bad for you,' Helen said with a smile, putting the books into a bag. 'That'll be eleven-fifty, please.'

When she'd gone, Helen picked up the four books the older woman had returned, thinking to put them back on the shelf. Remembering they hadn't yet been stamped with the Appleby logo, she looked towards the stairway. She could run up and hand them to Jess to do. But another customer approached the desk, so instead she slid the four books onto the shelf underneath. They could wait till later.

With Jess helping, Sarah finished unpacking the last of Mrs Clough's books a short time later and came downstairs. 'Here you go,' she said, handing Helen the A4 envelope. 'There were mostly receipts, one blank sheet of paper, and one five-pound note. An out-of-date one too, but he'll probably be able to change it in a bank.'

'Thanks for that.' Helen peered into the envelope, then sealed the top and tossed it under the desk. 'It was brilliant to get all those books put away. It's been so busy; I wouldn't have had a chance.'

'Glad I could help. Jess is upstairs finding a home for the last few books. She's a nice lass, isn't she?'

Nice? Helen wasn't sure. But then she wasn't sure of anything these days. She'd liked to have told Sarah the story of the theft, see what she thought of it. But she was afraid her sister would look at her in horror for offering Jess a room, no matter how temporary the arrangement was to be. So instead, she forced herself to smile and utter a mindless, 'Yes, very.'

'Right then, I'll go now, unless there's anything else you'd like me to do?'

'No, head off, and thanks again. It meant a lot to have you here, especially when the police arrived.'

'Hopefully, they gave that stupid cow a telling off for wasting police time.' Sarah reached under the desk and grabbed her handbag. 'Let me know if she contacts you to apologise.' She gave Helen a hug. 'I hope the rest of the day goes brilliantly.' Then she was gone, waving madly through the window as she passed outside.

Helen waved back, smiling slightly manically, the smile fading once Sarah was out of sight. It was a relief to be able to stop pretending, to let the worry about Dilly take centre stage in her head and furrow her brow.

'You're looking quite fierce,' Jess said, suddenly appearing in front of her. 'You okay?'

It was easier to share with a virtual stranger. There was no agenda, no past history to contend with, no toes to avoid treading on. She looked around to make sure her customers were busy, then turned back to speak in a low voice. 'I'm worried about Dilly's allegation. It might make trouble for me, have me recalled to prison.'

'No way.' Jess shook her head. 'You didn't steal it. It must have got tangled up in the books somehow.'

'Sarah thought maybe it had fallen in when Dilly was taping up the boxes.'

'There you go then, exactly what might have happened.'

Helen desperately wanted to believe it. The chain hadn't been broken, but perhaps the catch had been open. 'When you found it, was the clasp undone?' The fingers of hope that grasped onto this idea fell away when she saw the truth in Jess's eyes.

'I wish I could say yes,' she said.

Helen gave a rueful smile. 'Believe me, so do I.'

'What are you going to do?'

She didn't think she had a choice. 'I'm going to go and speak to her. I'm hoping when she got the medallion back, she apologised and said she'd made a mistake. If she didn't, I'm going to beg her to. Either way, I want to know why she dropped the medallion into the box because that's what had to have happened.'

'She put it in!' Jess sounded genuinely appalled. 'But why would she do such a thing? And then report you for having stolen it. It doesn't make sense.'

'That's why I want to speak to her.' Helen checked her watch. Another hour before she shut. Sixty minutes to wait before she could go and tackle Dilly.

'I'll go with you.'

'What?' Helen looked at Jess's earnest face. 'That's not necessary. You should go now, do something more interesting with your Saturday evening.'

'I don't think you should go alone. If this Dilly person deliberately put that piece of jewellery into the box, then she has it in for you for some reason. You need me there as backup. A witness, if you like, to whatever she might say. Or to whatever she might accuse you of.'

Jess was right. If Dilly had deliberately set Helen up, who knows what else she was capable of. 'Yes, you have a point, I suppose, but are you sure you want to get embroiled in my problems?'

'They're certainly more interesting than mine. Plus,' Jess added with a smile, 'if she deliberately set out to harm you for no reason, it sounds like she has some form of antisocial personality disorder, and that's of real interest to me.'

'You think she's a psychopath or something.' Helen remembered thinking Dilly had a Jekyll and Hyde personality. Maybe she hadn't been too far out.

Jess wagged her head side to side. 'The terms psychopath and sociopath are beloved by movies and books but they're not regarded as official diagnoses. But psychopathy and sociopathy describe traits that fall under the umbrella of antisocial personality disorder.' She grinned. 'You got me on my psychology soapbox there. It might simply be that this Dilly woman is a troublesome bitch.'

37

At six, Helen turned the sign on the door to closed and shut the blinds on the window. The last twenty minutes had been quiet, so she'd already counted up the takings. 'It's been a good day,' she said to Jess as she switched out the lights. 'When we've spoken to Dilly, I'll get us something to eat.'

'A pizza from next door?'

Helen put the alarm on and locked the door after them before she replied. 'Maybe we'll get an Indian for a change.' She walked briskly, Jess bobbing along beside her, throwing her curious glances. She was far too observant for her own good, Helen thought, increasing the speed of her step in the hope it would prevent unwanted questions.

'You don't like them, do you? Alex and Zander, I mean.'

All the speed walking had achieved was to put Helen out of breath. She slowed and turned to look at Jess in annoyance. 'Why do you think that? I've never said anything against them. They're good neighbours.'

'It's not what you say, more the way you say it. As if you're gritting your teeth at the same time.'

Helen probably was. But it wasn't the time to be going into detail about her suspicions of the pizza twins. She hoped her silence would end the conversation. But of course it didn't.

'They're having some issues with their heating system at the mo, and they wanted to know if it was causing you any problems. I said I'd ask you and let them know.'

'Problems,' Helen said, turning to look at her. 'What kind of problems?'

'Zander says that some days when they turn it on, it sounds like a demented drummer. It doesn't last long, he said, but every now and then, for no apparent reason, off it goes. "Bangydee bang bang," he said. I'm not sure if that's Cockney rhyming slang for something or if—'

'He said what?' Helen interrupted her, coming to a halt and turning to stare.

'Bangydee bang bang,' Jess repeated, looking surprised. 'Or something like that anyway.'

'Before that, what did you say before that?' Helen took a breath. 'I'm sorry, I sound a little crazy. Tell me again, what did Zander say?'

'Just that they were having problems with their heating system, that every now and then, it sounded like a demented drummer. It doesn't last long he said, but he was worried in case it was disturbing you.'

'The banging noises, oh my goodness!' Helen started to laugh, shaking her head, and laughing even harder when she saw Jess's look of concern. 'No, it's okay, it is genuinely funny.' She wiped a tear from her eyes, shook her head again and walked on. It seemed only fair to explain. 'I've been hearing noises, now and then, since I opened the shop. A knocking sound. It would go on a few times then stop. I haven't told you the story but it appears the previous owner collapsed and died in the stairwell. He'd tried to get help for days by knocking on the wooden step. He knocked so hard, and for so long, his knuckles were bloodied.'

'So when you heard the knocking, you thought the shop was haunted?' Jess's eyes were wide.

'No... yes... I'm not sure, but it wasn't just that. It was Zander who'd told me about the man, filling in the gory details about his bloodied knuckles, so when I heard the knocking, I got a bit suspicious.' She hoped to see the dawning of understanding on Jess's face, but it was still bemused. They'd reached the car by this stage. Helen glanced towards her home. She'd have liked to have gone in, opened a bottle of beer, and watched something mindless on TV. But she couldn't rest till she'd spoken to Dilly.

She clicked the fob to unlock the car and climbed in. It wasn't until they were on their way that she finished the explanation she could see Jess was waiting for. 'I thought they were trying to get rid of me.' She gave a quick glance to see if the light had yet dawned. 'You know, push me out, buy my beautiful, newly refurbished shop at possibly a knock-down price, then extend their pizza place into it.'

'But they said it had been for sale for years; they'd had every opportunity to buy it and hadn't bothered.'

'I know.' Hadn't she thought the same before she'd become riddled with suspicion? 'It was the knocking, and the break-ins, they all made me a little paranoid.'

'Understandable, I suppose,' Jess said.

But it was said in a tone of voice that told Helen she was being humoured, that Jess didn't understand at all. And suddenly, she desperately wanted her to. 'It's just that I've learnt to be suspicious of everyone's motives.'

'You were the victim of domestic violence; that must have left its mark on you. The fact you made that Toby guy pay for what he'd done to you doesn't mean it all goes away.'

Jess still didn't understand; how could she when she didn't know the whole story? Helen was suspicious of everyone's motives because she saw how easily hers had been swallowed. Everyone was an expert. The counsellors, Sarah, her parole officer, and now this young woman who hadn't a clue about anything outside the theories that were poured into her from books. They had no idea what she'd made Toby pay for. What Helen's motive had been.

No fucking idea at all.

38

Helen pulled up outside Dilly's house and turned to Jess. 'Maybe you should stay here.'

'I wouldn't be much good as a witness if I don't see or hear anything.' Jess nodded towards the house. 'I'll come in, but keep my mouth shut.'

Helen wasn't sure the younger woman was capable of keeping schtum, but she was tired and couldn't think of a good enough reason to insist that she stay in the car. Bringing her along had been a stupid idea; now she had to live with it. It was the story of her life. 'Right, let's get on with it then.'

She knocked on the door, timidly at first, then with more vigour, reminding herself that she'd done nothing wrong.

'Maybe she's out,' Jess said. She stepped around Helen to peer through the frosted glass, then rapped on it with the large, silver ring she wore on her middle finger. It made a loud cracking noise.

'Don't break the bloody glass,' Helen said, pulling Jess's arm away. 'Come on, let's get out of here.'

'No wait, I see something.'

They both stood in silence as the shadowy figure came closer, both stepping back with an indrawn breath when the door was wrenched open and Dilly appeared, her face drawn in lines of anger. 'I should call the police.'

'Please don't,' Helen said, taking a step forward. 'I only want to talk to you.'

'Ha! Not steal from me again?'

'I didn't take it. I swear. I don't know how it got into the box—'

Dilly held a hand up. 'You're a liar. I'm not sure you'd know truth if it bit you in the arse. But you'll pay for it. I told the police I wanted them to prosecute—'

It was Helen's turn to jump in, and she did, almost tearfully. 'But you got it back; why would you do such a thing? You know what it means for me.'

'I do, and just to be sure, I contacted that parole officer of yours. She was very grateful to me for alerting her.'

Helen had made it all so easy for her. She'd even given her Moira's name. 'I don't understand. We were friendly. You made tea for me.' She didn't know why but this one stupid thing brought tears to her eyes.

'Yes, and how did you repay me? You stole from me when my back was turned, using the very books you professed to love to hide it.'

'You're lying.' Jess's voice was quiet, but there was something in her tone that sliced through the air and made both Helen and Dilly turn to look at her. 'I can see it in your eyes, in the twitch of your mouth as you try not to smile. I'm guessing you know Helen didn't steal it because you put it there yourself.' She took a step closer so she was fully revealed in the overhead light. 'If Helen had stolen it, d'you think she'd have asked me to unpack the books? You don't think she'd have removed that frankly ugly piece of jewellery first? No, you put it there. The question is, why? Why do you want to destroy her?'

'Who the hell are you?'

'A friend.' Jess looked along the street. 'Now if you don't want your neighbours coming out to see what all the fuss is about. If you don't want them knowing what a conniving, lying old bat you really are, I suggest you let us in.'

To Helen's surprise, rather than shutting the door in their faces, Dilly stood back to allow them to enter. Jess didn't wait to be directed; she followed the light that drifted through the open door at the end of the corridor. 'Nice,' she said, looking around before pulling out a chair and sitting like one who was waiting for the main event to commence.

Dilly ladled on the sarcasm. 'Make yourself at home, why don't you.'

It was wasted on Jess, who sat back and crossed her legs. 'Thanks so much.'

Helen remained standing, bouncing slightly on the balls of her feet, as if in preparation to run away. She should do. Run and keep running from the hate she could see clearly in Dilly's eyes. Had it always been there? Well-hidden behind her kindly, friendly demeanour? This was why she'd set Helen up, why she'd rung the police, contacted Moira. Dilly hated her. It was a bizarre feeling to realise that someone felt that way about her and she'd absolutely no idea why.

'It doesn't matter what you say,' Dilly said, addressing Jess. 'The medallion was stolen from me and found in Helen's possession. They may decide it's not worth proceeding with a prosecution, but it's enough for that nice parole officer to consider recalling her to prison.'

Helen knew it would be. Moira would take great delight in telling her that she'd given her one chance and was unable to give her another. 'You know I didn't steal from you, so why don't you tell me what's going on.'

Dilly laughed. 'I suppose it doesn't matter if I do. I've started the ball rolling; it isn't going to stop.' She pulled a chair out from the table and sat.

When Helen continued to stand, Jess got to her feet, went over, took her by the hand and guided her to a chair. 'Sit, before you fall down.' She waited till Helen sat before taking the chair beside her and glaring at Dilly. 'Now, let's get on with whatever vitriol you're waiting to spill, please. We have a pizza waiting for us.'

'It's simple. I can explain in one four-letter word.' Dilly stared at Helen as she said it. 'Toby.'

The thought of returning to prison had already made Helen turn pale, but at this, the remainder of the colour faded from her face.

It was left to Jess to ask the question. 'You knew the man she killed?'

'The man she murdered, you mean. I'd only met him once, but I knew a lot about him from his mother, Anna, the woman I loved. His death destroyed her and ended our relationship, destroying me in the process.'

'No,' Helen shook her head. 'I never met Toby's mother, but I know her name wasn't Anna.'

Dilly sneered. 'You never bothered trying to meet her. If you had, you'd have known her given name was Diana, but she preferred to be called Anna.'

Helen remembered the wraith of a woman she'd seen in the courthouse. She'd discounted the possibility that she might be involved with what was going on. It seemed she was both right, and wrong. Toby had rarely spoken of his mother. He'd certainly never mentioned his mother's wife. 'I didn't have the opportunity to meet her. She and Toby had fallen out years before I met him.

They were back on speaking terms, but that was it as far as I was aware.'

'They were getting there,' Dilly insisted. 'And they would have made it if you hadn't murdered him.'

Jess brought the flat of her hand down on the table, startling both Dilly and Helen. 'He got what he deserved,' she said into the silence that followed. 'I've read up on the trial. Toby was a bully, a sadist. I saw the photographs of Helen's injuries. She was the victim and was only defending herself. It's crazy that she went to prison simply because she happened to have bought the knife a day before. Coincidences do happen.'

Dilly looked at her, her mouth twisting into a sneer. 'So young, so fucking stupid.'

'Leave her alone; she's only trying to help.' Helen's voice was thick with tears, heavy with weariness. 'She wasn't there that day, neither were you or Anna, so you're going to have to believe that I told the truth about what happened.'

'The truth? That you were a victim?' Dilly laughed. A raucous, loud, ugly sound that seemed to linger in the air. 'My biggest regret is that I didn't find out about you in time to go into that courtroom and tell the world what a piece of work you are. Anna only told me afterwards. After you were sentenced to four years. I remember she shrieked when she heard. Four years for Toby's life. It was crazy. It was only then that she told me what Toby had shared about his relationship with you.'

The inside of Helen's mouth had turned to sandpaper, her tongue caught on its abrasive grains. She tried to unstick it, to get the words out to stop Dilly talking. The chair screeched on the floor tiles as she pushed it back, got to her feet, and crossed to the kitchen. There were no cups or glasses to be seen so she turned on the tap at the sink, leaned over and drank from the stream of water, then turned it off and wiped a hand over her mouth. Pulling up the bottom of her T-shirt, she dried both face and hands as she walked back to the chair and sat. 'As well as being an abuser, Toby was a liar and a fantasist, so take whatever his mother told you with a large handful of salt.'

Dilly stood and walked over to a dresser. When she returned, she had a mobile in her hand. 'It's Anna's. She didn't want to be contactable, so she left it behind. When I'm feeling really lonely, stupid as I am, I listen to her voice telling me to leave a message. She recorded it in happier times. She was always a cheerful, almost joyful woman, and it's there in those few words.' She picked the phone up and pressed a few keys. 'She also kept every message she'd ever received. Never deleted anything.' Dilly looked up and caught Helen's gaze. 'Every WhatsApp message between her and Toby is here. It makes for an enlightening read.'

'If it's so enlightening,' Jess said, 'why didn't you take it to the police?'

'I did,' Dilly snarled. 'But it isn't my phone so they talked in circles about the difficulty in proving the authenticity of the messages, and the right to privacy yada yada yada. I couldn't persuade Anna to pursue it. By that stage, she'd withdrawn so much, we barely communicated any more.' She waved the phone again. 'But after reading these, I knew you'd lied. And then you get out of prison after two years! Where is the justice in that?'

Helen's eyes were glued to the phone. Had Toby really shared the intimate details of their relationship with his mother? She struggled to stay calm. 'Being out on licence isn't the same as being free.'

'Free enough to start your own business though, aren't you?' Dilly laughed unpleasantly. 'You have no idea how much I enjoyed helping you make it a success, knowing I was going to pull it out from underneath you at the end when I put you back in prison.'

She'd played it so well. Worse, Helen had helped her. She could see Jess, looking bemused, as if trying to make sense of it all. How could she when she didn't know all the facts? Helen thought of her bookshop. It was supposed to be her second chance. A new start for a fresh future. But could she really start again when the past lingered so painfully? When she'd never told the truth. *Perhaps it was time...*

'Your friend is looking a bit confused,' Dilly said. She turned to look at Jess. 'Let me read you a few of these WhatsApp messages and perhaps it'll help you to understand.'

...time to talk about what had really happened that night...

'I'll read one of the more explanatory ones from a couple of days before he was murdered.' Dilly shook her head. 'He wasn't shy about sharing with his mother.' She tapped the phone, squinted a little, and read, slowly, clearly, enunciating every excruciating word.

'Helen is lovely, Ma, but I don't see a future with her. It's the sex part; she doesn't enjoy it unless there's some pain involved. Really rough, you understand? She likes to be whipped. I'm not talking about gentle hits either; she likes it hard enough to leave marks. And it isn't a new thing; she's got scars on her back from older relationships. Sometimes, she winces when she sits back in a chair because her skin is so bruised and sore. It's getting a bit too weird for my liking.'

Dilly put the phone down and looked up to meet Helen's eyes. '"Hard enough to leave marks": would these be the same marks in the photographs that were shown in court? The ones they used to argue that you were the victim of domestic abuse?'

...it was time to confess...

I thought Toby loved me enough. I thought he understood my particular need. He certainly entered into it with gusto, hitting me just that little bit too hard, enjoying my pain just that little bit too much.

Over the years, there had been lovers who'd looked at me askance when I suggested we experiment with a little sado-masochism. When they did, I quickly laughed it off, referencing *Fifty Shades of Grey* and saying jokingly that perhaps these things were left between the covers of a book. But whereas I enjoyed sex with these men, and even managed an orgasm occasionally, it was when I had pain as a starter, as a side dish, as dessert, then, and only then, did I have a mind-blowing, earth-moving, groin-shuddering orgasm.

Perhaps if I'd met a decent man, things might have been different.

I might have settled for love.

But I met Toby.

A tall, good-looking man, he was well-spoken and fun to be with, even if his idea of fun was often as the expense of someone else's dignity. Was it that streak of cruelty that had attracted me? Perhaps I interpreted it as indicating a willingness to indulge my needs, as if the darkness I saw in him was equal to that within myself. It was only later that I realised Toby was, above all, mean.

On our second date, he dropped a less than subtle hint for me to cook him dinner. In my home. Sex wasn't mentioned, but we both knew what he meant. It had been almost a year since my last less than satisfactory relationship and I was attracted to him, so I thought, why not?

By the morning after, I understood one thing clearly. Toby's darkness was far deeper, more concentrated, more outwardly directed than mine. He approached sex like it was a battleground and I was a weapon he wielded. I don't think he deliberately meant to cause me pain; it was simply a side-effect of getting what he wanted.

'Did I hurt you?' he said, crushing me with the weight of his body so that even if I'd wanted to, I'd have had a hard job squeezing out an answer.

'I liked it,' I said, when he'd eventually rolled off me.

That was the beginning of our twisted relationship. The following evening, when I answered a knock on the front door, Toby was there, all his belongings in the two suitcases by his feet and the several refuse sacks on the backseat of his car. He was smiling in a self-congratulatory way. As if he'd pulled off a great deal. 'It took me longer to pack than I'd expected,' he said with a grin before leaning across to kiss me. 'I hope you haven't eaten; I thought we could go out for dinner to celebrate.'

Confusion must have been written clearly across my face, because he took a step backwards and shook his head slowly. 'You've changed your mind, have you?' He looked embarrassed, running a hand over his face and through his hair. He took a deep breath and let it out in a self-derisory laugh. 'I should have known it was too good to be true.' He picked up one of the suit-cases. 'Don't worry, I can go back to the house share. They won't have rented the room out yet.'

I swear there were tears in his eyes. He was *that* good a manipulator.

But even though I knew I was being a fool, and was absolutely sure there had never been any discussion about Toby moving in, I was reaching for the case he held and taking it from him. 'No, please stay.'

I ignored the self-satisfied glint in his eyes, ignored the warning light flashing inside my head.

Why had I been so stupid? Because I was lonely perhaps, and because in those early days, I thought his cruelty would be the answer to my particular sexual needs.

And it worked for a time.

It was months before I realised the truth. That Toby enjoyed inflicting the pain that gave me such pleasure, but he didn't like that I enjoyed it.

'You're sick, you know that, don't you?' he said one night, dropping the belt he'd used on my back with more force than usual, leaving me gasping with the pain from the welts he'd raised. That was the first time I'd seen disgust in his face but it wasn't the last.

'I'm sick but you're not. Is that what you're saying?'

He hit me then, his palm connecting with my cheek with enough power to knock me off the bed onto the floor. 'This is how you like it, isn't it?' he said, dropping on top of me, his erection hard, hot and insistent.

No, it wasn't. For me, pain was always the side dish, but for Toby, it was the main course. I wasn't stupid. I knew my desires were linked to my childhood, and to that sad conflagration of pain and pleasure learnt at my adored father's knee. I knew that I should get counselling. That my predilection for masochism could probably be cured. But my desires didn't hurt anyone, apart from myself, and I couldn't bring myself to talk about something that I'd carried with me for so many years.

I should have thrown Toby out after that first slap. I should have gone for help when I started to think that perhaps I was getting what I deserved. It wasn't that I explained everything away; I simply accepted it all: his increasing violence, his habit of helping himself to money from my purse, of borrowing my bank card and withdrawing money from my account with the pin number I'd been persuaded to give him.

It was strange because, in the end, it wasn't any of these things that made me snap. It wasn't even the look of disgust and derision on his face when he came into the kitchen that day.

'I can't bear your disgusting, warped desires any more,' he'd said, a sneer in every word, his eyes raking me, dismissing me. 'You're a pathetic slut who needs to get help, so I'm out of here.'

I remember my legs felt weak and I leaned on the counter behind, feeling the cold granite with my hands. It was pure coincidence that the knife I'd bought the previous day, one so sharp that I'd yet to decide where to put it, was sitting there. My fingers curled around the handle, almost of their own volition, and then it was there in my hand, gleaming steel.

Pure coincidence. I'd never planned to kill him. I certainly hadn't bought the knife with that intent. I'd told the police and the court the truth about that.

The lie I told, the big fat lie, was why I'd killed him.

The motive that everyone had swallowed.

I didn't kill him because he hit me. Or because he was stealing my money. Or even because he called me such vile, filthy names.

No, I killed Toby because he wanted to leave me.

40

———————

It was time to confess. Helen started at the beginning. Back to when a small child was so desperate for affection that she accepted it came with pain. Word after word, leaving nothing out, not all the men who'd happily agreed to her requests, not the ones who'd looked at her askance, not the months with Toby where he'd belittled, beat and manipulated her and made her feel useless and small. For the first time in her life, she told someone about her sexual deviancy. Oddly, it was the first time she'd called it that. Perhaps it was a night for truths. Her mouth grew dry as she spoke, but she didn't stop because she could feel the release of it all. As if she'd lanced a hideous boil. All the rot came out and left her feeling – freer.

She watched Jess and Dilly's face as she told her tale. Jess's eyes growing rounder in disbelief, her mouth slightly open as if she was breathing in the words. Dilly's eyes were still boring into her, her mouth still a harsh gash in her face, but Helen thought the anger was fading, just a little. She stopped to gather her thoughts before her final confession.

Jess jumped into the silence, reaching to grab Helen's hand and hold it tightly. 'It sounds like he was an absolute monster.'

Helen remembered his face that final day, the words he'd used, the way he'd looked at her. 'Yes, he probably was.' She pulled her hand away and used it to rub her eyes before looking at Dilly. The anger might be fading, but there was no lessening in the hate she saw there, and she hadn't heard Helen's final confession yet.

Finally, she was going to admit what she'd done. She took a deep breath, then holding Dilly's gaze, she said, 'You were right. I didn't kill him because he was a monster. I murdered him because he was going to leave me, and I couldn't face that.'

'I knew it!' Dilly snarled the words and sat forward with her clenched fist raised almost in triumph. 'You murdered him, destroyed Anna's life. Ruined mine. You should have gone to prison for a long time, shouldn't be free to start a fucking business and move on with your life.' She slumped back, shaking her head. Her voice was thick with tears when she said, 'It isn't fair.'

Jess glared at her. 'It isn't fair? Haven't you listened to what she said? She was neglected and damaged as a child and abused as an adult. Toby's abuse was a textbook case of coercive control. He used her somewhat unusual sexual needs as a weapon against her. Beat her with it, both physically and mentally.' She turned to Helen. 'Your father damaged you by warping the reality of pleasure and pain, but you adored him, and his death left you bereft. By the sounds of it, Toby filled his shoes perfectly. When he said he was going to leave you, you must have felt the same sense of abandonment, and you couldn't let it happen again, could you?'

Helen shut her eyes. Jess was speaking pseudo-psychological claptrap, wasn't she? There was no connection between the father she'd adored and the monster who'd invaded her life. 'I don't think...' Her voice faded. Was Jess right? Had her father been a monster too?

Helen felt Jess take her hand again, and took comfort from it as she opened her eyes. She met Dilly's gaze. 'I understand why you hate me now.'

Jess sniffed. 'She hates you because it forced her to face up to reality. That the woman she loved so desperately didn't love her. Isn't that the truth, Dilly?'

The three women sat silently for a moment. When Dilly spoke, her words were full of regret. 'I've never loved so intensely, so passionately. Anna was everything to me. I think when love comes to you later in life, it comes hard and is all encompassing. I thought that together, we'd get through Toby's death. I hadn't anticipated that she'd resent, even come to hate me, for those years she'd been separated from him.

'She said she didn't have enough space in her heart to mourn Toby and love me. She retreated into herself, spent her days in the library with her books. She'd left me long before she went to Wales. All I had were memories and those WhatsApp messages. I read them, reread them, and learnt to hate you with the passion I'd once had to love Anna.'

'I'm sorry.' Useless, empty words, but it was all Helen had. Toby had been an addiction. A harmful one. She still couldn't remember stabbing him; perhaps she never would. The mind had its own way of coping. 'If I'd told the court everything,' she said, 'I don't know if it would have made any difference to my sentence.'

'It might have made it shorter,' Jess said with a shake of her head. 'You're a seriously messed up woman.'

The anger that had lit up Dilly's face from the moment they'd arrived seemed to fade. 'For once, I agree with your annoying friend. I think they might have suggested you needed help.'

Helen laughed bitterly. 'I had counselling in prison, but I think it only works if you tell the truth and I didn't. This is the first time I've spoken about my problem.'

'I don't think your problem, as you call it, is unique,' Dilly said. 'Bondage, sadomasochism, masochism, they've all been around a long time.' She slumped down in the chair. 'You've painted a pretty hideous picture of Toby. Anna adored him, but I suppose she might have been biased. I only met him once, many years ago, and I didn't take to him. Or perhaps it would be more honest to say he didn't take to me. He didn't say it but I could see the word *dyke* in his eyes and in the twist of his mouth when he spoke to me. He refused to meet me again. Refused to meet his mother while she was with me. It broke her heart, but she was always sure he'd come around even as the years passed.'

'And he did?' Jess asked.

Dilly huffed a laugh. 'Not to Anna's relationship with me. Once a homophobe, always a homophobe. She was very cagey about it, but I think he finally contacted her because he needed money. He was her only child; she loved him regardless. He still refused to meet her, though; it was always WhatsApp messages. I think she clung to the hope it would eventually be more.'

The pain Helen had caused. 'Until I killed him.'

Dilly nodded. 'Yes, it destroyed her. When you were sentenced to four years, she showed me the messages he'd sent her about you, then withdrew into herself, almost vanishing before my eyes. She wouldn't talk about it, barely spoke to me at all in the last few weeks. All she did was curl up in that damn library and read.' She tilted her head towards Jess. 'Your annoying friend is right. She didn't love me enough, but if you hadn't killed her son, I'd never have known. I'll always hate you for that. For opening my eyes.' She got to her feet. 'I'll contact the police, tell them I made a mistake about the medallion. I am sorry. I thought causing you pain would help ease mine. It didn't.'

'I'm not usually adverse to pain,' Helen said with an attempt at humour. 'Physical pain, though – this psychological stuff makes my head spin.'

It was time to leave. She pushed to her feet, feeling heavier than she had only moments before. Confessing had freed her, but it hadn't erased what she'd done, hadn't made the burden of that any lighter. How could it when she knew it was thanks to her that Dilly and Anna's lives had been destroyed? 'Maybe it's a bad idea, but I would like to stay in touch, if that's okay? After all, you now know more about me than most people do.' In fact, these two women knew more about her than anyone did. It was a strange thought.

Dilly hesitated for a moment. 'I'm not sure that's a good idea.'

Of course it wasn't. Helen nodded, pressed her lips together and hoped the tears wouldn't come. Not yet. Later, she could open the floodgates.

'In fact, I'm sure it's not, but perhaps I'll pop into the shop one day, see what you've made of it.'

They'd never be friends. Helen didn't think she'd ever be forgiven, but there could be a level of acceptance between them. Perhaps that was enough. 'I'd like that.'

'I'll ring the police in the morning,' Dilly said, getting to her feet. 'I hope that'll be the end of it then.'

So did Helen. But she wasn't sure Moira would give up so easily.

41

Helen was lost in her thoughts on the drive home, so it wasn't until she'd parked outside the shop that she realised Jess was being unusually quiet. Had she been shocked by Helen's confession, disappointed that her feet were buried deep in the seedy side of life? Or perhaps Jess was of the opinion that booklovers had spiritual hearts that floated far above the mire, and that booksellers therefore should be above the gritty, sordid side of life.

The idea made Helen shake her head. Books were her antidote to the grim side of life, and they kept her afloat when the shit hit the fan; that was the reality of it. 'Let's get those pizzas to go, and have them at home with a beer.' She got out, surprised when Jess didn't move. 'You stay here then and I'll get them. What d'you fancy?'

'Pepperoni.'

No *please* or *thank you*. Perhaps Helen should be grateful. At least she wasn't being offered a psychological assessment.

She took a few minutes to admire her shop's window display. Tomorrow, she'd rearrange it. Change the word of the week to a new one. *Perhaps not serendipitous after all*, she thought, thinking of Dilly.

When Moira's grim face popped into her head, Helen stepped forward to rest her forehead against the window, the glass cold and soothing. It was a minute before she moved. When she looked back to her car, she saw Jess was still staring straight ahead. Whatever was wrong with her, Helen wasn't dealing with it that night; there wasn't any room left in her head for more angst. She walked to the pizzeria and pushed open the door, the warm, aromatic air inside immediately making her feel hungry. The few tables were full but there didn't appear to be anyone waiting for a takeaway.

'Hi, Zander,' she said. She felt a twinge of guilt for having suspected him and his brother of trying to push her out. 'I hear you're having trouble with your heating.'

He groaned. 'It's been Patrick Swayze, an absolute Lionel Blair.'

Helen hoped she was translating the rhyming slang correctly. 'Crazy and a nightmare, yes?'

'You're learning.' He jerked a thumb into the room behind. 'It makes so much damn noise, it's been frightening the customers. I meant to warn you, but that young lassie of yours said it wasn't bothering you.'

Someday, she might tell him about the knocking sound and how, for a brief moment, she thought it had been Reginald on the stairway with his bloodied knuckles. It might be better for future friendly relations to refrain from telling him her suspicions about him and his brother. 'No, it's not bothering me at all. Don't worry. Now, let me order so you can get back to your customers.'

Ten minutes later, she was heading back to her car, the pizza boxes warming her hands. 'Here we go,' she said, putting them in the back before climbing into the driver's seat. Jess glanced her way briefly, then resumed her stare of the road in front as they drove home.

It wasn't until they were sitting on the sofa, pizza boxes balanced on their knees, a bottle of beer in one hand, that anything was said, and then it was Helen who spoke. 'Great pizza.' Putting her beer down, she reached for the remote control. 'Let me see if I can find something worth watching.'

'No,' Jess said. She gulped beer from her bottle before putting it down. 'I'd like to talk to you.'

Helen wanted to drink her beer, eat her pizza, watch something mindless on TV. She didn't want to talk any more. She certainly didn't want to talk about whatever was bothering Jess, whatever was putting those worry lines on her forehead. Didn't want more grief, more angst, more fucking anything. 'Hasn't there been enough talk for one evening?'

She wasn't surprised when Jess shook her head and said, 'Do you think your parole officer is going to cause problems?'

Yes, Helen did. Regardless of Dilly's explanation to the police, she had, as she'd admitted, set a ball in motion. The missing medallion was on Helen's person when the police had called. She hadn't contacted them, or Dilly, to report the find. Saying that she'd 'intended to' wasn't enough. Moira might very well think the whole dodgy episode was sufficient to order her to be recalled to prison. And that would be the end of her dream. 'I already broke one of the conditions of my licence by staying in the shop without telling her. She wasn't a happy bunny. And then, stupidly, I forgot to phone her when I was supposed to and left a message that didn't impress her. This might very well be the last straw.' It appeared it was her day to face the truth. 'Without wanting to sound paranoid, I think she has it in for me now, so yes, I think she's going to cause me problems.'

'But you could keep the shop open, if you went back to prison, couldn't you? Your sister would help.'

Helen wasn't sure whether she was envious of Jess's belief in a happy ever after, or appalled by her inability to see things as they were. 'My sister has a job. She can't just chuck it to run the shop. And I couldn't afford to leave it shut. Not with things like council tax to pay, never mind the basic utilities. No, I'd have to face facts.' Maybe she could, after all, persuade Zander and Alex to buy it. The idea was almost amusing.

'You'll just have to make sure Moira doesn't have you recalled then, won't you?'

Helen took a sip of her beer, then kept the bottle resting on her lower lip as she stared at the woman sitting on the sofa beside her. Despite saying earlier that she was hungry, she'd only taken a bite out of a slice of pizza. She was guzzling the beer, wiping her mouth after every swallow. It appeared that whatever was bothering her was making her anxious. 'I don't think Moira is going to listen to any excuses I have to offer.'

Jess tilted her bottle back and gulped the remainder of the beer before turning to look at Helen. 'Was it hard for you to tell the truth earlier?'

It was Helen's turn to frown. 'Yes, of course it was. I've never told anyone about my childhood before, or about the way Toby treated me. But I wasn't trying to excuse myself for what I'd done; I just thought I owed Dilly the truth. It was, after all, thanks to me that she lost the woman she loved.'

'The truth.' Jess shook her head. 'To many people, it's an optional extra.' She picked up a slice of pizza, nibbled the end, and put it down again. 'You're a strange woman, d'you know that? And I'm not talking about your paraphilic disorder here.'

Helen knew she shouldn't ask but couldn't stop herself. 'My what?'

Jess put the pizza box on the floor and sat back. 'Having unconventional sexual needs and thoughts isn't unusual, but when they start to interfere with your life, when they put you at risk, or in danger even, they're a mental health issue.'

A paraphilic disorder. Having a name for it didn't make it any easier to bear, but perhaps it would make it easier to get help. It made Helen, suddenly, feel less alone. She shut the pizza box and tossed it on top of the other. 'So, in what other way am I strange?' She might as well know everything.

'For all you've been through, you're still stupidly gullible.'

Helen lifted a hand to her forehead. Gullible? Had she been? No, she'd been suspicious, paranoid even, about Zander and Alex, she'd had reservations about Dilly, and she was completely wary of Moira. So why was she being called gullible? She opened her mouth to argue, shutting it again when she met Jess's eyes. '*You* lied to me?'

'So many times, I was starting to lose track.' She picked up the beer bottle, remembered it was empty and pointed it towards the kitchen. 'I need another – you want one?'

Stunned, Helen merely nodded. Was she feeling so desperately let down because she'd met a better liar than she was?

'Here you go.' Jess handed Helen the opened bottle and sat beside her again, reaching out to pat her shoulder. 'Don't be too hard on yourself; I'm really very good at it.' She drank deeply. 'It's telling the truth I have trouble with, but after what you shared, I feel I owe it to you.'

'Go on then,' Helen said when seconds passed in silence. 'I assume you lied about not being involved in stealing my money.'

Jess shook her head. 'No, that was the truth. The lie was where I got the money from to replace it.' She laughed. 'I wasn't sure you'd believe me, but you fell for it completely. Seriously, you saw the other three women, each of them is about ten centimetres taller than me; did you really think I was going to go up against them to get a few lousy quid back?'

'You said you took it when you got the opportunity. That's why you had to leave your accommodation.'

'We attend the same university. They know my name.' Jess looked at her as if she still couldn't believe her naivety. 'You don't think they'd have got payback if I'd done something so stupid?'

Helen hadn't given it any thought at all. She'd been too grateful to get the money back to question its provenance. Now she did. 'So where did you get the money? And why lie about it all? I didn't know your names; it isn't as if I could have chased you down.'

Jess raised her beer bottle and smiled. 'I got it from your parole officer, the delightful Moira Manson.'

42

Helen couldn't take it in. She must have misheard. Had to have done. That or she was dreaming. Yes, that had to be it; her life was one bloody nightmare after the other.

'It's the truth,' Jess said. 'When we left the bookshop that Wednesday, the other three went off still giggling about pinching your money, and I went to get the bus. The books you'd sold me, in one of your paper bags with that seriously cringe logo blazoned across it, were on the seat beside me at the bus stop. Moira came up to me, looked at the bag, looked at me as if weighing me up, then asked if I'd like to earn some money.'

Helen was so dismayed by Jess referring to her logo as being *seriously cringe* that it took a few seconds for the rest of the sentence to sink in. 'She offered you a job?'

Jess sniggered. 'You think she's so full of Christian charity that she'd offer a job to someone who was obviously scraping by, do you?' She sucked at her beer. 'No, I don't suppose you do, yet you're right, kind of. She was offering me a job, but not the kind I'd be able to add to my CV.'

'If you're waiting for me to guess what it was, you'll be

waiting a long time. Unless...' Helen's eyes widened '...she wasn't propositioning you, was she?' She couldn't imagine her stickler-for-the-rules parole officer doing such a thing, but then she couldn't imagine her stopping to offer a job to a stranger either.

'Yuk, no!' Jess did an exaggerated shiver. 'What she wanted from me was much more interesting.'

Helen guessed she wasn't pausing for dramatic effect or to drag out the big reveal. She could see it in her eyes; she was suddenly afraid that telling Helen might be worse than not.

'You've started now; you've no choice but to tell me the rest.'

Jess looked at the bottle she held, swished the contents, took another swig. 'I'm telling you because I think you deserve to know what's going on, although I don't know all of it. You're a good woman, even if you don't believe that yourself. Right,' she said, 'here goes. Moira wanted me to get close to you, to get friendly. She said she'd make it worth my while.'

It would have been easier to believe Moira had made sexual advances because this... this made no sense at all. Why would she have wanted Jess to become 'friendly' with Helen?

'I don't understand.' She cringed at how pathetic she sounded. 'Did she say why?'

Jess shook her head. 'She wanted me to tell her where you went, who you met, if you'd any meetings with anyone in the shop. Stuff like that.'

It made no sense whatsoever. 'And she didn't say why she wanted to know?'

This was met with a gruff laugh. 'You've met her; you know what she's like. Intimidating and a bit scary, and I don't scare easily. So, no, I've no idea why, but her money was good. She gave me three hundred quid upfront and promised me another seven. That's a grand, so forgive me for not turning up my nose at it.' She see-sawed a hand. 'Mind you, I had to pay you out of that three hundred so I didn't have a lot left.'

'You paid me with money you got from my parole officer for spying on me?' Helen's head was reeling so she wasn't sure why she found this quite so distasteful.

It was obvious that Jess found her attitude amusing. 'Filthy lucre still pays the bills.'

Ignoring her, Helen searched through conflicting thoughts and ideas for anything that would make sense. 'I don't understand why she'd want to know those things about me.' She frowned, finding one thought and going with it – hadn't she been convinced Zander and Alex were trying to force her out? Perhaps it was a case of right idea, wrong guilty party. 'Unless she has her own notions of owning a bookshop and wants mine.'

'I don't think so.'

There was something in Jess's tone of voice that made Helen sit up and turn to face her. 'You know something, don't you?'

Jess tapped the beer bottle against her front tooth, the sharp noise loud in the silence. When she took it away, her expression had changed, more resolute, harder. 'I've no proof, but I think it was Moira who broke into your shop and here too.'

Helen laughed. 'That's ridiculous! Why would she do such a thing?'

'I think she's looking for something.'

'Looking for something,' Helen parroted. 'Like what?'

'No idea.'

'Well, why are you saying that then?' Helen shouted, exasperated with a conversation that seemed to be going around in circles.

Jess sighed. 'There's more I should tell you. She wanted to know when it would be safe to go into the shop without fear of you walking in on her. She's there now.'

'What?' Helen jumped to her feet. 'How?' Then she slapped her forehead hard, as if trying to knock some sense into it. Gullible? No, she was simply stupid. 'You gave her the spare key?'

Jess didn't bother attempting to lie or look embarrassed. 'The lure of the filthy lucre again. Yes, I did. It wasn't hard to find; you'd labelled it so neatly.'

'But the alarm. It hasn't gone off.'

'You mean the one with the code nine eight seven six?' Jess looked at her sadly. 'Seriously, there's no point in having an alarm if you're going to let all and sundry see you tap in the code, is there?'

There didn't seem any point in arguing that Helen hadn't allowed *all and sundry* to see the code, just Jess, a woman she'd stupidly trusted despite everything. 'Right, so she's in the shop now. Looking for something.'

Jess checked her watch. 'I'm guessing so.' For the first time, she looked a little embarrassed. 'She did say she wasn't going to do any damage, so I didn't think it'd be any harm really. And she promised me the rest of the money this week.'

'You didn't think it would be any harm!' Helen glared at her.

'It probably isn't any consolation, but if I'd known then what I know now, I wouldn't have agreed.'

'I don't want your bloody pity!'

Jess shrugged. 'It's not pity; it's empathy. There's a huge difference.'

There was, and Helen could see the truth in Jess's eyes. 'You'll be a good psychologist,' she said as anger drained away. 'Right, Moira, what am I going to do about her? I could ring the police, have her arrested for trespass.' Helen reached for her phone, stared at it for a moment and dropped it on the sofa beside her. 'If she was arrested, they'd just assign me someone else, wouldn't they?'

'It stands to reason.'

'I might even get someone worse.' Helen gave a snort. 'Although I'm not sure that'd be possible. No,' she got to her feet, 'better to go and catch her in the act, then I can use it for my benefit.'

'Right,' Jess said. 'I'd better come too to play the trusty side-kick again. Robin to your Batman. Anyway, you might need a witness.'

Helen looked at her. 'If you come, she'll know you've told me and won't give you the rest of that money.'

Jess put her beer down and got to her feet. 'It might surprise you, because it sure as hell surprises me, but it seems I do have some morals tucked away.' She stretched and yawned. 'It seems to me that you're due a bit of good luck and a happy ever after, so let's go find out what the cow is up to.'

43

Helen parked the car a little distance from the shop and switched off the engine. Lights were still blazing from the windows of the pizzeria next door, but from where she sat, there didn't appear to be any shining from the interior of the bookshop. It wasn't until they were closer, neither of them speaking, that she could see a faint, bright line around the edge of the blinds. Not a torch, the light was steady. Probably one of the table lamps. What the hell was Moira searching for?

'You okay?' Jess whispered, then giggled. 'Not sure why I'm whispering; it isn't a bloody James Bond movie.'

'Let's get this over with.'

Helen reached the door first and took out her keys, hoping Moira hadn't locked the door from the inside and left the key in situ. They were in luck, she had left the key in the lock, but she'd carelessly forgotten to turn it. Helen pressed the handle and pushed open the door a little before sliding her hand in to move the overhead bell out of the way.

'Where—' Jess started, slapping a hand over her mouth when

Helen gave her arm a sharp dig and held a finger over her lips to warn her to be quiet.

The light was coming from the lamp on the desk. There was no sign of Moira, but when Helen listened intently she could hear a faint sound coming from upstairs. Shutting the door quietly behind them, she locked it and pocketed the keys, nodding when she saw Jess's grin. Then, walking on the balls of her feet, she crossed to the stairway and started a slow ascent.

When Helen peered around the banister at the top, she saw Moira in the storage room. She'd obviously decided that turning on the overhead light might cause suspicion and was using a torch to search the boxes. On her knees, she was totally engrossed in what she was doing and oblivious to the eyes watching her. Helen had given no thought to what she'd do when she came face to face with her but in the end, it was simple.

Holding a hand up to keep Jess where she was on the stairway, she crept forward, keeping to the shadow of the wall until she reached the door. Then, in one quick movement, she reached for it, pulled it shut and turned the key in the lock.

'Go you,' Jess said, joining her.

They both jumped back when the door was hit from the inside. 'Who's there? Unlock this door immediately, or I'll ring the police.'

Helen raised an eyebrow. 'You go ahead and do that,' she said, pitching her voice loud and firm. 'When they arrive, you can explain why you're trespassing on my property. I may be out of prison on licence, but I have rights.'

'What are you going to do?' Jess whispered. 'You can't keep her locked in there forever.'

'Why not? I'm betting nobody knows she's here.'

Jess looked horrified for a moment before laughing uncertainly. 'You're joking. Aren't you?'

'Fuck's sake, of course I'm bloody-well joking!' Frustration, and the feeling that her life was spiralling out of control, was making Helen angry again. She stood close by the door and said, 'I want to know why you're here. And why you paid someone to spy on me.'

'Let me out.' Moira banged the door again. 'I can explain.'

Helen laughed. Loudly. Letting it roll around the space. If she sounded a little manic, well, all the better. 'You're in no position to make conditions. Explain first, then I'll consider whether I should let you out or phone the police myself.'

When there was no answer, she crossed to pick up a stool and brought it back. 'I'm making myself comfortable, so take your time. We have all night.'

'It's not what it seems. I'm acting in your best interest.'

'Paying someone to spy on me is in my best interest? You'll forgive me for thinking that's a load of cobblers.'

'You've been misinformed.' Moira's voice was surprisingly calm. 'Yes, I did pay someone, but it was to keep an eye on you so you wouldn't get into trouble. I know how much this shop means to you and I wanted to make sure you were given every chance.'

'Really? So that's why you broke in here last week, and why you broke into my home. And before you try to tell me I'm talking nonsense, I have proof. Photographs that show you breaking and entering.' She heard Jess's gasp and held up a hand. 'I also have a signed statement from Jess Milgate that says you asked her to keep you informed of who I met, and where I went. What I want to know is why, and what the hell you were expecting to find when you came here tonight.'

She was relaxing back against the door and jumped when Moira started to bang it so loudly, it rattled on its hinges.

'Let me out!' She sounded less calm now. 'I'll have you arrested for keeping me prisoner.'

'As soon as you tell me what you were looking for, I'll let you out. Simple as that.'

'I was just checking that you weren't selling anything dodgy.'

Helen laughed and relaxed back against the door again. She knew desperation when she heard it, and Moira was desperate. She exchanged a grin with Jess, who'd sat on the top stair and looked to be enjoying the show. 'Anything dodgy? It's a second-hand book store, not a printing press for radical or terrorist propaganda. So let me ask you again, what were you looking for?' When there was no answer, she got to her feet. 'Right, I'm off to make a cup of tea. I'll be back in a bit.'

'No, wait!'

Helen heard a note of fear in the voice with a twist of pleasure.

'You going to tell me what's going on?'

'Okay, right, I'll tell you.'

Helen heard her moving about in the room. 'Anytime soon.'

'I was looking for a book, okay. A book.'

Helen frowned. 'It's a bookshop, we have lots of them, so you'd better narrow the field down a bit.'

'The Friday night when I helped you carry in those boxes of books, remember?'

Helen considered the question. It didn't appear to be a trick. 'Yes, I remember.'

'I'd opened the second box, but you came back before I was able to pick up the book I saw inside.'

It was like getting blood from a stone. 'What book are we talking about?'

'A book of short stories, by Hemingway, called *In Our Time*.'

'Okay. But I still don't understand; why did you want it so desperately that you were willing to break the law to get it?'

'Do you have it?'

'No, I'm guessing it was sold.'

'When? I came back the day you opened. I was your first damn customer. It wasn't on the shelves; I searched for it. And then I broke in to find it and couldn't. I hoped you'd taken it home for safekeeping, so I went there—'

Helen slapped a hand on the door. 'You mean you broke in!'

'Whatever,' Moira said dismissively. 'I thought you must have it hidden away and were waiting for someone to come to value it. That's why I hired that stupid Jess girl. Much bloody good she was. When did you sell it?'

'I'm not sure. There were books on the shelves upstairs. It wasn't really open for customers but I did let a few go up. One of them must have bought it. I don't look at the titles when customers bring books to the desk.'

'You sold it for two quid.' There was anguish in Moira's voice.

'Yes.'

'You stupid, stupid cow. Do you know how much it's worth? Do you know anything about rare books? No, of course you don't; you're just a stupid second-hand bookseller. I'll tell you, shall I? It was a 1924 edition of the book. Do you know how rare it is? Well, I'll tell you, shall I? Bloody amazingly rare. Only three hundred were ever published. The last time one went for sale, it sold for £300,000. Do you know what I could do with that money? I'll tell you, shall I? I could give up this crappy job, move to Spain, retire.' She slammed a hand on the door, making Helen jump again. 'And you, you fuck-wit, gave it away for two quid! Now, let me out of here.'

'I'll let you out on one condition.'

There was no answer.

'Dilly has withdrawn her complaint. There was no truth in it anyway; she'd planted the piece of jewellery to frame me. I want you to assure me that it goes no further. Plus, that you don't give me any more grief for the remainder of my licence. At the end, I'll give you the copies of the photographs, and the signed statement. Deal?' When this was greeted by silence, she slapped a hand on the door. 'Deal?' She hoped Moira wouldn't ask for proof of the non-existent photographs or statement. If she did, she'd have to brazen it out.

'Right, okay, we have a deal. Now let me out of here.'

Helen waved to Jess and pointed to the bathroom, waiting until she was out of sight before unlocking the door.

'Right,' Helen said, pushing it open to face a rather dishevelled Moira. 'Now, get out of my shop. I'll still have to see you, but it'll be on my terms. In my home, not here. A minute on the doorstep, no longer.'

Moira didn't bother to reply. Holding her nose in the air, as if she hadn't just admitted to breaking and entering with the intent to steal, she strode off, her stilettos tapping each tread as she descended. A minute later, Helen heard her shout. 'Unlock the bloody door, you bitch!'

'I'm the bitch,' Helen muttered as she went down to let the visibly angry Moira out of the shop. 'Bye now, please don't come again,' she said as the woman brushed past and almost ran to her car.

When she turned Jess was there, a huge grin splitting her face. 'Bloody hell, you played that well.'

'I surprised myself.' Helen rubbed her suddenly tear-filled eyes. 'I think it worked, though.'

'Hell, yes, you won't see her again until you have to. I loved the bit you said about a minute on your doorstep. Ace that was.'

Helen wasn't really listening to her. She was looking around her shop. With no more paranoia about Zander and Alex, no more worry about the break-in to taint it, it already felt better. She glanced to where Jess was buttoning her jacket. Perhaps Helen would get help for her condition... what had the budding psychologist called it? Para-something or other. She couldn't remember. It didn't matter; she'd find someone to talk to who would know.

'You must be gutted, losing out on that book,' Jess said, coming to stand beside her. She put an arm around Helen's shoulder. 'We should go home. I'm thinking I could manage that pizza now, and a couple of beers. I think we deserve them, don't you?'

'We do.' Helen slipped an arm around Jess's waist and pulled her closer. 'Thank you for being with me. Not just this evening, but earlier too. It meant a lot.'

Jess stood back. 'I've been feeling guilty about my arrangement with Moira for a while, but earlier, when you told your story, I knew I couldn't go on with it. I was already impressed by your determination to get past all the shit that was being thrown at you and now that I know exactly how much, well, I'm amazed.'

'I amaze myself sometimes,' Helen said. She nodded towards the door. 'You head home, stick the pizzas in the oven to warm up, open a couple of beers. I want to stay here a bit. I'm going to leave the car where it is and follow you in a few minutes.'

'You sure you're okay?'

'Certain. Go, I'll just be a few minutes.' Helen gave her a gentle push, and when she'd gone through the door, locked it behind her. She wasn't taking security lightly in future.

Crossing to the desk, she sat on the stool in the circle of light from the lamp and took out her mobile. 'Hi, Sarah,' she said when it was answered. 'I wanted to thank you again for coming this morning. You've been so supportive; I'm not sure if I've ever thanked you enough.'

'You don't need to thank me. I've been waiting for an opportunity to say...'

Helen heard an indrawn breath and braced herself for what was to come.

'...how proud I am of you for putting what happened behind you and making a success of your life. That's the first thing. The second...' Another indrawn breath. 'This is hard for me; I'm not good at talking about my feelings. I dismissed you when you spoke about our childhood; I shouldn't have, I should have admitted how jealous of you I was back then—'

'Jealous? Of me?' Helen wondered if the world had tilted on its axis because nothing was making sense.

'You were such an adorable kid, all rosy cheeks and lips, like a bloody cherub. Everyone admired you. If we were out together, people would stop and comment on how gorgeous you were. Meanwhile, I was a gangly, buck-toothed, skinny mess. And our father...'

Helen pressed the phone to her ear, but when the silence lingered, she said, 'What about him?'

'He adored you. Only you. He more or less ignored me and Doug. We desperately wanted his attention, his affection, but he only had eyes for his darling little Helen.'

'I didn't know.'

'I think it's why Doug and I clung to each other.'

In the memory of Helen's childhood, her siblings were monsters, her father a saint; how wrong she had been. The prison counsellor had tried to get through to her, had tried to tell her that her siblings weren't to blame for her childhood problems, that they'd been children, older than she, but still children. It hadn't been their role to rear and protect her. The counsellor didn't know the half of it. 'I wish I'd known how you felt. You should have said.'

'You were ten years younger; you wouldn't have understood. You might have looked like a cherub but goodness, you were a brat. If we took you with us, you cried because we went too fast, or you got bored, and you'd whine to Mum. She'd tell Dad and he'd leather us for upsetting you. If we didn't take you, you cried, and it ended up the same way. Doug and I couldn't win.'

It dawned on Helen then. She'd been the monster. All this time, it was her reflection she'd been seeing. 'You must have hated me.'

Sarah laughed. 'I'm not sure children have the capacity to hate, but we certainly resented you. But that was then; we're not children any more.'

That was then. Sarah had left a troubled childhood behind. Perhaps Doug had too. Helen had dragged it with her.

'We should have talked about it years ago,' Sarah said. 'If we had, we might have been closer growing up, but we've never been big talkers, have we?'

Helen hadn't been ready to talk. She was now. Meeting Dilly and discovering the ramifications of Helen's one senseless act of violence had changed that. In confessing the truth about that horrendous night, it had freed up something in her head that allowed her to see other truths: her paraphilic disorder – she'd checked the name with Jess – and her father's warped parenting.

'We'll do better now,' she said. She would. She'd keep building her relationship with her sister and reconnect with her brother. 'How about next Sunday, I'll take you and Devon for lunch?'

'No, save your money; come here, I'll cook something special. Then I'll get rid of Devon to the pub and we can sit and have a good old natter.'

A home-cooked meal with her family. 'That sounds perfect.'

'I hope you're having a well-deserved rest now.'

'Pizza and beer with Jess.' It was almost true, or it would be soon. 'Oh, and you might think I'm crazy, but I'm going to ask her to stay.' She held her breath and waited for her sister's comment.

'I think that's a brilliant idea. I liked her; she'll be good for you.'

Helen laughed. 'Yes, but I gave you an edited version of how we met. On Sunday, I'll give you the unedited one and fill you in on everything else. She's been Robin to my Batman; I think you'll like her even more by the end.'

When she finished her call, she reached underneath the desk for the books she'd put there that afternoon. The ones that nice woman had brought back to replace with four others, an idea that had worked in Helen's favour. And there it was. *In Our Time*, by Ernest Hemingway. 1924 printed clearly on the cover. In perfect condition. And because Helen had taken them straight from the boxes Moira had opened, there was no Appleby logo stamped on a page to devalue it. If only the parole officer knew the favour she'd done her.

There were no dog-eared pages. No damage to the cover. It was almost in mint condition. Moira had said the last one had sold for £300,000.

Helen hoped she was right.

44

Monday morning, Helen was waiting behind her desk with her laptop open in front of her. She'd sent an email to Sotheby's, including several photographs of the Hemingway book. Although it was unlikely she'd hear from them for a while, she kept refreshing her emails, just in case. Between checking that and waiting for Jared to arrive, it wasn't surprising she was feeling so jittery.

He'd rung almost every day to ask if she'd been through all his grand-aunt's books, and if she'd found anything interesting. The first couple of times, she'd explained that she was too busy. The third and fourth time, it was a blunt, 'Not yet, now sorry, I have to go.'

On Saturday, she'd sent him a message to say she'd finished and had an A4 envelope ready to hand over when he called in. Then she'd switched her phone to silent. He'd rung twice and she hadn't answered. Finally, he'd sent a message:

Is it okay to call around tomorrow to pick it up?

Her reply was blunt:

> Sorry, I don't work on Sunday. I'll have it ready
> for you on Monday.

And here she was waiting for him to show up. It would have been nice to have had Jess playing Robin to her Batman again, because she was predicting a very unhappy Jared. And she knew unhappy people could be irrational.

She was staring at her laptop when the jingle of the doorbell alerted her and she looked up to see him coming through the door. She'd thought he was handsome the first time she'd seen him, had thought he was a charming kindred spirit as they'd chatted. But now she knew better: he was a good cover, bad book. She should have known when his grand-aunt had said he intended to throw her precious books into a skip.

'Good morning,' she said as he ambled towards her. As if he wasn't in a hurry. As if he wasn't desperate to get his hands on the envelope that rested on the shelf by her knee.

'Morning.' He waved a thumb over his shoulder. 'I thought you didn't open till nine thirty.'

'No, nine. Every day.'

His smile was sardonic. 'Except Sunday.'

'Except Sunday,' she agreed. Reaching under the desk, she pulled out the A4 envelope and handed it to him. 'I've kept it safe for you.'

He didn't snatch it from her hand, but Helen didn't miss the uneasy mix of expectation and anticipation that flickered across his face as he reached for it, and she knew immediately that she'd been right. He was hoping to find a copy of his grand-aunt's will inside.

'How's business?' he said as he played with the envelope,

fingers tugging at the glued-down flap. Trying to play it cool, yet obviously desperate to rip it open.

She'd been worried how he'd react when he saw the contents, but she needn't have been. He wasn't going to open it in front of her. Perhaps he was afraid he'd give himself away. 'Business has been very good, thank you. How's your grand-aunt?'

He shook his head. 'She's keeping me on my toes. The move to the retirement apartment is happening next week. She's resigned to it now, but it hasn't been easy.' His fingers were still fiddling with the flap of the envelope.

Helen, noticing them, kept her eyes fixed on his face. 'She's lucky to have you to help. Please tell her I said hello and that her books have found new homes.' She wondered what he'd say if she told him she was hoping to sell one of them for hundreds of thousands of pounds. He might demand its return, say it had been added to the boxes by mistake. It might be a wise move on her part to ask Sotheby's for anonymity.

He'd managed to open the flap of the envelope, and she could see he was itching to have a look inside, his eyes flitting down to it even as she continued to talk, amusing herself by holding him captive. How anxious he was to get away, how desperate to open that envelope. Hoping to find a copy of his grand-aunt's will inside.

He wouldn't.

But he'd been right; it had been tucked into one of the books. One of the four that the lovely Mrs Evans had bought, and brought back in exactly the same condition, including the document that had been slipped between the dust jacket and the front cover of one.

Helen had taken it out and read it, smiling when she saw what the amazing Mrs Clough had done. She'd left the bulk of her money, almost four million pounds, to the National Literacy Trust.

She hadn't forgotten her grand-nephew, but Helen was sure he wasn't going to be happy with the fifty thousand he'd been left.

Helen almost smiled at the speed at which Jared made his escape when a customer came through the door to claim her attention. He didn't bother to wait till he was out of sight, opening the envelope as he walked past the window, close enough that Helen could see his expression change from expectation to anger. The receipts she'd collected were tossed in the air, fluttering behind him as he stormed off.

It was better that he didn't know the truth.

Perhaps she was being unfair to him. Perhaps he'd have continued to be nice to his grand-aunt regardless of how much, or little, she was leaving him, but Helen wasn't willing to risk it.

This way, he'd continue to live in expectation and would have to keep being nice to her.

It was what that wonderful, book-loving old lady deserved.

MORE FROM VALERIE KEOGH

Another book from Valerie Keogh, *The Mother*, is available to order now here:

https://mybook.to/MotherBackAd

ACKNOWLEDGEMENTS

My twenty-ninth book and my eleventh with the fabulous Boldwood Books. A big thanks to all the team there, especially my amazing editor, Emily Ruston, copy editor, Emily Reader, proofreader, Shirley Khan, and marketing executive, Niamh Wallace.

The writing community is so supportive but a special thanks goes to Jenny O'Brien, Anita Waller, Judith Baker, Pam Lecky, Keri Beevis and Diane Saxon, who are always there and who I was pleased to mention in this book.

As always, a huge thanks to all the bloggers who share their reviews and to everyone who picks up one of my books.

Thanks also to my wonderful family – my husband, Robert, my sisters, brothers, nieces and nephews.

You might be interested to know that Ernest Hemingway's *In Our Time*, was first published in 1924. Inside, there was a woodcut portrait of Hemingway. Unfortunately, during the printing process, this bled through to the next page, ruining more than half the print run. Only 170 of the 300 printed were deemed suitable to sell. The remainder were given to friends and reviewers.

In 2023, a rather worn copy of *In Our Time* fetched $277,200 at auction.

I love to hear from readers. You can find me here:

Facebook: www.facebook.com/valeriekeoghnovels

Instagram: www.instagram.com/valeriekeogh2

BookBub: www.bookbub.com/authors/valerie-keogh

And you can sign up for my newsletter here: bit.ly/Valerie-KeoghNews

ABOUT THE AUTHOR

Valerie Keogh is the internationally bestselling author of several psychological thrillers and crime series. She originally comes from Dublin but now lives in Wiltshire and worked as a nurse for many years.

Sign up to Valerie Keogh's mailing list here for news, competitions and updates on future books.

Follow Valerie on social media here:

facebook.com/valeriekeoghnovels

x.com/ValerieKeogh1

instagram.com/valeriekeogh2

bookbub.com/authors/valerie-keogh

ALSO BY VALERIE KEOGH

THE

Murder

LIST

**THE MURDER LIST IS A NEWSLETTER
DEDICATED TO SPINE-CHILLING FICTION
AND GRIPPING PAGE-TURNERS!**

**SIGN UP TO MAKE SURE YOU'RE ON OUR
HIT LIST FOR EXCLUSIVE DEALS, AUTHOR
CONTENT, AND COMPETITIONS.**

SIGN UP TO OUR
NEWSLETTER

BIT.LY/THEMURDERLISTNEWS

ALSO BY VALERIE KEOGH

THE

Murder

LIST

THE MURDER LIST IS A NEWSLETTER DEDICATED TO SPINE-CHILLING FICTION AND GRIPPING PAGE-TURNERS!

SIGN UP TO MAKE SURE YOU'RE ON OUR HIT LIST FOR EXCLUSIVE DEALS, AUTHOR CONTENT, AND COMPETITIONS.

SIGN UP TO OUR NEWSLETTER

BIT.LY/THEMURDERLISTNEWS

Boldwood

Boldwood Books is an award-winning fiction publishing company seeking out the best stories from around the world.

Find out more at www.boldwoodbooks.com

Join our reader community for brilliant books, competitions and offers!

Follow us
@BoldwoodBooks
@TheBoldBookClub

Sign up to our weekly deals newsletter

https://bit.ly/BoldwoodBNewsletter

Made in the USA
Las Vegas, NV
02 March 2025

18943366R00164